# Rock Your World

## B Crowhurst

*I would like to dedicate this book to anyone who's ever had an idea or a dream and wondered if they could...*

*You can.*

# Chapter 1

## *Abbie*

I sit in my last class of the day listening to the rain fall against the window. English Lit is usually my favourite class but today my mind is wandering. Something about the sound and smell of fresh rain always distracts me. It's so mesmerising. I tune back into my teacher in time to hear her ask the class, "Had Romeo and Juliet known their fate, do you think they would have still begun their romance?"

I stop and think about that for a minute, bringing my mind back to task. *That's a really good question, isn't it? would you embark on a great love affair if you knew ultimately it would end both your lives? Would you even have a choice?* I try to imagine what it would be like to be that in love with someone; so in love that you would rather die than live without them. The hopeless romantic half of me thinks I would like to find out one day. The overthinking anxious half is terrified of the idea.

"Class dismissed," the teacher announces from the front of the room. I realise I was so wrapped up in my own thoughts I didn't even hear if anyone answered her question. I wonder if anyone thinks the same as me?"Where you at today, Abz?" My best friend gets up from her desk next to mine and looks at me with concerned blue eyes. Louisa is the only person who calls me Abz, it started when we were little.

"Sorry, I'm just really tired I guess." I shrug as I lift my backpack over my shoulder and walk out with her. "The end of term can't come quick enough; these deadlines are killing me!" I honestly don't think Louisa has any idea what it's like to worry about school.

"You give yourself way too much of a hard time you know? Cut yourself some slack and try to have fun. F-U-N remember that?" She stretches the word and widens her eyes to emphasise her point.

I roll my eyes at her but really, I do wish I could be more like Louisa. She's so carefree and always smiling. She never really worries about anything and she's so confident. I wish I could be that way too. Me, however, I'm a painful over-thinker and self-critic. I set my own bar so incredibly high that I can never reach it and spend most of my time beating myself up for it.

"You are still coming tonight, aren't you?" Louisa senses my hesitation and sticks out her bottom lip whilst making sad eyes at me.

"I don't know Lou, I've got so much work to do, I..."She interrupts me before I can think of any more reasons not to go to the party with her.

"Abbie Grace Daniels you promised me that you would come with me to this party! It's going to be the best one of the year! Everyone is going to be there!" She stops walking in the middle of the corridor and puts her hands on her hips almost tripping over a group of Year Nines coming along behind her.

"Fine," I say as I blow out a defeated breath. "You full named me so I know better than to argue with you. You clearly mean business, I'll be there."

"Perfect, I'll pick you up at eight." With that Louisa turns and walks down the corridor sporting a face-splitting grin with her brown curls bouncing as she goes. *Damn, I really do need to stay home and finish my assignment.* I let out a sigh as I head out the door. *What will I even wear?*

***

Just after eight, I hear Louisa sound her horn to let me know she's outside. I take one last look in the mirror before I turn to pick up my bag. I settled on a pair of dark, snug jeans with black heels and a simple black halter neck top that has an open back. My dark blonde hair is down and hangs in loose waves below my shoulders. I don't wear a lot of make-up generally but tonight I have a single sweep of black eyeliner across each lid and light lip gloss. I feel satisfied that I have achieved feminine but understated. I'm not one to draw attention to myself or the way I look. Most of the parties I've been to before are full of girls who are trying way too hard with their short skirts, cleavage-enhancing bras and foundation so thick you could dent it with your finger.

"Tell me again why you're so excited about this party?" I ask Louisa as we pull onto the enormous driveway and park the car.

"Because this is Harry's house, you know the guy from our Sociology class? His parents are out of town. He's invited the whole of Year Twelve! Rumour is he has a pool in the back garden!" She literally bounces up and down in the driver's seat with excitement. "I bet he'll have booze here and everything...not that I'll be drinking obviously!" she says as she jangles the car keys at me.

I think I like the sound of tonight less and less the more Louisa tells me. "Just don't hook up with some guy and abandon me again like last time." I grumble as we start to get out of the car. I look over at Louisa as she silently crosses her heart before marching off toward the house.

Looking up at the enormous house in front of me I can't believe how spectacular it looks. Harry's parents are clearly loaded. I think I heard someone say once that his parents are both lawyers which is probably just as well. With all the things I've heard about Harry's parties, he may well need a good lawyer one day!

These types of parties are a fairly regular occurrence at our school. It's quite prestigious and so there are many kids whose parents have an abundance of money and incredible houses, but are never around to actually parent their rogue teens. So, these wild house parties are the consequence. I'm not one of these kids. I had to work my butt off to get into this school and my parents carry the burden of the fees around their necks, so I *continue* to work my butt off to prove I deserve my place. I never used to even dream of attending these parties, but as the school year went on Louisa has worn me down and I've tagged along with her for the last few.

"Hurry up, Abz!" she yells. I do my best to keep up with her without falling on the gravel driveway in my heels. As we approach the front door, I can tell the party is already in full swing. The music is blaring so loud it makes my chest thump. The house is stunning inside but smells of beer and teenage boys. I stare up at the incredible chandelier above us in the hallway. *Their hallway is bigger than my lounge!* Louisa links her arm with mine and drags me towards the kitchen as she squeals and waves at some guys she knows. I internally eye roll. *This is going to be exactly like last time.*

Several hours later I'm sitting outside by the pool. *Yes, the rumours were true. there is indeed a pool.* I haven't seen Louisa for over an hour. *Typical.* I chatted with a few friends from my Psychology class earlier in the night before almost everyone at the party got too drunk to hold a proper conversation. Now I'm just bored. I've known pretty much everyone at this party since we all started school five years ago. Most of them I have no desire to stay in touch with once school is over and we all go off into the big wide world. Louisa is different, we've been friends since nursery. We are not at all alike, but maybe that's why we work.

Looking around the garden I breathe in the night air. The garden itself is beautiful, with fairy lights in the trees and modern sculptures dotted across the lawn. Its beauty, however, is ruined by the rowdy, drunken group of boys throwing each other in the pool and the multiple steamy make-out sessions that are taking place on various garden loungers. You know the type of drunk teenage snogging that is just a big messy grope fest? Then a fistfight breaks out over by the kegs, it would seem Jenny, from Politics, has been flirting again and her boyfriend, Steve, starts throwing punches. *Nothing ever changes.*

I decide to walk to the far end of the garden to try and get away from the noise and clear my head. I had a beer earlier which is now starting to take effect. I notice a gap in the perfectly manicured hedge that seems to lead to another part of the garden. As I put more distance between myself and the loud music, I feel much better. *I really can't stand dance music; totally not my scene.* I follow the gravel path that leads away from the main garden and down a few steps. I'm glad no one can see me as I must look ridiculous trying to navigate these steps in my heels. *These shoes were a mistake.* It's then I realise I can hear an acoustic guitar playing. *Now we're talking! Where is that coming from?* I round the corner of the hedged pathway and find it opens into a beautiful courtyard with an oak tree in the middle. More fairy lights hang in its branches, and lanterns decorate the edge of the space.

That's when I see him. The most incredible pair of chocolate eyes look up at me from under tousled brown hair. The guitar music stops just as I realise that Mr Chocolate Eyes was the one playing the guitar. He's sitting on a bench under the tree with the guitar on his lap. A tight black t-shirt that makes no secret of his more than adequate biceps and a pair of faded jeans hug all the right places. I swallow hard and press my lips together to make sure my jaw hasn't hit the floor. Then, just when I thought the view couldn't get any better, his face breaks into the most breath-taking smile I've ever seen. I think I forget to breathe for a second and my heart adopts a new rhythm all of its own.

"Not your kind of thing either, eh?" he asks, not letting the smile fade from his lips. *I think you're exactly my kind of thing.* I say to myself. Then I realise that although my brain is doing overtime, my lips and face are doing absolutely nothing. I have been rendered a silent, gawking idiot. He lets out a small chuckle and says, "The party music I mean."

"Right, yea of course. Err no not really, it's not my kind of music," I stammer as I try to string a coherent sentence together.

"And what is your kind of music...?" he stands and reaches to shake my hand as he waits for me to fill in the end of his question with my name. His eyes twinkle and that smile takes my breath away all over again.

"Abbie or sometimes Abz. Abbie Grace Daniels," I clarify as I take a step forward to take his hand.

"Lovely to meet you, Abbie Grace Daniels," he says as he takes my hand and shakes it. A shock of electricity starts at my palm where his hand holds mine and runs right through my body straight to my groin. *Holy shit, what was that?* He's so close I can smell his aftershave and it makes me dizzy.

"I'm Jake Greyson." He looks straight at me with those deep brown eyes and smiles again. I nod shyly in response as he releases my hand and I take a step back to try and regain some control over my senses. *Get it together Abbie!* I mentally chastise myself for my appalling lack of coherence.

"So, you haven't answered my question yet." He looks at me with a hint of amusement dancing around his lips. *Oh god, how embarrassing, he must get this reaction from girls all the time. I mean look at him!* I subtly clear my throat and swallow. *Talk to him, you idiot!* I am literally screaming at myself inside to do something other than stand and stare at his beautiful face.

Before I know what's happening, words just start pouring out of my mouth. "I'm sorry, I had a beer earlier and I think it went straight to my head, so I came out to get some air and get away from the music and all the idiots in there, but these shoes are killing me. I really shouldn't have listened to Louisa. Then I heard your guitar and wanted to see where it was coming from, and then I was so surprised that I was a bit speechless and, now oh my god I'm completely rambling and can't shut up apparently." *You. Fucking. Idiot.*

Jake laughs and flicks the hair out of his eyes. He puts one hand on my shoulder. *There goes that lightning bolt of electricity again.*

"Well, Abbie, that was a lot of information for a guy to take in in one go." He beams that megawatt smile at me again and I think he's genuinely amused at my idiocy rather than irritated.

I let out a sigh and bite my bottom lip. Something I do when I'm nervous, apparently. Louisa pointed it out to me before our mock exams last year.

"Can we start over?" I peer up at him shyly from under my lashes and I realise how much taller than me he is, even with these stupid heels on.

"Hi, I'm Abbie and I am definitely not crazy, despite how it may seem, and in answer to your question I love Indie rock mostly." I hold my breath and wait for a response.

"Me too," he says and holds my gaze for a second longer than necessary. "Would you like to sit with me?" He gestures to the bench for me to take a seat and then sits on the other side with his guitar back in place on his knee.

I relax ever so slightly and regain some sensible thought processes. No easy task when I can't get past how hot he is.

"So, where are you from, Jake? I've known everyone at this party forever, but I've never seen you before." *I would definitely remember*, I add in my head.

"I just finished school in London. I was in a pretty good music programme there. Harry's family have been friends with my dad since we were little, so we've come for the summer." A flicker of emotion crosses his face, but it's so quick I'm not sure what it was.

He starts to play the guitar and I instantly recognise the song. "I love this song." I smile as I watch his fingers work their magic.

"Well, you're full of surprises Abbie Grace Daniels." He doesn't stop playing, but he looks right at me and smiles a sexy, lopsided grin. "No one else has ever heard of this song." He looks impressed. All I can think about is how sexy it is to hear him say my full name.

"Carry on, it's amazing." I sit and watch him transfixed while he plays the rest of the song. I can't quite believe the surreal situation I find myself in. Watching quietly, I drink him in getting totally lost in the moment listening to the guitar, watching his expert fingers strum the strings and marvelling at the way his arms flex in his t-shirt as he plays. I realise then that the song is over, and he's finished playing. He puts his hand on the fretboard to still the strings as he looks at me.

"It's getting kind of cold out here. Want to go and get a drink?" I shiver as his words caress me, and I'm pretty sure it's not from the cold.

"Sounds great, but please don't laugh at me trying to walk along the path in these shoes. They were a major error in judgement."

I'm embarrassed just thinking about trying to walk in them in front of him. Before I realise what's happening Jake has dropped to his knees in front of me.

"Well, I'll just have to carry them for you." He gives me that look again, when he looks up at me through his unruly hair. That look of melted chocolate in his eyes that turns my insides to molten lava. And just like that, I have lost all ability to think or speak again.

He gently starts to take off my left shoe. His fingers brush along my ankle as he undoes the buckle and then down the top of my foot as he slides my shoe off. *Holy fucking shit.* I can feel my toes curling and my heart racing. This has to be the single most erotic moment of my life so far. *Granted my experiences in this area so far have been non-existent, but still.* He then repeats the action again with the other shoe, all the while his eyes never leave mine. I think I've forgotten how to breathe this whole time.

"Let's get you that drink, shall we?" he asks as he stands up with his guitar slung over one shoulder and my black heels in his hand. I nod, and stand up before realising that I have to get over the gravel path barefoot before we get to the grass again.

"Err Jake..." Just as I'm about to point out my predicament, he comes to the same realisation at the exact same time and a mischievous grin spreads over his face.

"Not a problem," he says and he picks me up in one swift movement and throws me over his shoulder fireman style! I squeal in shock and laugh uncontrollably as he marches down the path with me unceremoniously hanging over his shoulder. *Thank god I didn't wear a skirt!* I can't help but notice how his pecs feel against my thighs, he is rock solid.

Once he gets to the grass, he gently sets me down on my feet. As I straighten up his face is only inches from mine. He's so close I can feel his breath on my lips. I look into those beautiful eyes and hold my own breath as I become only too aware of his hand on my lower back where he put me down. It feels like heat is radiating from the point where our bodies meet and it's like nothing I've ever experienced before.

"Aaaabbz!!" Louisa's high-pitched screaming breaks through the magic of the moment. Jake reluctantly moves his hand and steps away as I turn to see what has got my friend in such a frenzy. I tear my eyes away from Jake and turn to see Louisa marching across the grass towards me with her bag and mine tucked under her arm.

"I've been looking everywhere for you!" she scolds. "Where were you?" She doesn't even seem to notice Jake standing there which tells me something is definitely wrong. Louisa always notices a good-looking guy. "You know what? It doesn't matter. We have to go. Come on!" She pulls me by the arm back towards her car.

"Wait, what? Why? What's going on?" I'm asking Louisa, but my eyes are on Jake. I don't want to leave, not now.

"Someone tipped the police off about the

party. There was a complaint about the noise and now they're on their way. We can't be caught here with alcohol when they do, Abz! You know my dad will kill me!" She tries to pull me towards the car as she explains.

I know she's right. My parents would be less than impressed if they knew this party had no parents present and copious amounts of alcohol. I don't turn seventeen for another few weeks, I'm one of the youngest in the year.

Reluctantly I take one last look at Jake and give him a weak smile as I take my shoes from him.

"Sorry, we really have to go." I feel a sudden sense of panic that I may never see him again. The thought of that is almost worse than the fear of getting in trouble. *This is crazy, I only just met him!*

We turn and run across the grass back to the car. As Louisa starts the engine and pulls away, I look back and see that Jake is still watching me. His eyes never leave mine as we drive away. He runs his hands through his hair as he watches and an emotion I can't place crosses his face. *Bye Jake.*

# Chapter 2

## Jake

I can't take my eyes off her as she leaves. I don't think I've ever seen anyone so beautiful in my life, and the best part is she clearly has absolutely no idea how stunning she is. This party was lame until she showed up and now, she's gone. Escaped into the night like fucking Cinderella – literally! I mean she almost forgot her shoes!

I run my hands through my hair as I watch the car turn out of the drive and disappear. *Why do I feel so deflated? I meet girls all the time, but not like her.* Most of the girls I talk to are so fake, with their 'trying too hard' outfits and their 'come fuck me' eyes. Abbie is none of those things. Her lack of confidence is endearing and actually quite refreshing, I feel this overwhelming need to want to take care of her but at the same time, she seems to have a direct line straight to my dick. The very fact she wasn't trying to be sexy makes her sexy as hell. *I have to see her again.*

At that moment I decide I'll talk to Harry. He goes to school with her, I'm sure he can make it happen. *Harry, shit!* Abbie's friend said the police were coming to break up the party. I better go help him sort this shit out.

I walk back towards the house in search of Harry and find him in the kitchen trying to rid the worktops of any evidence of alcohol.

"Jake man, where you been? The police are on their way." Harry looks pissed off as he shoves handfuls of empty cans and plastic cups into a bin bag.

"Yea, I heard. Your dad's the best lawyer around, he can make this go away, right?" I ask as I scoop up more cans.

"Not this time, bro, I promised my old man I wouldn't do this again. He's done bailing me out." Harry shoves drunken party goers out of the kitchen as he tidies.

Harry and I have known each other all our lives. He's a good friend, he just makes terrible choices most of the time. Although we've never lived that close to Harry and his parents, we have always stayed in touch. We used to go on holiday together every year as kids, but I haven't been there much for Harry over the last couple of years. My schedule was so intense while I studied that I never had time to leave London. I'm hoping to put that right while we are here for the summer.

The doorbell rings and Harry freezes. "Shit," he says as he ties a knot in the bin bag.

"Stay here, man. I got this." I slap Harry on the back in encouragement and go to answer the door.

I take a deep breath and open the door, "Good evening, Officer." I turn the Greyson charm up to maximum effect and hope for the best. *It can't hurt, right?*

***

Several hours later, Harry and I are just cleaning away the last remnants of the party.

"Listen, thanks again, man." Harry gives my shoulder a rough squeeze as I bend down to retrieve what turns out to be a lacy thong from the gap in the sofa cushions. *Classy.* I shove it in the bin bag as I smile at Harry. "I owe you one," he says.

"Ah don't worry about it. It's no big deal. I told the copper the party was my idea and you and your dad were out of town. He seemed like he couldn't be bothered with the paperwork so was happy with the promise of me turning the music down and being on my best behaviour." I grin at Harry, pleased with myself for how smoothly I pulled that off.

"I appreciate it Jake, my dad will go ape shit if he knows this happened again." Harry puts the last bag of rubbish outside the door and scans the room.

"Just an idea dipshit, but why don't you stop throwing these wild parties and pissing off your parents?" I ask, somewhat sarcastically.

Harry chuckles and rubs his chest. "I have a reputation to uphold. The ladies love it." He smiles a wolfish grin and opens himself a beer as he flops onto the sofa. "Anyway, I didn't see much of you during the party, where were you? D'ya get laid?" He wiggles his eyebrows in amusement.

"Na man, nothing like that." I pause before saying, "There was this girl, though." I run my hands through my hair in frustration at how she was there one minute and gone the next.

"You must take classes with her. Any chance you can put in a good word, mate?" I try to sound casual, but I'm desperate to see her again.

Harry lost interest the minute I said I didn't get laid and is now busy scrolling through Facebook on his phone. "Who is it?" he asks without even looking up from his screen. I didn't realise he was still listening to me.

"Abbie Daniels." Just saying her name stirs something inside me. *What is it about this girl?* I suddenly have Harry's full attention.

"Abbie? As in Louisa's friend Abbie? You're shitting me! You spoke to her?" he looks genuinely shocked.

I nod, waiting for Harry to elaborate.

"She's smoking hot man, but she doesn't even talk to guys, let alone date them. She's so elusive, like a fucking unicorn. The kind of girl everyone dreams about but no one's ever been there." Harry shakes his head in a mixture of shock and amusement.

I wonder if what Harry says is true. *How can that be possible? how can someone look like her and yet have never been with a guy?* The possibility of being all her firsts makes me excited and ner-

17

vous at the same time. Being a reasonably good-looking guitar player means everyone assumes I play the field and lost my virginity ages ago, but that actually couldn't be further from the truth. Everyone just assumes, and I don't correct them.

"Well, she spoke to me. I need to see her again, man. Can you sort something out?" I can't even try to act casual.

"Whatever you need my friend." Harry claps me on the back as he gets up and heads for the door.

"I'm going to bed. I'll message some people and sort something out." Harry yawns and leaves the room.

As I get ready for bed, all I can think about is her. Standing at the sink brushing my teeth in the mirror, I keep replaying meeting her repeatedly in my mind. The way she looked at me through those stunning long lashes and the incredible way she smelled still has my head spinning.

I finish in the bathroom and flop down on the bed, staring up at the ceiling. It's really comfy. I love staying at Harry's, it feels like home, strangely. I guess it's because Dad and I move around such a lot that Harry's house is one of the few constants I've had in my life. I lay there for ages, my mind full of thoughts of Abbie until I eventually drift off into a deep sleep.

*** 

I wake to the smell of bacon and

coffee. *Mmmm, that smells so good.* Harry's parents must be back. Julie makes the best breakfast and the smell makes me realise how hungry I am. I shower in a hurry and jog down the stairs to find Julie and Mac sat at the breakfast table with a very hungover-looking Harry slumped in his chair. My dad is nowhere to be seen. *Figures.* He's probably either still upstairs in bed or out in someone else's bed.

"Morning, love." Julie smiles warmly at me as she gets up from her breakfast. "What can I get you?"

"It's ok, stay there and finish your breakfast. I can help myself."

Julie sits back down, and I pour myself some coffee and grab a bacon sandwich off the counter. Julie is amazing, she's the closest thing to a mum I've ever had and she's always fussed over me like one of her own. I join them at the table and start eating my bacon sandwich. *It's superb.* Harry hasn't touched his yet. He's sitting with his head in his arms on the table.

"It's nice to see you didn't take part in whatever alcohol-fuelled debacle my son did last night, Jake. Maybe in a couple of years, Harry will also have more sense than to spend every weekend pickling his liver." Mac looks at us both over his morning newspaper as he throws disapproving looks at Harry. Harry doesn't look up to notice though, he's still got his face buried in his arms on the table.

I think Harry said he was going to tell his parents he went out drinking with friends to explain the hangover but I can't remember the cover story so I just shrug and smile politely at Mac who returns to his paper.

After breakfast Harry slopes back off to bed while I help Julie clear away the dishes. Once Mac leaves for his usual golf session, Julie comes and stands next to me at the sink.

"Thank you, Jake. I know Harry threw another party last night and it would have been you that got him out of trouble and made sure the house was clean so Mac wouldn't know. You're a good friend to him." She squeezes my forearm in appreciation and gives me a warm smile.

I turn to Julie. "How did you know?"

She chuckles as she picks up her handbag. "You two may fool Mac, but a mother always knows. Let's just say there were a few clues you missed in the tidy-up. Have a lovely day, darling, I'm off out now. If your dad comes back, tell him there's food for him in the fridge."

"Thanks, Julie," I say as she turns and leaves through the back door.

I climb the stairs and wander down the endless hallway to Harry's room. He's lying on his bed listening to some sort of god-awful club music. Harry and I have never agreed on our taste in music.

I take a seat in his huge leather gaming chair and swing on it.

"You didn't even seem drunk at the end of the party last night, man. What's up with you?" I look around his room as I wait for his response.

*He's such a fucking slob.* I feel sorry for the cleaner who has to pick up his shit every weekend.

"I know, I was fine. It's the tequila shots, man. They crucify me come morning." He throws his arm over his face in mock desperation. "I'll be fine by lunch."

I chuckle at him and shake my head. "So, what's your plan for me seeing Abbie again?"

"Actually, I did have a brainwave on that one, hence why I've had to lay back down." Harry laughs at his own joke, then sits up and pulls his phone from his pocket. "It just so happens we have a group assignment for Sociology, so I will message Louisa and organise a group study session for everyone here." He looks rather pleased with himself.

"Everyone? How big is the group?" I feel a sudden pang of jealousy at the thought of having to share her with a group of people.

"Err, there'll be six of us and you're welcome, doofus!" Harry throws a pair of balled-up socks at me before tapping away on his phone sending out the group message.

"I noticed your dad hasn't come home yet." Harry takes a more sombre tone. I know that look; it's sympathy. It's the same face everyone makes when they talk to me about my selfish asshole father. "Any idea where he is?"

I shrug and look at the floor. "No, probably in bed still with some prostitute or someone else's wife, I should imagine." I blow out a sigh. "It doesn't fucking matter. All the time he's out, he's not giving me a hard time. Every cloud and all that." I try to make light of the situation, but talking about my dad makes me uncomfortable.

"Anyway, you know your mum knows about the party last night, don't you?" I change the subject as quick as I can.

Harry laughs. "That sounds about right. Nothing gets past that woman. She's cool though. She never rats me out to Dad."

"Your mum is more than cool, she's an absolute legend." Everyone thinks Harry's mum is great. She's so laid back and easy-going. It makes no sense that she married someone like Mac, who is always one stressful situation away from a coronary.

"Alright, calm down. That's my mum, you keep your eyes and your dick to yourself." Harry looks disgusted, but I know he's only joking. I've practically grown up with Harry's family. Julie is like family to me; I could never think of her that way.

"You're such a dick, shut the fuck up." I throw the sock ball back at him and get him right between the eyes. "I'm going to play guitar in my room, catch you later."

# Chapter 3

## Abbie

**N**erves get the better of me as I arrive at the massive, gated driveway to Harry's house for the second time this week. Dad is dropping me off for a study session for our group Sociology project. It seems odd to me I had never been to Harry's house until last weekend, and now we are here again. Maybe Louisa has a thing for Harry? It was her who told me this had been arranged.

I thank Dad for dropping me off and climb out of the car. I take a deep breath and head towards the house. I'm really nervous. Jake said he is staying here for the summer. *I wonder if he's home?* I've thought about nothing but him since the party. I took extra care getting ready today in case he's here. Part of me desperately hopes he is but it terrifies the other part because I have no idea what to say to him. He's so gorgeous that he reduced me to a jabbering idiot when we met. I'm determined not to be like that this time. *I can do this.* I look down at my outfit to check everything is as it should be as I approach the front door. I wore tight, faded, ripped jeans with a plain white t-shirt and Converses. I have my straight hair down with some lip gloss, and my signature single sweep of eyeliner over each lid. *Here we go.*

I ring the doorbell and wait. I can hear Louisa inside already; she answers the door with a huge smile and pulls me in for a hug. Louisa's outfit choices are always bolder than mine, but I guess if I had a figure like hers, I'd want to show it off too. *If you've got it, flaunt it, right?* Today she's wearing denim shorts that make her legs look like they go on forever and a bright pink top with spaghetti straps that clings to all her feminine curves.

She takes my hand and leads me down the hallway towards the sound of more voices. We walk through into the kitchen; it looks even more stunning in the daylight without empty beer cans strewn all over it. There is a large island in the middle of the kitchen where some of the others already sitting on high stools. The counter top looks like some sort of glossy marble and there is every type of mod con known to man in here. It's like the kind of kitchen you'd expect a top chef to own. *I wonder if they even cook in it?*

I realise I'm one of the last to arrive. Harry is leaning against the counter and now talking to Louisa. I can tell by the way she keeps twirling her hair around her finger that she's into him. *I thought as much.* I make a mental note to make sure I ask her about Harry later when we're on our own.

A girl called Steph is sitting at the counter laughing and flirting with Miles. I like Miles, he's quiet and actually pretty funny, but Steph is a total bitch. I have as little to do with her as possible, but unfortunately, she was grouped with us for this assignment. She's so fake; we are here for a study session and yet she has turned up looking like she's auditioning for a glamour shoot. There's more boob out of her top than in it and with a skirt that short it will be a miracle if I make it out of here without having seen her underwear. I internally eye-roll at the sight of her. *She really pisses me off.* Austin is the only one from the group not here yet, and I can't help but notice there's no sign of Jake in the house yet. I'm not sure if I'm disappointed or relieved.

I stand awkwardly in the doorway, not wanting to interrupt Harry and Louisa, but definitely not wanting to sit with Steph. Luckily, Louisa senses my discomfort and saves me.

"Abz, have a drink, there's juice or Coke on the side and we're ordering pizza. Just let Harry know what you like before he texts it through."

"Ok, thanks." I grab a can of Diet Coke and pull the ring. I take a seat on the stool next to Louisa and sip my drink. Looking up, I see Jake come through the doorway into the kitchen wearing a tight white t-shirt with a band logo on the front and black shorts. *Holy shit, he's even hotter than I remember.* I force myself to swallow my drink before I spit it everywhere. He looks straight at me and smiles that ridiculously sexy smile of his. I feel my cheeks flush as I smile back.

"Everyone, this is my friend, Jake," Harry

announces as Jake makes his way over to the fridge and takes out a carton of milk. Jake nods at the group before draining the carton of milk, his eyes on me the entire time.

"Jake, this is Louisa, Miles and Steph and I'm pretty sure you've already met Abbie." Harry grins cheekily at Jake. *I wonder if Jake talked to Harry about me?*

I take my eyes off Jake long enough to look round the group as they are all introduced to him. It's then I realise Steph is practically drooling at the sight of Jake. Miles having quickly been forgotten.

"Nice to meet you, Jake. Harry said you're in a band, is that right?" she purrs at him as she thrusts her chest out even further. *As if he could have missed the Grand Canyon sized cleavage she has on display.*

"Yeah, that's right," Jake says dismissively without even looking at Steph. He's still watching me from across the kitchen. I feel self-conscious and look down at my lap. When I look up Jake is walking straight past Steph and Miles and comes over to where I'm sitting. He picks up one of the text books I've put on the counter and fans the pages with his thumb.

"So, what is it you guys are doing today?" The question could be for anyone, but he is still looking directly at me. My eyes dart over to Steph. *She looks really annoyed; she's not at all used to being ignored.* Then I look back at Jake realising he's waiting for me to answer his question.

"Err, it's a group Sociology assignment

about what attracts people to one another." I remember to breathe as an afterthought. *Why can I not function around this guy? I'm as pathetic as Steph.*

Jake's eyes seem to twinkle even more in amusement, he leans in closer to me and drops his voice so only I can hear. "I see, well I'd be very interested to hear what you find."

Before I can think of anything witty to say back, or anything at all in fact, he turns and starts to head back out the door. "I'm going for a swim," he calls over his shoulder to Harry as he walks out.

"I vote we sit outside and study," Steph says as she reapplies more lip gloss. "The view is amazing." She looks at me and smirks. She is obviously talking about Jake. *Back off, bitch.*

"Na, the wi-fi signal isn't great out there, let's go to the dining room. Anyone got an issue with pepperoni before I send the order through?" Harry asks as he starts to gather up the books we need and take them to the dining room.

It takes forever for everyone to get organised and ready to study. Louisa is too busy flirting with Harry and Miles is looking more bored by the minute. We got a message to say Austin wasn't coming because he is sick, which leaves him sat between me and Steph. Steph is busy texting and chewing gum instead of having pizza with us. Apparently 'that would be a disaster for her figure.' *Give me a break. A girl has to eat!*

Finally, we start the assignment and I'm

given the task of taking notes. Miles is talking about laws of attraction and he's actually quite smart. I write frantically trying to keep up with him. Just then I see Jake outside from the corner of my eye. I stop writing mid-sentence and turn to watch him. He walks across the garden towards the pool wearing the same black shorts, but he's now shirtless. *Bloody hell, he's every teenage girls' fantasy.* I rest my chin on my hand so I know my mouth is closed as I watch him. I can see every muscle in his chest and arms. He has the most incredible tan. I can see there's a small tattoo on his upper left arm but he's too far away to make it out. *I wonder what it would be like to trace my fingers over those muscles and tattoo?* I watch as he breaks into a jog and dives effortlessly into the pool. *He definitely works out.*

When he resurfaces, his hair is all wet and drips run down his face and along his strong jawline. He runs his hands through his wet hair and his chest is glistening wet. *Jeez, this is more than I can handle.* He turns and ducks back under the water as he swims lengths. It's then I realise I had totally forgotten I was in a room full of people and meant to be listening and taking notes. Everyone is staring at me. Harry and Louisa look amused, Steph just glares.

"Welcome back, Abbie." Harry chuckles, clearly amused by my blatant ogling and daydreaming. "Something more interesting outside?"

"Err no, sorry." I must be the brightest shade of scarlet because my cheeks are burning with embarrassment. I pick up my pen again, realising I wasn't even holding it anymore. "Carry on, Miles," I say as I drop my head to carry on with the task in hand.

Over the next hour, I put all my efforts into not looking out the window at Jake. I keep my head down as I write, in an attempt to block out the temptation. This assignment is worth a lot of marks. *I really need to focus.* I have managed to keep up with the note taking, but my mind keeps wandering back to Jake. *Is he still in the pool? Is he still wet and shirtless? Stop it, Abbie, concentrate.* This entire study session has been an internal struggle between the sensible half of me who knows I need to focus and the other side of me that's been awoken by Jake. The side of me that can't stop fantasising about this guy I've barely met.

Finally, the study session comes to an end and everyone breaks off for a well-earned rest. Steph mutters something about having better things to do with her time and leaves. *Thank God.* I stretch in my seat; my neck is aching from taking notes for so long.

"Abz, are you ok to hang here with me for a bit longer?" Louisa tries to sound casual, but her eyes are gesturing to Harry.

"Sure, I'm just going to find the bathroom." I stand and stretch again. *I really must sit up straighter when I work.* Louisa smiles and grabs a slice of cold pizza.

"Ok, meet us in the lounge," she says as she takes a bite.

I realise as I head up the stairs and along the hallway that I have absolutely no idea where the bathroom is. *I should have asked Harry before I wandered off. This place is like a maze.*

Most of the doors to the rooms are shut, so I assume they are bedrooms. *I wonder which one is Jake's?* The next door ahead of me on the left is slightly ajar, so I think there's a fairly good chance this is the bathroom. I push it open gently and find a room with at least six different guitars lined up on stands along the far wall. *Whoah, they're incredible!* I've always loved guitars and wished I could play, but I don't have a musical bone in my body. So instead, I just admire those that can. *These must be Jake's.* I take a step into the room to get a closer look. There are four electric guitars and two acoustic. One of them is bright red with silver edging and another one has intricate swirling artwork across it. I get closer so I can touch them. They are polished to a beautiful shine. I run my fingertips gently down the strings of one when I hear someone clear their throat from behind me.

*Holy shit.* I turn to see Jake standing in the doorway on the other side of the room, wearing just a towel around his waist and leaning on the door frame. He's still dripping wet and shirtless, but this time he's clearly just got out of the shower. The sight is even sexier up close.

"Like anything you see?" he asks, grinning at me in that mischievous way that he does.

Once again, I'm rendered speechless and have to put all my energy into keeping my eyes on his face and not letting them roam over his perfect torso.

"The guitars," he nods his head to the guitars behind me. "You said before that you like that kind of music." He must know the effect he has on me and is playing on it.

*Stop being a loser, Abbie, and talk to him. He's just a guy.*

"Sorry, I didn't mean to be nosey. I was looking for the bathroom when I saw your guitars. It's an impressive collection." I drop my eyes to the floor and bite my lip. I don't even know where to look. *What is appropriate in this situation?* This is totally uncharted territory for me. Jake on the other hand seems more than comfortable standing there in nothing but a towel, having a casual conversation.

"Thanks," he holds my gaze as he talks. *He's so intense.* "So, are you guys all finished with your studying?"

I nod at him, still struggling to pull my thoughts into any kind of order.

He stands up off the doorframe and takes a step closer to me. "And what did you learn today about attraction?" He's looking at my lips now as he talks. *This isn't in my head; he knows exactly the effect he has on me and is playing with me.*

I can't help but smile, though. His grin is so infectious. *How can someone be so mischievously cheeky, but intensely sexual at the same time?* I manage to draw up some courage from way down deep somewhere and answer him.

"Rather a lot, actually." This time I allow

my eyes to unashamedly roam over his chest and back up to his eyes. *Ok, where has this flirty bravery appeared from? This is so unlike me.*

"Well, give me five minutes to get dressed and you can tell me all about it." He rearranges the towel with both hands before turning towards the wardrobe. *Eyes up, Abbie.*

"Oh, and Abbie… the bathroom is the next door along," he says from the wardrobe.

"Right, yes, of course. See you in a bit." *How embarrassing.* He practically just asked me to leave so he can get dressed in peace without me staring at him. I hurry out of the room as my cheeks return to a familiar shade of crimson.

\*\*\*

Over the next few hours, I totally relax. I sit with Louisa, Harry, Miles and Jake while we talk, laugh and joke. I feel so comfortable and have had so much fun that I've almost forgotten how attracted to him I am. *Almost.* There is so much more to him though than just his looks. He's hilarious and clearly very talented. I've learnt all about his band and his life in London.

Louisa and Harry have been getting on well. *That's an understatement.* They have openly flirted the entire time, but it's kind of sweet. She's barely looked at anyone else.

"Louisa, we need to leave in about ten for the cinema," I remind her.

"Ok," she reluctantly gets up and everyone takes that as their cue to gather their stuff.
Jake stands and touches my forearm. "Be right

back," he murmurs, and my arm tingles where he touched me.

I go back to the dining room and gather up my books in my bag, grabbing my phone and purse. *Where are my shoes?* I thought I took them off by the front door as I came in, but they're not there. Checking the kitchen, I still can't find them. I go back to the now empty lounge and look under the sofas. Everyone must be outside saying goodbye. *Where the hell are my shoes?* Then I spot my Converses neatly sitting under the bookcase over the far side of the room. *That's weird, I didn't even come over this side of the room.* I go over and pick them up.

I sense Jake come up behind me. I don't know how I know it's him; I just do. He has a certain presence. He's standing so close we're almost touching, but not quite. I feel his breath against my neck as he whispers in my ear. "I see you found your shoes. I didn't hide them well enough." Goosebumps spread from my neck where his breath touched me all the way down my spine. "The longer it took you to find them, the longer you'd have to stay."

A nervous smile crosses my face. Inside I'm doing cartwheels at what he just said, but I try to play it cool. I turn slowly to face him. Our faces are only centimetres apart.

"You hid my shoes so I'd be here longer?" I ask before biting down on my lip and staring into his eyes. He nods silently, his eyes never leaving my lips. I hold my breath and wait for him to kiss me. *Please kiss me.*

Right on cue Louisa bursts into the room completely oblivious to the perfect moment she just ruined – again! *For fuck's sake.*

"Oh great, you found your shoes. Come on, let's go or we'll be late for the film." With that, she spins and bounces out of the room.

I sheepishly look back at Jake. I don't know what to say or do now. Louisa just deflated the moment like a balloon after a birthday party. Now I feel awkward. *Would he have kissed me if she hadn't come in?*

He gives me a lopsided smile and runs his hand through his hair. *God, I love it when he does that.*

"So, maybe I could take your number? Louisa can't interrupt a text message, can she?" He laughs but looks almost nervous asking me. *That can't be true. He's so confident.*

I hand him my phone so he can save his number to it and he does the same. As I take his phone, I notice his background picture is of an album cover I love. I smile to myself as I type in my number.

"Why are you smiling?" he asks with a twinkle in his eyes.

"I love this band." I gesture to his phone screen as I hand it back "But do I need a reason to smile?" I can't help it when I'm around him; he's so infectious.

"No, not at all. You should do it all the time. It's beautiful." If at all possible, I think my smile gets even bigger. Jake gets more perfect by the minute.

"ABBIE!" Louisa shouts from somewhere down the hall.

"I have to go," I say to Jake reluctantly. "It was nice to see you again."

As I turn and leave, I can feel him watch me walk away.

"I'll text you," he calls after me and I smile all the way to the car.

# Chapter 4

## Jake

Now that I've seen Abbie again, I have this weird sense of calm. She's like Chicken Soup for the Soul. Ever since I met her at the party, I had felt agitated and anxious to see her again and now that I have, all's right with the world. Surely, it's not normal to be so affected by someone so fast, is it? I hope I played it right. I was surprisingly nervous, but I didn't want her to know that. Girls want confidence, not pussies. But they don't want arrogant pricks either. *Ugh. Who the fuck knows what girls want?* I probably should have toned down the nudity though. It was only the second time we've met. Still, it's not my fault she wandered into my room while I was showering, is it? Hiding her shoes was a lame move, but I wasn't ready for her to go. She was blatantly checking me out though, and she smiled a lot today. I'm going to take those as good signs. That smile of hers does things to my insides.

I take my phone out of my back pocket, really wanting to text her. *Is it too soon?* I have no idea how this works. *Play it cool, man.* Looking at the clock, it's been three hours since I watched her sexy arse walk out of here. Her film is probably finishing about now. *One text can't hurt, can it?*

**How's the film? Jx**

She texts straight back, another good sign.

**Boring actually. What you been up to? X**

*Hmm, what shall I say back? Oh, sod it, I'm laying all my cards on the table.*

**Thinking about you. You never did tell me what you learnt about the laws of attraction today. Jx**

Well, it's out there now, may as well flirt up a storm. I hope she's smiling as she reads this. There's a delay this time. *Shit. Maybe that was too much too soon. Man, navigating girls is hard.* My phone vibrates:

**Like attracts like. If you want something badly enough then with the right mental attitude you can make it yours... or so the theory says x**

I grin like an idiot. I like this more confident side of Abbie. The side when she relaxes and isn't nervous. I saw a glimpse of her earlier. I know she's in there.

**I whole-heartedly agree. Jx**

I put my phone down then pick it back up. I'm going to invite her to my gig on Saturday.

**My band are playing at The Rose pub on Saturday. Just a small gig to keep us sharp over**

the summer. Would you like to come? Jx

Sounds great. What time? X

*I just asked out Abbie Daniels, and she said yes*. I would high five myself if I could. *Does this count as a first date?*

7ish. See you then. Jx

I feel ten feet tall right now. Today has left me with a warm, content feeling. *God, I'm such a sap. Where have I left my balls?* Saturday's performance needs to be top-shelf. I might text the boys and arrange a rehearsal.

Just then I hear a door slam downstairs and raised voices. *Dad's back.* I haven't seen him for several days. This is what he does, just disappears for days on end. I've never heard him argue with Mac before though. I head down the stairs to listen in. As I approach the kitchen, I can hear Mac whispering angrily.

"You have to tell him, Harvey. You can't keep doing this to him."

I push the door open and they both go quiet. "Tell who what?" I look between them both with my arms folded across my chest.

My dad's a big guy, but I think I have the edge these days, much to his annoyance. "What are you arguing about?" I look at Dad.

Mac mutters something about this being between us and excuses himself from the room.

"Nothing you need to worry about." he says dismissively. *Man, he really pisses me off. He's only been back two minutes and he's already ruined my good mood.*

"Where have you been all weekend?" I ask, still glaring at him with my arms folded.

He smirks at me as he grabs himself something to eat from the fridge. "That's none of your concern Jake, I'm the parent round here, not you."

"Could have fooled me," I mutter angrily.

His temper flashes and, he raises his voice. He's always been erratic and unpredictable. *He's a freakin' nut job.*

"Remember who you're speaking to, Son. You might think you're all grown up these days, but I'm still your father and you will show me some respect!" He's so angry, he's practically spitting the words at me. *Whatever has gone on with him and Mac has got him rattled.*

"Respect has to be earned… *Dad.*" I emphasise the last word for sarcastic effect and turn my back on him before leaving the room. I hear banging and crashing in the kitchen as I walk away. No doubt he's taking his frustrations out on Julie's crockery. *Arsehole.*

This is how it's always been with me and Dad. We've always clashed and butted heads. I've always resented him for moving us around so much and him never being there for me. I think if truth be known, he resents me too for being left with me when Mum died. I was only little. I don't really remember her. I've only ever known it to be me and Dad. I sometimes wonder how things would have been different if she hadn't died. *It's probably for the best, she'd only be as mis-*

*erable as I am living with that selfish bastard.*

I head back to my room. It's probably best to just let this blow over, whatever it is. I pick up my favourite acoustic guitar and play. It's my go-to response for most things. Playing has always made me feel better, or helped me escape, whichever I need. I think about Abbie while I play; she is fast becoming my new happy place. She looked so beautiful today and she does it without even realising it. She's just naturally gorgeous, even when she's not trying to be. The complete opposite to that other bimbo here today. I can't even remember her name, but she was dressed like a hooker and fluttering her eyelashes at me. I meet girls like that all the time in London. Do they not know how ridiculous they look? She literally had everything hanging out on display for all to see and yet I couldn't have cared less what was squeezed into that trashy outfit. Abbie on the other hand doesn't make any show of her incredible curves, but they lure me in all the more because of it. She's so easily flustered and embarrassed too, which is quite adorable and good fun. I've decided bringing a flush to her cheeks is my new favourite thing to do.

I consider texting her, but I don't want to come on too strong, too quick. Saturday feels like a lifetime away until I can see her again. My thoughts are interrupted by a knock at my bedroom door.

"Can I come in, sweetheart?" Julie's gentle voice asks from the hall.

I put the guitar back and open the door

for her. She looks concerned, but still greets me with a smile.

"Sorry Julie, was I playing too loud?" I ask as she comes in and sits beside me on the bed.

"No darling, it was wonderful as always. I just wanted to check in with you and see how you're doing. I heard what happened with your dad." She gives my arm a reassuring squeeze. She really is the nicest person.

"I'm fine thanks, Julie, just Dad being Dad. Sorry if he broke anything downstairs."

"You're such a sweet boy. Always thinking of others. Try not to be too hard on him darling, everyone is fighting battles no one else can see." Julie always sees the good in everyone, even when you have to look really hard.

"I think it's just me he's always at war with." I have little empathy for my dad's shortcomings as a father.

"It might surprise you, Jake, but he's not always the monster you think he is." She waits for a response, but I just play with the edge of my duvet.

"As long as you're ok, darling, I'll leave you to it." She gives my arm another squeeze before leaving the room.

I stand little chance of getting any sleep right now. My mind is way too busy from all of the day's events. *I need to go for a run.* I head down to Harry's room to see if he wants to join me. I find him sat on his bed with his headphones in. *Listening to crap again, more than likely.*

I mouth and motion with my arms, "Want

41

to go for a run?" He nods.

Harry and I have fallen into this pattern since I came to stay. We often run together first thing in the morning or late at night. We both like to keep our fitness up. Harry plays football and loves the attention his six-pack gets him from girls. Me, because performing in the band and lugging all the gear around is surprisingly physical, so it helps to stay in good shape.

We jog down the long gravel driveway and out onto the street, keeping a steady pace. As we round the corner Harry's phone beeps and he smiles as he reads the message. I raise an eyebrow in question.

"That smile only means one thing, bro. Who's the girl? Is it Louisa? You two seemed pretty friendly earlier." I know I won't have to probe him; he tells me everything. Often way more than I need to know.

"Yeah, she's pretty cool. Great pair of tits." He laughs as we keep running. *Typical Harry, all the class and decorum of a caveman.*

"Is it serious?" I know the answer before I even finish the question but you never know, one day he might surprise me.

"Of course not. Just a bit of fun."

"Does she know that?" I ask him. I'm starting to sound a bit out of breath now. We've run a fair distance.

"Yeah man, I won't make that mistake again. I told her this is just a summer thing."

Last year Harry broke a few hearts over the course of the summer and the girls teamed up and got their revenge by way of chilli flakes in his football shorts.

He grabs his crotch as he runs. "It makes my dick burn just remembering that."

I laugh out loud as we jog up the hill. "Race you back" I shout as I break into a sprint. I don't stand much chance of winning; Harry is so much faster than I am, but it feels good to push myself. As predicted, he overtakes me with ease and sprints back to the house. I bring up the rear a minute or two later, seriously out of breath.

\*\*\*

The next few days come and go without incident. I throw myself into my rehearsals with the boys, and I'm feeling good about Saturday's gig. I haven't seen much of Dad, which is always a bonus; he's fucked off somewhere again. I don't know why Julie and Mac put up with him. He literally treats their house like a hotel when we stay.

There's only one more day until I get to see Abbie again. I've been counting down the days. *I really need to get a grip. This girl has me by the balls already and she doesn't even know it.* We've exchanged a lot of messages over the week, just casual chit chat mostly with the odd bit of flirting here and there. She lives such a normal, settled life. It must be nice to have grown up in one place with people around you that you can rely on. She plans on going to Uni when she finishes school and getting her teaching degree. I wish I had a plan like that. My main ambition in life is to not end up like my old man. Other than that, I guess I'll just have to wait and see what life throws at me. Music is my passion, that's what I love, but I know there's no guarantees I can make any money out of it.

When I get back from rehearsal, dinner is on the table and everyone is sat down to eat. Even my dad. Julie smiles at me and gestures to the empty seat.

"We saved you a plate darling, we've only just started. Hope you're hungry," she says. Dad doesn't even look up.

"Thanks Julie, it looks delicious." I take my seat at the table and start to eat the carbonara which Julie knows is my favourite.

"How was rehearsal man?" Harry asks with a mouthful of pasta. Julie swats him on the arm to remind him of his manners.

"Yeah, it's sounding good. I think the boys are finding it a strain to keep travelling down here from London all the time but it's not for much longer."

Dad looks up and wipes his mouth on his napkin as if he is about to speak. He never has anything to say about my band. He's never even been to a gig. All my guitars I have saved for and bought myself.

"We won't be going back to London after the summer, Jake." he says, flatly.

*Here we go again. Where are we going this time?* This is exactly why I never plan for the future.

"Where are we going then?" I stab my fork into my pasta and twirl it round aggressively as I wait for him to answer.

"I haven't ironed out all the details yet so I can't say for sure, but it won't be London. There's a potential business investment I may need to pursue in the States." He says it so matter-of-factly as if he's just suggested we get ice-cream.

"The States?" I roll my eyes and scoff. "Not this again, you've been threatening to move us overseas for as long as I can remember." Julie and Mac keep their eyes on their food trying not to get involved.

"Just don't get too comfy, Jake. We aren't staying." He stands up and goes to scrape his plate.

*As if I ever could. I don't stay anywhere long enough.* The longest we've ever stayed in one place was London for the past two years while I finished my music programme. Other than that, we have always moved. I attended six different schools as a kid, which made making friends and keeping them hard. Harry and his family have been my only constant.

After dinner I head up to take a shower. I text Abbie to see what she's doing. I get this gnawing feeling down deep somewhere that pursuing things with Abbie might not be for the best if we're going to up and leave again, but I shake the feeling away. Just as I'm about to step under the water she texts back. I probably shouldn't be as pleased as I am right now.

## Watching tv in bed x

The mental image makes me smile and gives me something to think about as I let the hot water run over me.

# Chapter 5

## Abbie

It's Saturday night and I've just arrived at The Rose. I look around the pub trying to see Jake. Feeling like a fish out of water, I try to fight off the rising sense of panic that's building. I hate walking into places on my own, but Louisa already had plans. *Suck it up.* I decide to go to the bar and order a Diet Coke. That'll give me something to do while I calm my nerves and look for Jake. I'm not old enough to order anything stronger, so that will have to do. I stand at the bar and wait my turn. The pub is busy and loud so this could take a while.

As I search for my purse in my bag, I feel a pair of strong, muscular arms wrap around my waist from behind and my whole body breaks out in goosebumps. *Jake Greyson.*

"You're here," he says in my ear before kissing me on the cheek from where he stands behind me. His close proximity is making me dizzy. *Will I ever be able to think straight around him?*

I turn to look at him and smile. He's wearing a checked shirt rolled up to the elbows over his t-shirt and a pair of black jeans. His hair is all messy and gorgeous, like he just got out of bed. His eyes are alive with mischief as usual, but there's an extra buzz of excitement about him. Maybe this is how he is before he performs.

"Let me get you a drink." He gestures to the barmaid. She smiles and flutters her eyelashes at Jake as she heads straight over to take his order. *Ugh. Funny how you didn't notice me standing here, silly cow.* I don't know why I'm surprised; I imagine Jake gets this kind of reaction wherever he goes.

Jake orders himself an energy drink before turning to me.

"Just a Diet Coke please." I say to him. While the barmaid disappears off to get our drinks, Jake leans in and tucks a loose strand of hair behind my ear.

"You look lovely," he says while his fingers linger in my hair. "I'm glad you came."

"Thank you, me too." I changed my outfit three times before finally settling on a pair of cropped black leggings and a lacey grey top that hangs over them. I've never been to anything like this before, so I didn't know what was the right thing to wear. Looking around though, I think I've managed the right mix of casual and dressy.

Jake takes a long swig of his drink before setting it down on the bar. "We'll be playing soon. Are you going to be ok on your own? We can get you a space right next to the stage so I know where to find you."

I smile at his thoughtfulness and nod appreciatively.

\*\*\*

Watching Jake perform on stage has got to be the single most sexy thing I have ever witnessed. He's so confident and powerful up there. I stare in awe as I watch him play the opening song. *That voice.* It's enough to bring any girl to her knees. I don't think there's a single girl in here not undressing him with her eyes right now, wishing they could be that guitar. He handles it like a pro.

Jake looks around the crowd as he sings and plays until his eyes settle on me. He breaks into an earth-shattering grin and winks at me. *Dear God.* My insides flip over and my groin tingles in appreciation. He's playing with so much force that he's glistening with sweat across his forehead and the muscles in his arms are straining his t-shirt. *I think I've actually died and gone to heaven.*

I watch like this for the next five or six songs, totally lost in my own desire. *I hope no one can tell just how turned on I am right now.* I fidget in my seat a little, remembering that I am in a crowded pub and glance down at the table to double check I haven't been dribbling this whole time. Taking a piece of ice out of my glass, I pop it in my mouth hoping to cool the heat in my face.

By the time the last song ends, Jake is pumped with adrenaline and the atmosphere in the room is electric. He has the whole pub eating out the palm of his hand. The room breaks out into applause and cheers. There are even some shout outs for an encore.

With the room still shouting and applauding, I stand up to go in search of Jake. Going through the door that must lead round the back of the stage, I walk down the corridor; I see him at the other end with the rest of the band. He catches sight of me and immediately puts down the bottle of water he's chugging. He winks at me and smiles, holding his arms out for me.

As I approach, I say, "Jake, that was absolutely incredible!" but he cuts me off picking me up and spinning me round in the air. I squeal in surprise and as he lowers me to my feet, his mouth finds mine, and he brings me in for the most heart-stopping kiss. *Our first kiss.* His tongue unashamedly explores my mouth. He's still a little breathless from his performance. *Or maybe our kiss?* His t-shirt is damp with sweat and he smells like the most divine mix of sweat and aftershave. Not a combination I ever considered sexy before, but right now it's glorious. The adrenaline and excitement clearly still coursing through his veins from performing. *I love how much he loves it.* He continues to kiss me as his breathing and heart rate begin to return to normal. His hand's buried in my hair, keeping us as close to each other as possible. *Wow, I've been kissed before... but never like this.* There is something so raw about Jake.

All too soon, he slows his tongue and gently licks across my bottom lip before kissing me on the lips. *Bloody hell, I can't even think straight.*

"Thank God, Greyson, I thought you were never going to put her down." I tear my eyes off Jake to see one of the other band members put his hand out in greeting.

"Hi, I'm Dan, you must be Abbie."

I step back from Jake so I can shake Dan's hand. I feel a little embarrassed now I realise they all saw that. "Yes, nice to meet you."

I give Jake a quizzical look. "You talked about me?"

He smiles in response.

"Correction. He never *stops* talking about you." Dan laughs. Jake gives him a playful punch on the arm, but doesn't deny it.

"Well now, you've finished sucking face, any chance you can actually help us pack up, Greyson?"

\*\*\*

I spend the next week on some sort of euphoric high from my kiss with Jake. I've either been floating around the house in a world of my own, or staring out the window at school. It's a good job there are only three more days of term left and that most of the big assignments are done, because I can't concentrate on anything. Jake has messaged me every day since, and we have spoken on the phone a couple of times. We have plans to see each other later today.

"Hello love," Mum walks into the lounge where I'm sitting. The tv is on, but I'm not watching it. I'm scrolling through job ads on my phone trying to find weekend work.

"Hi Mum," I look up from my phone to see she's brought me in a mug of hot chocolate with cream on top, just how I like it. She takes a seat next to me on the sofa.

"How's the job hunting going?" she asks as she flicks through the tv channels.

"Nothing so far. Everyone wants someone with experience. How are you supposed to get experience if no one gives you a start?" This is something that really frustrates me.

"I know love, try not to lose heart. Something will come up. So, tell me more about this Jake you've been texting all week." She's trying to look like she's watching tv and not at all interested, but I know Mum, she's *very* interested.

I can't help but smile at the mention of his name. "He's nice. I met him through a friend at school."

I tell Mum all about him and she pretends

to casually listen, but I know she's making mental notes on everything I'm saying.

"He plays the guitar you know." I throw into the conversation.

Mum raises her eyebrows. "Oh, that's exciting... good with his hands then." She jokes.

"Mum!" I shout, shocked. I'm still getting used to how openly she talks to me about boys as I've gotten older.

"Well, have a lovely time tonight angel." Mum says as I get up to go and get ready.

***

Jake meets me outside the cinema, and he greets me with a smile and a kiss. The kind of kiss that makes your insides melt. He's chewing gum and I can taste the mint on his breath.

"Remind me again what this film is about?" I ask him as we get in line.

He takes my hand and his fingers thread through mine. I love the gesture, but the physical contact makes it hard to think straight.

"I have absolutely no idea." He grins as he strains his neck to read the snack options without letting go of my hand.

"Why are we seeing it then?" I laugh.

Jake leans in close and wraps his arms around me. "I have no intention whatsoever of watching this film. There are far more interesting things to look at... like my girl," he whispers in my ear before kissing just below it.

*His girl.* The words have my heart racing and my pulse thumping. He makes me so nervous, but in the best way.

True to his word, Jake barely looks at the screen the entire time. He sits in the dark watching me. He never breaks contact the whole way through, either holding my hand, kissing me, or tracing his fingertips up and down my thigh. *What did I ever do to deserve this guy? He's so damn hot, but it's more than that; he makes me feel like I'm the only one in the room. What on earth does he see in me?*

As we leave the cinema hand in hand, I see Steph heading towards us with some guy I don't recognise wrapped round her. *Ugh, please keep walking. I don't want her to ruin my night.* She immediately sees Jake and smiles. I swear she straightens up to subtly stick her chest out further. *Seriously?*

"Oh Jake, so nice to see you again," she gushes and rests her hand on Jake's forearm. He doesn't react in any way other than to squeeze my hand a little tighter. "I almost didn't recognise you with your shirt on." She giggles at her own joke. This is clearly an attempt to make her date jealous and me uncomfortable. *She is unbelievable.* Her date raises his eyebrows and looks between Steph and Jake in question.

"Jake was in a pool the last time we saw each other," she clarifies "Jake's a guitarist Scott, isn't that awesome?" She places her hand on this guy's chest as she speaks, but doesn't take her eyes off Jake.

Scott doesn't say anything. He just glares at Jake. Steph's attempts to rattle him are clearly working. I unintentionally clear my throat and Steph then looks me up and down.

"Oh Abbie, I barely noticed you there. How nice of Jake to take you out while he's in town before he goes back to London for bigger and better things." *What. A. Bitch.* I would love nothing more than to smack her in the damn face, but I don't.

With that, Jake turns to me and pulls me in for a kiss. He presses tight up against me and makes a real show out of how much he's enjoying it. When he breaks away, I'm out of breath.

"Actually Steph, there is *nothing* better. I already found the best." He looks at me and squeezes my hand. "You guys enjoy your night."

He smiles politely at Steph and Scott before leading me away by the arm, leaving Steph standing there with her mouth open like a fish. I'm not sure who's more shocked; her or me. As we walk away arm in arm, I can't stop smiling. *Jake just stood up for me in front of Steph.*

Jake drives me home and walks me to the front door in the dark. "Thank you for earlier," I say to him, looking at the floor. I'm not sure what to do at the end of a date. I've never been dropped home before.

"What for? It was a terrible movie." He laughs and shoves his hands in his jean pockets.

"It was, wasn't it?" I laugh too. "But I didn't mean that. I mean what you said to Steph. She's a real bitch to me."

Jake takes a step closer to me and strokes his fingers across my cheekbone and down my face. "I meant what I said. Never let anyone make you doubt your worth, Abbie." He kisses me goodnight and leaves me tingling all over as he turns back down the drive towards his car.

I watch him drive away as I open the front door. *I don't know what this feeling is, but I've got it bad.*

# Chapter 6

## *Jake*

"**F**uck yeah!" I high five Dan as we finish playing the new song. It sounds good... I mean really good. Since I met Abbie, lyrics just keep pouring out of me. I've been so productive I don't think the boys can keep up. People always say the best songwriters draw from their pain and sadness, but I seem to find the opposite to be true. My life has been a painful shit show for years and my songs are alright, but now I have something good in my life, someone that actually brings me happiness and I seem to have so much more to say.

I've written this latest song for Abbie, and I want to play it when she comes to watch us next. The boys were not at all sold on the idea when I first suggested it. They rolled their eyes and swore a lot but then they heard it and decided it's actually pretty fucking good.

Tomorrow is Abbie's birthday, and I want to make it special. Her parents have invited me over for dinner, which is terrifying. I've never done the whole 'meet the parents' thing before. Abbie says they're cool with us but I can't imagine they're thrilled their daughter is dating a slightly older guy with no real prospects, who mostly survives on his guitar skills and charm.

I help the guys pack up from rehearsal and head home. I know the travelling is hard on them while I'm here, but I don't know what to tell them. I can't even definitely say I'll be coming back to London because the way Dad's talking, we won't be. I try to shove the thought further back into my mind. No use worrying about it yet, I guess. I just want to enjoy the summer with Abbie. I take my phone out and text her.

### Pick you up at 1pm tomorrow? Jx

Her reply is almost immediate.

### Where are you taking me? X

I think for a minute. I like to make her laugh. She's so beautiful when she laughs.

### To heaven and back. Jx

I can picture her laughing as she reads this to herself.

### Well now you've set the bar real high... x

Now I'm the one smiling. She's sassier in her messages. I like it when a little bit of confidence shines through and she relaxes.

### I won't disappoint. Jx

\*\*\*

I knock on Abbie's door at eleven. I've packed a picnic in the car with Julie's help. She came down to see what all the noise was while I was clattering about in the kitchen earlier, only to discover that I have no friggin' clue how to put together a picnic. She really came through. She even found me a blanket and basket to pack it all in rather than the rucksack and hoodie I had originally planned on using. *I guess that's the kind of things mothers do to help you.*

Abbie's mum opens the door and smiles. "Hello Jake, come in." I follow her into the lounge as she talks. "Abbie won't be a minute. Wardrobe malfunction, I believe." She gestures for me to take a seat which I politely accept.

Abbie's dad walks into the room saying, "Don't embarrass her before she's even left the house. Nice to meet you, Jake," as he sticks out his hand. I stand and shake it.

I'm instantly struck by how warm and friendly they are. If they have any reservations about Abbie spending time with me, they certainly don't show it.

Abbie quietly steps into the room. She looks absolutely breath-taking. She's wearing a white summer dress that shows off the slight tan she's acquired over the past week. I've never seen her in a dress. I can't help but notice what incredible legs she has, but I can't check her out, not here. It's taking all my self-restraint to keep my eyes on her face with her parents in the room.

"Ready?" she asks. I nod at her and pick up my car keys. I know I'm grinning like an idiot since she came into the room. I can't help it.

"What time would you like us back for dinner, Mrs Daniels?" I ask as we head to the door.

"Oh please, call me Sally. I'll probably have dinner ready for around six. Have a lovely day together." She waves us off as we get into the car.

Once I see the front door close, I lean over to Abbie as she finishes buckling her seat belt and kiss her on the lips. "Happy Birthday." It's so hard to focus on anything other than her when she's around. She's like a magnet drawing me in.

"Thank you. So where are we really going?" She looks excited. I hope I live up to expectations. The problem with being a cocky shit is you have to live up to it and deliver. *No pressure.*

"You'll see." I grin at her as I pull out into the traffic. It's not a long drive, about twenty minutes or so. She chats the whole way there about her birthday presents and past birthdays. She's had such an amazing childhood. I love listening to her talk about her family. As she talks, I absentmindedly trace circles on her thigh. Her skin breaks out in goose bumps, but I can't tell if it's because of me or the air-conditioning.

We arrive at our destination; a stream Harry and I used to play in as kids. I remember it as being an idyllic place, a real picture postcard setting. I only hope it's as I remember it. We park in the layby off the country lane and I collect the picnic basket out of the boot before taking Abbie by the hand. It's really warm and sunny, which is perfect. I lead her down a small path in the bushes that leads to an opening next to the stream.

"Jake, this place is beautiful. How did you know about it?" she asks as she looks around. I spread the blanket out on the grass and we take a seat.

"Me and Harry used to play down here when we were little. I came to stay a lot during the summer back then with my dad. See that tree over there?" I point to a twisted willow tree that hangs over the water almost horizontally. "There used to be a tyre swing in that tree and we would take turns to run and jump onto the tyre and see who could swing across and jump off the other side of the stream without getting wet."

Abbie laughs. "And how often was that successful?"

"Almost never." I unpack the picnic and spread it out on the blanket.

"Wow, you said you wouldn't disappoint. This is incredible," she says as she looks at the assortment of food and drink.

"Well, I will confess to having help. Harry's mum saved me from the margarine and jammy mess I was creating."

Abbie screws her face up in mock disgust. "Well thank goodness, who even puts jam and margarine together?"

I laugh at her mocking me and raise an eyebrow. "Oh, so you think you can get all cocky because it's your birthday, do you?" I tease.

She smiles flirtatiously at me as she bites her lip and shrugs her shoulders. I still don't think she has any idea how sexy she is. I grab the can of squirty cream Julie packed for the strawberries and shake it at her. "Run," I say to her deadpan.

Abbie squeals with laughter as she jumps up and runs through the grass away from me. I don't even try to run after her to start with. I just watch her, mesmerised. *Fucking hell, that arse in that dress.* I rearrange my jeans to try to hide just how turned on I am. I take off at a jog and catch her up with ease. I pick her up round the waist from behind and she screams as I bundle her to the ground. She is giggling and breathless as we lay in the grass together. I pop the lid off the cream with one hand and she laughs even harder and protest. She tries to take the can from me but fails.

"Jake, no. It's going to be so col... Aaaahhh!" She screams as I squirt whipped cream all over her exposed thigh where her dress has ridden up in our scuffle.

"Shit that's freezing!" she laughs, still out of breath from running. I manoeuvre myself so I'm kneeling between her legs and drop down. I slowly lick the cream off her legs with my tongue, watching her while she watches me. I swear to God it's the hottest damn thing I've ever experienced. Abbie's breathing starts to steady and her cheeks flush. She watches me intently as I swirl my tongue around her inner thigh licking up the cream. Her eyes darken with desire, a side of Abbie I've not seen yet.

I know I need to do something to break the intensity of the moment. I don't want to expect too much too fast. I finish lapping up the remainder of the cream while she watches me intently and then slowly kiss her leg as I come to a stop.

"Ready for lunch?" I ask her, trying to sound casual as I sit up.

We eat the picnic food and enjoy the sunshine for the rest of the afternoon. Before we head back to Abbie's house, we take a walk along the stream and I tell her stories of all the antics me and Harry used to get up to here. We pass by a few cottage style houses along the edge of the creek which I remember from when I was a kid. Abbie stops walking and looks at the last one in the row. It's white with brown beams and has a porch with some sort of flowering plant growing up it.

"I want to live in a house like that one day," she says, looking at the house.

I tuck a loose strand of hair behind her ear that is blowing in the breeze. I get an uneasy feeling in the pit of my stomach. I never think about what the future holds, there's never been any point. But Abbie has hopes and dreams, and I suddenly feel responsible not to let her down. I push the troubling thought down as far as it will go.

*** 

Dinner at Abbie's is surprisingly laid back. It seems my first impression of her parents was accurate. They ask me about my life and seem to listen with genuine interest as we eat and they tell me embarrassing stories from Abbie's child-hood, much to her embarrassment. I can't think of a time when I've felt as happy and relaxed as I do around Abbie and her family.

After dinner, Abbie's parents tell us they're going out for a bit. That seems odd on Abbie's birthday, given what devoted parents they are. *Nothing like my dad.* It was Mrs Daniels who invited us for dinner and now they're going out.

Mrs Daniels hangs back after her husband has already gone out to the car.

"Be good angels, and if you can't be good, be safe." She says as she kisses Abbie on the fore-head and leaves. Abbie looks mortified and has gone the brightest shade of red. *I do like Mrs Daniels; she reminds me of Julie.* This is obviously her not-so-subtle way of giving us some privacy.

I take Abbie by the hand and lead her up the stairs to her bedroom, where I dumped my bag earlier. "I want to show you something." I say as we get to her room. She's gone unusually quiet and seems really nervous. I take her in my arms, gently kissing her on the lips to try to put her at ease.

"I got you something for your birthday." I say stroking her cheek. She smiles and seems to relax a little. Reaching for my bag, I take out the small parcel I wrapped earlier and hand it to her. *I hope she doesn't think this is lame.* She unwraps the parcel and opens the small black box. She holds up the silver chain in the air to reveal what is hanging from it.

"It's the plectrum I was playing with the night we met." I explain as she admires the shiny black piece of plastic that hangs from the chain. "I had it made into a necklace." Her face breaks into a breath-taking smile. *Thank fuck.*

"Oh my God, Jake, it's absolutely perfect." She cries as she throws her arms round me. She hugs me tight and I breathe in the smell of her hair. She smells like coconut shampoo. I take the chain and do it up round the back of her neck for her, sweeping her hair to one side in the process.

"I'm glad you like it." I say as my eyes settle on her lips.

"I love it," she whispers as I lean in and kiss her. Softly at first, but then harder and more urgently. I could honestly kiss this girl forever. Her tongue is doing incredible things in my mouth and in this moment, she is all I can think about. *Hell, who am I kidding? She's all I ever think about.*

Without breaking contact with her lips, I slowly lay us both down on the bed side by side. My tongue is eagerly exploring her mouth and I put my hand in the back of her hair to deepen our kiss even further. Our bodies are pressed so closely together I can feel how nervous she is. She is trembling all over. *Don't mess this up.* As we kiss, I take my hand from her hair and gently rest it on her breast. I feel her breathing catch in her chest.

"Is this ok?" I ask her gently. She nods silently and kisses me again. I rub and knead her breast as we continue kissing and I feel her nipple harden against my touch under her top. *Man, she is so hot. I want her so badly. I don't think I've ever been this turned on.*

I make a conscious effort to angle my hips away from her slightly as we lay pressed up against each other. My erection is making my jeans tight and uncomfortable, I'm sporting so much wood right now, but I don't want to scare her or rush her. I slowly move my hand so it's now under her top and slide it inside her bra. She moans into my open mouth as I squeeze her full breast that fills my hand perfectly. *Fuck, I could come just from hearing that noise alone.*

I break our kiss and begin trailing gentle kisses down her neck as I continue to run my fingers over her erect nipple. *She is so God damn beautiful it hurts. Is now the right time to tell her I'm a virgin too?* I can tell she's nervous. Maybe that would make her feel more at ease? *No Jake, no one wants to hear the guy they're with is a rookie.* I'm at war in my own head. *Don't let her know you're as terrified as she is. You need to be a fucking man and do this right.* All this deliberating in my head is a real buzz kill. *Great, now I've scared myself and my hard on is fading fast with nerves.*

I take my hand out of her bra and trail my fingertips down to the waistband of her jeans. I undo the button with ease and pull open the zip. She is more than trembling now, she's shaking.

"It's ok," I whisper against her neck, but I'm not sure whether it's for her benefit or my own. I slide my hand inside her jeans and I can feel how wet she is. *Fuck, this girl turns me on in every way.* My erection comes back with a vengeance. I start to move my hand slowly inside her jeans when Abbie freezes and pulls out of our kiss.

"Jake, stop," she says in a panic. I look at her terrified eyes, she looks like a deer in headlights.

"What's wrong?" I ask her gently. I know how I handle these next few minutes will be what defines me in our relationship as a horny prick or a gentleman. I'm determined to be the latter.

"I'm sorry, I'm not ready." She bites her lip and looks at the bedsheets. Tears are threatening to spill from her eyes. I remove my hand from inside her jeans and gently bring her chin up so she has to meet my gaze.

"You have nothing to be sorry for. We've got all the time in the world." I can see her visibly relax at my words and she plants a soft kiss on my lips.

"Thank you for understanding." She sighs and snuggles her head into my chest. We lay like that for the next hour or so watching a movie, and I think she may have fallen asleep.

"Abbie?" I stroke her hair and try to lift her off my chest. "It's getting late. I have to go, baby." She sleepily leans up off me and rubs her face. A tired smile creeps over her lips

"That's the first time you've ever called me that," she says as she sits up. "I like it." She yawns.

I get up off the bed and grab my bag. Abbie follows me to the door. "I'm sorry about earlier, Jake. It's not you." I put a finger over her lips to silence her. *She doesn't owe me an explanation.*

"Happy birthday, gorgeous." I run my finger over her bottom lip before giving her one last deep kiss and heading out the door.

# Chapter 7

## Abbie

I take a deep breath and have one last look in the mirror. Tonight's the night. Everything is arranged for me to stay at Harry's with Jake after the gig. My parents think I'm staying with Louisa. It's not a complete lie; she will be at Harry's too.

I have pulled out all the stops to try to give Jake a night to remember. We've never talked about how many girls he's slept with and I'm not sure I want to know. *But look at him*. He's sexy as hell, so the list must be long. I need to try to make the other girls he's been with pale into insignificance. *I can do this.* I totally blew it on my birthday and panicked. I will not let that happen again.

Louisa has been helping me all day. She knows how important tonight is and has helped me tap into my 'inner rock chick' in hopes of it giving me the confidence I need. I have to say, I think it's working. I feel like I could take on the world right now. I'm wearing tight black leather trousers with black boots. I have a black bra on with a sheer black top over it, which you can see through completely. It took Louisa all day to convince me on this part, but I'm glad she did. *This outfit is next level.* The gig is in an underground pub tonight, so anything goes where fashion choices are concerned. Louisa did my makeup with a tad more eyeliner than normal and glossy lips. My hair is down and slightly back-combed to give it extra volume.

I hear the taxi beep outside.

"Ready?" Louisa asks as she links her arm with mine. "He won't be able to take his eyes off you."

I smile at my wonderful friend. "Thanks for today, Lou. Let's go."

When the taxi pulls up at the address Jake gave, we are in the middle of an industrial estate. It's so dark and there's no one around except the bouncer on the door. The pub entrance is just a doorway between tall, derelict factories with broken windowpanes. *This place is scary. I'm so glad I didn't come alone.*

We're under-age but Jake assured us we won't get ID'd on the door because he's put us on the guest list and he plays here regularly. We get out of the taxi and get into the pub with no trouble. I've never seen anywhere like it before. It's like a weird mix between a nightclub and a pub. There's no club music playing because there's a full line up of bands playing tonight. Jake's band is headlining. I think we may have missed the first band as we are much later than arranged. Louisa said this outfit is worth the wait. *I'm hoping she's right.*

As we push our way through the crowds of people, I notice the walls are decorated with crazy neon patterns and pictures that glow under the UV lights. *This place is so trippy.* Louisa pushes her way through to the bar and orders some drinks, but it's so loud I have no idea what she said. Apparently, they don't ask for ID once you're inside. *It gets dodgier here by the minute.* A few minutes later she hands me a plastic pint glass full of something dark in colour.

"What the hell is that?" I ask as I take it from her.

"Snakebite." She smiles as she takes a sip of her own. "To give you courage."

"Or kill me." I eye the drink suspiciously. This evening seems to be fraught with danger. I wish I didn't worry and overthink everything all the time. Life would be so much simpler.

"Less thinking, more drinking," she says, and she drains a third of her glass. Louisa knows me so well.

*Oh geez. Here goes nothing.* I take a mouthful and find it's actually not that bad. It tastes a bit like blackcurrant. I'm not even going to ask what's in it. Tonight is about doing, not thinking.

Louisa looks up from her phone. "Harry and Jake are over by the stage. He's just finishing his sound check."

I follow Louisa through the crowd to find the boys. I see Jake before he sees me. He's concentrating on tuning his guitar. Harry sees us fighting our way through the crowd and taps Jake on the shoulder to get his attention. Harry's jaw almost hits the floor; he's never seen us dressed like this. Jake looks up and does a double take when he makes eye contact. His Adam's apple visibly bobs as he swallows. *Nailed it.* He immediately lifts the guitar strap over his head and puts it down so he can put his arm around me. He smiles sexily as he leans in. He doesn't even try to hide how much he's checking me out.

"You look incredible, babe." He has to half shout at me to be heard over the amps. He kisses my neck just below my ear and his hand travels down to feel my behind. "How am I ever going to concentrate on my set with you looking like that?"

I smile at him. *This was exactly the effect I was hoping for.* I put my arms around his neck and see Louisa over his shoulder give me an air high five. As I kiss Jake, a guy I don't recognise comes and taps him on the back.

"Sorry to interrupt dude, but you guys are up next." Jake nods at him and lets me go.

"Stay with Louisa and Harry while I'm on stage. The wolves will be circling with you in that outfit." He kisses me on the cheek and grins as he heads up onstage.

I watch Jake's band perform for the rest of

the night from my space in the front row. I'm more than happy to be an outright groupie. I sing along, jump around and just generally lose myself in the music. It's been a great night and I think the multiple snakebite drinks I've consumed have helped. The room is buzzing and Jake has the crowd eating out the palm of his hand. He really is a glorious sight to behold. He's given it his all tonight and is gleaming with sweat. His t-shirt is wet and his forehead glistening.

The song ends, and Jake then takes the mic. The crowd goes quiet. I don't think there's a single person in here not giving him their full attention. The girls want to be *with* him and the guys want to *be* him.

"This is our last song of the night. It's a new song, we hope you like it. I've written it for someone very special." He looks directly at me and winks. My insides clench and my heart stops. *Could this guy be any more perfect?* I listen to the song, entirely mesmerised. It's much gentler than their other songs, but the crowd is loving it. I'm close to tears the whole way through, I can't take my eyes off him. *I can't believe he wrote a song for me and sang it in front of all these people.*

When the final song ends, everyone cheers and goes wild. Jake thanks everyone and says goodnight as they leave the stage.

Harry leans in to me and Louisa so we can hear him over all the cheering. I had been so lost in the show, I almost forgot they were even here.

"I've got a taxi waiting to go back to mine. We'll meet Jake out the front." We both nod and follow him through the crowd to the exit.

When we get back to Harry's. Harry and Louisa say goodnight and disappear off down the hall to Harry's room. We make our way to Jake's room and he closes the door behind us. I'm still running on snakebite and adrenaline from such an incredible night. I barely feel nervous at all about what I'm about to do.

"Listen Abbie, I want you to know there's no pressure... " Jake starts to say, but I stop him mid-sentence by putting my finger over his lips just like he did on my birthday.

"I know," I whisper against his neck as I trail kisses down to the neckline of his t-shirt. *I'm running this show tonight.* I want to be sexy and confident for him. I run my hands over his chest, feeling every inch of hard muscle. *He really is heavenly.*

"Abbie, I need to tell you something." He looks uncomfortable under my gaze. I don't say anything, just wait for him to continue.

"I haven't done this before either," he says with embarrassment. I let out the breath I didn't realise I had been holding. *Thank goodness that's all it is.*

"Why didn't you tell me before?" I ask him gently as I reach up and run my hands through his hair.

"Because I didn't want you to think I was a pussy," he admits. I've never seen him like this. He's always so confident and carefree, but right now he's showing me his vulnerabilities.

I run my hand down his body with purpose and grab hold of his dick through his jeans. "You're definitely not a pussy, Jake Greyson," I whisper darkly, in hopes of conveying just how much I want him right now.

I'm even surprising myself tonight. *What was in that snakebite?* I'm enjoying my newfound confidence, though. He crashes his mouth to mine and pulls me in for a passionate kiss. His tongue forcing its way into my mouth and melding with my own. I feel him harden in my hand.

He steps back and sits on the edge of the bed. He holds my hands and is about to pull me down beside him, but I stop him. *I don't want him to try to look after me through this. I want to blow his mind.* I stand between his legs in front of him and pull the opaque black top I'm wearing over my head so I'm standing in front of him in just my black bra and leather trousers. He reaches around behind me and unclips my bra and lets it drop to the floor. He edges forward so my breasts are close to his face and gently kisses each one and cups them in his hands.

"You're so beautiful, Abbie," he says as he runs his tongue up and down between my breasts. I pull his t-shirt up and he helps take it off. *I don't think I'll ever get sick of this sight.* Time seems to stand still and speed up all at the same time over the next few minutes. We continue to undress each other and explore each other's bodies with our hands until we are laying stark naked together. He leans up on one arm and uses the other to trace his fingertips up and down my arm as he looks at me.

"If you want to stop at any time Abbie, promise you'll tell me?" He really is the sweetest guy. Always putting my feelings first.

"I promise." For the first time tonight, my nerves start to take hold. *I'm about to have sex with Jake Greyson.* The enormity of that statement sinks in and settles into a nervous ball of energy in the pit of my stomach. My breathing gets faster and I can hear my pulse thumping in my ears. He leans over and rolls a condom on from the nightstand before resting over me on his strong forearms.

"Are you ready, baby?" he whispers, looking into my eyes but seeing into my soul. Now it's actually about to happen, I don't know which one of us is more nervous. I can feel his arms trembling as he holds himself over me. I nod in response and with one firm but gentle movement he slides inside me. I cry out from the initial sting and he holds perfectly still giving me time to adjust to this new sensation. He kisses me tenderly. I can't help but think about all my friends telling me how my first time would be awful, but Jake is so gentle and attentive. I'm overcome with the emotion of how perfect this feels. Tears threaten to spill over as the enormity of the moment consumes me. I blink them back and hold it together, not wanting to scare him or ruin the moment.

He then starts to slide in and out, building a steady rhythm. I can tell he's holding back from fear of hurting me. He kisses me and I kiss him back harder to show him I'm ok and he begins to relax and build momentum. I open my eyes and I can see he's getting close. He closes his eyes and moans my name as he starts to thrust into me harder. *Holy shit, this is incredible!* With one final push, he finds his release and comes inside me in a rush. He collapses on top of me breathless and we lay like that for ages. He stays inside me and just holds me silently until our breathing regulates. He kisses my forehead as he pulls out from inside me. I instantly feel empty with him gone.

When I come back from freshening up in the bathroom, Jake is sprawled across the bed on his back, fast asleep. He is still naked, covered only by the sheet thrown over his bottom half. *He is absolute perfection.* I climb into bed next to him and snuggle into his chest before drifting off to sleep myself with a smile on my face.

# Chapter 8

## *Jake*

It starts to pour with rain as Harry and I jog back towards the house at the end of a long run. I pushed myself tonight, and it feels good. I can feel my calves burning.

"Ah shit," Harry moans. "My new trainers are getting wet."

I laugh, shaking my head. "Sucks to be you man, I can't imagine what it must be like for that to be your biggest problem today." I'm only joking, but Harry lives a seriously privileged life and has no idea how good he's got it.

"Come on, things aren't so bad for you. I mean, you're banging Abbie Daniels for fuck sake. Life could be worse." Harry is preoccupied by his wet shoes and looking at them as we approach the house.

"Shut up man, I'm not 'banging her' as you so eloquently put it. There's more to it than that. We... " I stop talking and jogging at the same time, causing Harry to run into the back of me where he wasn't looking where he was going.

"What the hell, man?" Harry protests at my

sudden halt, but I signal to him to be quiet and point to a car parked at the end of his drive. My dad is talking to someone inside it. We duck around the corner so we can watch without being spotted. The car is a black BMW with blacked-out windows, not the kind of car generally used for friendly visits to a neighbour. I can't see who Dad is talking to inside or how many people are in there, but Dad keeps looking back at the house as if checking no one is watching. Harry looks at me with raised eyebrows. We both know my dad is involved in some shady shit, but we have no idea what and he has never brought his 'business' to Harry's house before. After a few more minutes of quiet talking, dad gets in the back of the car and it drives off down the lane at speed.

Harry blows out his cheeks as we step out from around the corner. "Shit, man, what was that all about?" he asks. It's more of a rhetorical question, he knows I'm clueless when it comes to my dad. We have as little to do with each other as possible.

I run my hands through my now soaking wet hair. "I don't know, but it didn't look good. How did I end up with such a prick for an old man? Seriously, why can't he ever think about anyone other than himself?"

Harry gives me an encouraging slap on the back and grips my shoulder. He knows there's nothing he can say to make any of this any better. "Come on, let's go. I'm fucking drenched."

When I get back up to my room, there's a message on my phone from Abbie.

**Thank you for a wonderful night. No regrets? X**

How can someone as beautiful inside and out as her be insecure? Why on earth would I have any regrets? I have thought about nothing else all day since we woke up together this morning. I'm the luckiest guy on the planet to have had her share my bed last night. I've had to try *not* to think about it because every time I do I get a raging hard on. Abbie had this confidence and determination about her last night that was sexy as hell. Granted, I'm sure the alcohol had given her courage, but she was incredible. I hope I gave her the first time she deserves, and that I wasn't a let-down. If I was, she didn't show it.

**Hell no! You? Jx**

I realise my knee is bouncing up and down as I wait for her reply.

**Not a single one x**

I smile with relief. Abbie is spending the day with me here tomorrow as Harry's parents are dragging him off to look around prospective Universities. *Tomorrow is going to be a good day.*

\*\*\*

"Come on Abbie. What on earth are you doing in there?" I call towards the house. She went in to change so we could go for a swim, but she's taking forever. *How do women spend so long changing outfits?* I've been waiting in the pool for her since we got back from our walk.

"Coming." I faintly hear her shout back. I do a couple more lengths while I wait. I come up for air at the far end of the pool and look back at the house to see Abbie emerge from the doorway. She has a towel wrapped around her and is walking towards the pool with a nervous expression.

"What's wrong, babe?" I ask her as I wipe water out of my eyes.

"It's this new bikini, I've never worn it before." She bites her lip and looks down at her feet.

"What's wrong with it?" I make my way across the pool to where she's standing.

"It's err, a bit smaller than I realised." *How is this making her blush when I've already seen her naked?* I smile encouragingly at her.

"It sounds perfect." This seems to give her the confidence boost she needs, and she smiles shyly as she drops the towel. *Holy. Fucking. Hell. I swear to God she just gets hotter and hotter.* She is wearing a white bikini that accentuates her incredible curves and does not leave much to the imagination. She steps forward out of the towel at her feet and instead of edging into the water like I thought she would, she dives straight in head first. *That's my girl; full of surprises!*

When she comes back up for air, I take the opportunity to grab her by the waist and dunk her back under the water. She screams and laughs as she tries to move out of my reach. *She is so beautiful when she laughs.* Abbie bobs about in the water just out of arm's reach as she tries to get her breath back. Her wet hair clings to her shoulders and splays out into the water, and her wet skin is sparkling in the sun. It's the perfect moments like this when I'm happy with Abbie that the gnawing feeling in the pit of my stomach comes. The one that makes me feel sick thinking about what will happen at the end of the summer. *How could I ever leave her?* The fleeting moment of worry must have reached my face because she moves closer to me and puts her hands on my chest.

"You ok?" she asks as she traces the outline of my pecs with her fingers. *I am now.* I think to myself. Every time she touches me, she sends an electric current straight to my dick. I don't want her to know how much I worry about leaving. I don't want to taint the perfect summer we're having, so I bury the thought down and go back to ignoring it.

"Couldn't be happier," I say into her mouth as I take her in my arms and kiss her. Her incredible wet curves are pressed up against me under the water with only that tiny bikini of hers between us. She wraps her legs around my waist as our kiss becomes deeper and more urgent. She grinds against my hard length as she gently sucks on my bottom lip. *Fucking hell, I'll explode right here in the pool if she keeps this up.* I run my fingers from her neck down her spine to her perfect bum and squeeze.

"Let's go inside." I suggest breathlessly and she nods in agreement. She's as close to losing control right now as I am and I don't have a condom out here.

When we get up to my room, I unwrap the towel from around her in a hurry and throw it on the floor. I walk her backwards towards the bed as I kiss her neck and that spot just below her ear that makes her moan with pleasure. My fingers find the strings that tie her bikini bottoms at her hips and pull them until they undo and fall to the floor. She starts to pull at the waistband of my swim shorts as I reach around to unclip her bikini top. We fall on to the bed tangled in each other. The bedding is getting soaked beneath us but I couldn't give a shit right now. My hands roam all over her flawless skin as she runs her hands through my hair and pulls just the right amount, so I'm suspended somewhere between pleasure and pain. *I need to be inside her.* This is different from the other night. I was careful and cautious, and we were both nervous with the pressure of it being our first time. This is more urgent, more passionate, more primal.

"Make love to me, Jake," she whispers in my ear. *Fuck, I don't need telling twice.* I grab a condom from my bedside table. I watch her while I roll it on. Her hair is spread out across my pillow and her breasts rise and fall with her fast breathing. *She's so fucking perfect.* Without hesitation or holding back this time, I slide inside her and do as she asks. I make love to her… hard. Then I do it all over again.

It's several hours before we emerge from my bedroom. I would have happily never left there again, but we've worked up an appetite.

"How do pancakes sound?" I ask her as we head down to the kitchen.

"Mmm perfect," she says. She has scooped her hair up on top of her head in a wild bun and her cheeks are still pink from our afternoon's exertions.

"That's lucky because that's about all I can do well in the kitchen." I gather the ingredients I need from the fridge and mix the batter. Abbie sits at the counter and watches me with intrigue.

"How did you learn to make pancakes?" she asks as she passes me the whisk.

"After Mum died, I had a childminder for a while. She used to make the best pancakes. I just watched and learned, I guess." I shrug casually and continue mixing, realising this is the first time I've spoken to Abbie about my childhood.

"What happened to your mum, Jake?" she asks quietly. "You don't have to tell me if you don't want to, if it's too private." She adds quickly.

I stop what I'm doing and go over to where she's sitting. I stroke her cheekbone with my thumb so she meets my eyes.

"I think we've shared enough for there to be no secrets between us, don't you?" She blushes in response. I don't want her to tiptoe around talking to me about my parents. People have done that my whole life and I don't want Abbie to. I'm prepared to tell her anything she wants to know.

"Mum died when I was four. She suffered a sudden brain aneurism. I don't remember her fully, more the idea of her, really. It was totally unexpected from what I know, but Dad and I have never spoken about it." I stroke my hands up and down her thighs in a soothing kind of way and give her a quick kiss on the cheek before returning to the bowl of batter.

"What, never?" she asks in surprise.

"Nope, not since the day of her funeral. I remember that day, so many people were crying, but I just stood there. I didn't know what to feel. After we got back, Dad never mentioned her name again. By the end of that week, every last trace of her was gone from the house. I don't even have a photo." I just stare at the mixture as it goes around and around in the bowl. I've never said these things out loud to anyone before.

"I'm so sorry, Jake." I feel her come up behind me and wrap her arms around my middle. She snuggles into my back and just holds me. It's so nice, no one's ever done that before. Abbie's voice brings me back to the present.

"Why does your dad move you around so much?" I can't believe she even remembers me telling her this the first time we met. I pour the pancake mix into the pan as we talk.

"I honestly don't know. We talk to each other as little as possible. He always seems to be chasing *business deals*." I use air quotes to accentuate my point. "Whatever the fuck that means." I decide not to tell her I suspect whatever he does is illegal. *No need to worry her.*

I can't see her face to try and read her expression, she's still nestled into my back but I can tell she's thinking about what she wants to say next.

"Does any of this scare you, Jake?" she asks quietly behind me.

"Any of what?" I turn around to face her and give her my full attention.

"Us," she says, biting her lip and looking at the floor. *More than you know.* I think to myself.

"Should it? Does it scare you?" I lift her chin with my finger so she looks at me. She has such incredible eyes. I'm not sure I'll ever get used to all the ways in which she's beautiful.

"I've just never felt anything so…" She pauses, searching for the right word. "Intense. I think about you all the time," she confesses. Inside I'm smiling and high-fiving myself, but I can tell she's worried about telling me this, so I decide to try to lighten the mood.

"Abbie... are you trying to tell me that I rock your world?" I ask her playfully. I raise my eyebrows and pretend to play a power chord on an invisible air guitar. She immediately bursts out laughing.

"Something like that." She laughs. Mission accomplished; her gorgeous smile is back.

The pancake batter looks ready so I decide to go for the flip. I toss it in the air and catch it again expertly.

Abbie laughs. "Wow, I'm impressed."

I give her my most charming smile and take a theatrical bow.

"Now comes the important part... what would you like on top?" I ask as I look for suitable toppings in the cupboards.

"Hmmm, definitely you," she says. I turn around and give her an over-the-top shocked face.

"Did you just openly say something flirty?" She giggles and looks away.

"Maybe," she says, giving me a sexy half-smile.

"Maybe?" I move towards her and make it obvious I'm going to tickle her. She screams and runs around the counter away from me, but I'm faster and tickle her so hard she can't breathe.

Amongst our laughter and wrestling I'm suddenly aware of the front door banging.

"What are you doing?" Dad's voice cuts through the air like a knife. Abbie immediately stops laughing and drops her hands away from me in embarrassment.

"Making pancakes," I tell him bluntly. *You don't intimidate me, arsehole.*

"Well, it doesn't look like that's all that's going on." He snaps louder than necessary. I can tell Abbie is already uncomfortable. *Great first impression, Dad.*

"Dad, this is my girlfriend, Abbie." I don't know why I'm even bothering with the niceties. He doesn't give a crap. It's more for Abbie's benefit.

"Girlfriend?" he scoffs. "We've only been here five minutes, Jake."

*Who does this fucker think he is?* I'm about to say something about his shitty attitude towards Abbie when she introduces herself.

"It's nice to finally meet you, Mr Greyson." she says politely. *Wow, she's a better person than I am. He doesn't even deserve for her to acknowledge him.* Dad just looks at her, expressionless. The smile Abbie had attempted for his benefit is fading fast under his unreadable glare.

Then he snaps his eyes from her to me and says, "Well, don't get too attached. We're not staying, remember." With that he turns and leaves the kitchen without so much as a backwards glance. Abbie is standing there looking at the empty doorway as if she can't quite process what just happened.

"I'm so sorry, baby." I hug and kiss her to try and make her feel better. "It's not personal, he's a fucking arsehole to everyone."

We eat our pancakes together, but I can't help but notice that Abbie is unusually quiet for the rest of the afternoon. She's barely said a word since Dad left the room and her usual sparkle isn't there.

I put my hand over hers on the table. "What's wrong, gorgeous?"

When she looks up at me, I can see she's upset but trying not to show it. "What will happen at the end of the summer, Jake, when you leave?" *Shit.* This is the conversation I've been hiding from. The reality I don't want to face.

"I don't know, but I know it won't be over. We'll make it work." I try to sound as confident as possible, even though I'm not sure how.

"How though? You don't even know where you're going and I have to stay and finish my last year of school," she says, sadly.

"We've never gone outside of the South East, so I'll never be more than a few hours away and I drive so I'll be able to come back all the time." I feel as unconvinced as she looks.

"Besides, it won't be long before I can become financially independent from Dad and then I won't have to follow his sorry arse anywhere.

I can be here with you, or wherever you want to be." I realise as I'm saying these things that I really do mean them. It suddenly hits me like a ton of bricks the extent of my feelings for her. The thought of being separated from her makes me feel sick. *I think I'm in love with her.*

This seems to be enough to put her mind at ease for now. She wraps her arms around me and rests her head on my chest.

"Let's just enjoy what time we have together now and worry about the rest later." She tries to sound uplifting, but I can't miss the edge of sadness in her voice.

"Everything will be fine, baby, I promise." *I hope I'm right for both our sakes.*

# Chapter 9

## *Abbie*

"Right, spill," Louisa says as she eyes me over her enormous milkshake. We're sitting on the comfy chairs in my favourite coffee shop. It's at the back of a book shop. The smell of coffee and books together is the best combination.

"Spill what?" I grin at her. I don't know why I'm acting dumb; we both know what she's referring to.

"Err, well, the fact that I have barely seen you in *weeks* because you've spent every possible minute with Jake would suggest there is something to tell," she says as she spoons marshmallows off the top of her milkshake. "That and the stupid grin on your face… so come on, out with it, I want every last detail."

I can't help it. I know I'm grinning like an idiot. "Oh Lou, he's so incredible." I can't believe how I sound. Like some lovesick school girl ,which I guess technically I am? *Such a cliché.*

Louisa rolls her eyes, but I know she wants the gossip. "So aside from the obvious hunky packaging he comes in, why is he so incredible?

Why this guy over all the others that have tried and failed over the past year or so?"

I stir my coffee as I think about her question for a moment.

"I don't know what to say, I could list you all the reasons why I like him so much and you'll probably just throw up in your mouth." We both laugh at that. Louisa doesn't really do sentimental. "But the main reason I guess is he just makes me feel like no one else matters."

Louisa looks at me for a second as if I've grown two heads. "Have you swallowed a romance novel or something? How worried should I be?" She squints at me as if assessing me.

I laugh at her silliness. "No, it's all good. *I'm* all good... better than good." I feel my cheeks flush as I remember just how good some of my recent days with Jake have been.

"Fucking hell, he's really good in bed, isn't he?" Louisa suddenly blurts out way too loud.

I choke on my coffee and start to cough. I try to 'sshh' her but I'm still coughing up latte. At least the redness in my face now could be down to that rather than the embarrassment.

"Well?" she asks impatiently as I compose myself. Smiling from ear to ear I confirm it is in fact very good. *Not that I have anyone to compare him to, but how could it be better than this?* The next half hour or so is spent answering Louisa's relentless questioning. She really is unbelievably nosey. I decide not to tell her that I was also

Jake's first. That's not my information to share.

"So anyway, what about you and Harry?" I ask her to try and deflect the conversation away from me. "What's the story there?"

Louisa shrugs her shoulders. "Same as usual. You know me, I love the chase and a pretty face." She laughs at her own rhyme.

"So, nothing serious then?" I clarify.

"Nope. I will miss that bum of his though when I'm done." I roll my eyes at her ridiculousness. Louisa never stays with anyone long before she gets bored and moves on to the next one.

"There's a party tomorrow for one of the football guys, why don't you and Jake come?'

"Actually Lou, I can't. Jake is taking me camping to a music festival." I get an excited, nervous feeling in my stomach just thinking about it.

She raises her eyebrows at me in surprise. "Wow, this really is a big deal. Are your parents ok with this?"

"Yeah, they like Jake and they're cool with it. Speaking of which I need to go pack." I say as I start to stand up and grab my purse.

Louisa pulls me in for a goodbye hug. "Don't forget to pack your good undies."

*\*\**

By the time Jake arrives to pick me up I have packed and repacked four times. I am definitely over-thinking this. *Damn Louisa and her under-*

*wear advice.* I came to realise that underwear wasn't my only problem. *What pyjamas do you wear camping with your boyfriend? How do you balance sexy with not freezing your arse off in a tent?*

When I open the door to Jake, I burst out laughing. "What are you wearing?"

He has neon paint stripes across his cheeks and he has waxed his hair into a crazy mess. He has sunglasses with electric blue frames and a bright yellow vest on that shows every ripple of his chest. A far cry from his usual monochromatic wardrobe choices.

"It's a music festival." He shrugs casually, as if this is explanation enough for his eclectic outfit. *This weekend is going to be fun.* I love how he gets this buzz of energy when he's excited about something.

It takes several hours to get there and then several more to get the tent up. Neither of us has the faintest idea what we're doing so by time it's done it has started to get dark and we can hear the festival is in full swing.

"Well, that was hard work." I pant as we put the final tent peg in. I stand back to admire our handiwork. "Can we go have fun now?" I'm quite excited now I'm here and can feel the buzz from everyone around us. The ground shakes a little from the thump of the music and we can see all the strobe lights flashing down the hill.

"Wait, one more thing," Jake says as he rummages through his rucksack and pulls out two small pots of neon paint.

"You're not ready." He pulls me closer by the wrist so I'm standing in front of him. He takes two fingers and smears them through the paint. *That's oddly erotic.* Then he paints two stripes across my cheeks to match his. He re-applies more paint to his fingers and repeats the process but this time paints two bright pink and orange stripes over the curves of my breasts. "Perfect," he says admiring his efforts. "Let's go."

I honestly don't think I've ever had as much fun as I do over the next few hours. The festival is insane. We work our way through various tents with stages showcasing all kinds of music and enjoy so many different types of food and drink; many of which I have no idea what they even are. I've never been anywhere like this before and it's incredible.

We have eaten, drunk, danced, and laughed so much that my face and ribs ache. We are now in a tent which is totally blacked out except for the UV which makes our body paint glow. We aren't the only ones covered in stripes. Many people are wearing glow in the dark clothes or accessories and have also decorated themselves. *Now I get it.* Jake and I are dancing together, I can't see him in the pitch black, I just know he's there from the tell-tale orange streaks across his cheeks and the feel of his rock-hard abs as he grinds up against me from behind as we dance.

*Just when I think Jake has given me the sexiest experience of my life, he goes and does something even hotter.* There is something about the total darkness and us moving together along with the music that is so sensual and arousing. *I never want tonight to end.*

We dance like this until the early hours of the morning, totally lost in each other and the atmosphere. Eventually Jake shouts in my ear over the music, "You ready for bed, baby?" The anticipation of what is still to come makes my stomach flip. I nod and he leads me by the hand out of the tent.

"I'm just going to find the toilet before we go back to our tent." He kisses me on the cheek. "Wait here, don't go anywhere."

I stand firmly planted on the spot where I am and wait for Jake, I start to shiver realising how cold it is out here now I've stopped dancing. Lots of people are all still moving around the site, mostly making their way back to their tents as the music ends. It's quite amusing watching groups of people staggering about, clearly having had too much to drink.

"Hey beautiful." An unfamiliar voice comes from behind me and makes me jump. I turn to see two guys approaching me and I instantly feel uncomfortable.

"What's a lovely thing like you doing out here all by yourself?" The two men have walked right up to me and are standing way too close.

They're so close I can smell the alcohol on their breath and I can see how glazed their eyes are. *Shit.* I panic but I don't want them to see how scared I am.

"I'm waiting for my boyfriend; he'll be back in a minute." I try not to let my voice give me away.

The two men smirk and sneer at each other. "That's what they all say, darling"

One of them steps even closer so he's right in my face and unashamedly rakes his eyes over my body. It makes me feel sick and I'm fighting the urge to cry. *Please hurry up Jake.*

The other man produces a small clear plastic bag from his back pocket and hands it to the one who's in my face. *Fuck, there are pills in that bag.* I can feel the panic rising.

"How about you take one of these and come have a good time with us?" He moves his hand towards me like he's about to touch me. I flinch and step backwards away from him.

"N-no thank you," I stammer as I try to put as much distance as I can between me and them. My manners still prevailing even in the company of these scumbags.

"Oh, now come on, don't be like that." The other one says. He hasn't looked at my face once, his eyes are fixed on my breasts. I can taste the rising bile in my throat. They move towards me again and I suddenly realise there is hardly anyone else about. *Double shit.*

"No. Please leave me alone." I sound scared now, I can't pretend anymore. I start to look around for the best direction to run in.

"The lady said no." Jake's voice breaks through the darkness assertively. *Thank God.*

I look past the two men to see Jake standing behind them with his arms folded across his chest and a murderous look on his face. I've never seen him look like this. They turn to look at him lazily.

"Oh, you are real?" one of them says to Jake with mock surprise. "We assumed she was just playing hard to get." They snigger at each other, making my skin crawl. I can see Jake's jaw tense as he tries to control himself.

"Yes, and I'm here now so you need to move along," Jake says without expression.

"Come on mate, we're only looking for a bit of fun." One of them slurs taking a drunken step toward me. "We can all share this fine piece of arse." He waves his arm, gesturing at me as he looks me up and down again.

Jake squares up to him and gets right in his face. He towers over the both of them. He's much taller and broader than they are.

"I've been nice so far, now you need to fuck off," he says through gritted teeth. I can see the muscles in his forearms straining as he clenches his fists.

"Jake come on, let's go." I tug at his arm to try to get him to back down and leave quietly. Jake's face softens when he hears my voice and he un-clenches his fists. He glares at them both one last time before turning to leave. As we start to walk away, one of them calls out to Jake.

"Enjoy fucking your slut girlfriend tonight. She's clearly gagging for it!" Before I can stop him Jake spins back around, closes the gap be-tween them and punches him square in the face. I'm pretty sure I hear his nose crack. I gasp and put my hands over my mouth as the guy staggers back, clutching his face.

"Maybe now you'll learn some manners," Jake says. He takes my hand and we start to march back towards our tent leaving the two men tending to his face in the dark.

When we get back to the tent, Jake runs his hands up and down my arms.

"You're shaking, you ok, baby?" He looks at me with concern. I don't know what shocked me more, the encounter with those vile men or the fact that Jake punched him.

"I'm just cold." I try to play the whole thing down. I don't want it ruining our perfect week-end. As he runs his hands up my arms, I can see his hand is swollen and starting to bruise. I take it in both my hands and bring it to my lips kiss-ing each knuckle in turn.

"It was kind of sexy, you know," I say as I con-tinue to kiss the back of his hand.

"What was?" His gorgeous brown eyes are like dark chocolate in the dimly lit tent.

"You coming to my rescue like that." I look up at him through my lashes and place his hurt hand on my face.

"Oh, it was, was it?" He looks amused and increasingly aroused. All traces of his earlier anger long gone.

I step closer so I'm pressed up against him as I nod. "Like my knight in neon armour." I giggle and kiss him as I put my hands in his hair. He moans against my mouth and my knees go weak. I hastily pull his vest top over his head to reveal his perfectly sculpted chest. I trace my fingers along the outline of the heart-shaped tattoo on his upper arm, something I fantasised about doing when we first met.

"It's for my mum," he says softly, answering my unspoken question. I nod and kiss the outline of the heart shape on his upper arm.

We continue undressing each other until we are naked on top of the sleeping bag. There's something about the small space we're in and the cold night air that seems to heighten all my senses. Our hot breath is visible in the space between us as we breathe more heavily. The neon body paint has smeared and mixed with sweat as we rub against each other. We've done this multiple times before, but something feels different tonight. It's as if there's a deeper connection. Jake doesn't break eye contact once as our bodies meld together and we find our rhythm. Jake strokes my hair and runs his fingers down to where the necklace he gave me sits at my collarbone. When we reach our climax, I feel Jake shudder as he holds me tighter and I'm suddenly overcome with emotion. Tears spill over and run down my cheeks. Jake sees them as he lifts himself off me.

"Abbie, what's wrong? Did I hurt you?" He kisses away my tears with concern.

"No of course not," I whisper "I just… " I know what I want to tell him but I can't bring myself to say it out loud. *Just say it Abbie*. I can't make my lips move.

"Abbie… " he waits for me to look at him. "I love you," he whispers against my skin. "I love you so much."

Fresh tears brim over from my eyes as I look at him. He looks as nervous as I feel.

"I love you too, Jake," I whisper back as I press my forehead to his. I don't think I could ever be as happy as I am at this moment. *He's everything.*

# Chapter 10

## Jake

The following morning, we pack up our camping stuff and spend the day together before heading home. It's the perfect end to a perfect weekend. Watching Abbie's face light up as we discover quirky little shops in tucked away lanes is priceless. Every time I look at her and see the faint pink smudges still visible just above the edge of her top, my mind wanders back to last night. I'm so in love with this girl, there's no going back now. I'm all in. She occasionally rubs her fingers across my still sore knuckles. Thinking about what those fuckers wanted to do to my precious girl makes my blood boil.

By the time I drop Abbie home, it's the evening. I kiss her goodbye on the doorstep and tell her I love her. Now I've told her once I can't stop saying it. I drive home, trying to come up with a plan for how I can stay near Abbie. *Maybe I can stay at Harry's for a bit and find a job?* I'm exhausted, it's probably best to think about this tomorrow after some sleep.

When I get home, it's dark and the house is quiet, so I assume everyone is in bed. I try to be as quiet as I can as I go through to the kitchen to get a glass of water. I'm aware of a figure sat there in the darkness. It's Dad. *Fuck, he scared the crap out of me.*

"Where have you been?" he demands.

"Camping." I snap back. *Here we go. Why does he always have to ruin everything?*

"I've been trying to reach you. Where's your phone?" I can barely see his face in the dark, but I can tell by his tone he's pissed off.

"It died. I can't exactly charge it in a field, can I?" I grab a glass from the cupboard and go to the sink.

"We're leaving, Jake. First thing in the morning. Go pack your stuff," he says, coldly.

"What the fuck? Why? Where are we going this time?" *He can't be serious.*

"Watch your language. I have a business offer I have to deal with, and it's urgent. We leave for the US tomorrow." His tone of voice doesn't change at all. I don't think he ever feels anything.

"What? Like hell I am." My mind is racing a hundred miles an hour. *I can't just up and leave the country, not now.*

"Jake, don't make this difficult. Go pack your stuff and get some sleep. We have an early flight." He stands up as if the conversation is over. Like this is a perfectly normal conversation, and he's said all he has to say. *This can't be happening.*

"This doesn't make any sense, why America? Why now? What the hell am I even meant to do in America?"

The questions come pouring out louder and faster as I try to make some sort of sense of the situation.

"Lower your voice, everyone is asleep," he hisses through gritted teeth. "I told you I have to go for a business deal and you'll do the same thing you would have here. Look for a job." *He is such an arsehole.*

"I'm not leaving." I can hear my pulse thumping in my ears, I'm so worked up. *How did I end up in this parallel universe? I was so fucking happy this morning.*

Dad sighs, I see the outline of his shoulders rise and fall in the dim light. "If this is about the girl... I told you not to get too attached."

"Her name is Abbie. Dad, I love her." I run my hands through my hair in desperation. *I can't leave her, I can't.*

"You're nineteen years old Jake, you don't know what love is," he says dismissively.

I'm so angry I'm shaking. I start to lose my temper and raise my voice.

"What would you know about love, you selfish prick? You've never loved anyone other than yourself."

I know instantly I've crossed the line. Dad flies at me in rage. He grabs me by the neck of my t-shirt and pins me to the wall. He raises his fist to me and I close my eyes, waiting for the blow. He has never hit me before, but I've really pushed him this time. I hold my breath but the punch doesn't come. I open my eyes and look at him. He's shaking with anger and glaring at me, but he slowly lowers his fist.

"Your mother, Jake! I loved your mother so God damn much." His voice is so quiet as he whispers his admission.

"When she died, so did I." He lets go of me and steps back, looking at the floor. Neither of us speak for a minute while I absorb this new information and we both control our breathing. I haven't heard him utter her name since the day of her funeral. The air is heavy with all the years of unspoken words.

"Every time I look at you, I see her." He can't bring his eyes up from the floor as he speaks. I realise in that moment why my dad has always seemed like such a distant, self-absorbed dick. I was young and so consumed by my own grief when Mum died, it never occurred to me that Dad was hurting too. *It still doesn't excuse all the years of neglect and shitty parenting. I was just a kid.*

"Dad, I... " He cuts me off. Just like that his guard goes back up, and he shuts off the emotion he just gave me a glimpse of. He looks at me again now he has composed himself.

"Jake, you will do as I ask. We leave for America in the morning and you *will* be on that plane. I have my reasons, but the less you know, the better. This is not up for discussion."

He turns and leaves the room without looking back. The conversation is over. *How am I supposed to leave Abbie behind? How am I going to tell her? I can't bear the thought of breaking her heart, of breaking my own heart.* I pace the room, running my hands through my hair. I pick up a vase from the windowsill and throw it at the wall.

"FUCK!" I shout as I let go of it and it smashes on the other side of the room. I sit on the edge of the sofa with my head in my hands. *This can't be happening.*

I take out my phone to message Abbie. I don't even know what to say to her. *We've just had the best weekend together. I told her I loved her for God's sake, and now I have to tell her I'm leaving.* I type a message out three times but delete it each time. In the end I simply put:

**Are you still awake? Jx**
**It's pretty late, so she's probably asleep.**
**My phone pings straight away.**

**Yeah I am. I can't stop thinking about**
**this gorgeous guy I spent the weekend**
**with. He rocks my world! x**

*Shit. I feel like the biggest arsehole in the world.* I type back:

**I need to see you. Can you let me in**
**without waking your parents up? J x**

Her reply is instant:

**Easy tiger. Can't stay away eh? x**

Any other night, the thought of sneaking around with Abbie in the dark would make me all kinds of horny, but not tonight. I can feel a lump in my throat just thinking about what I'm about to do. I don't correct her. I just need to see her and get this over with. *It hurts already.*

**Be over in 10. Jx**

When I arrive at Abbie's I go around to the back of the house. The utility room is about as far from her parent's room as possible so I know that's where Abbie will be waiting for me. I can see the light on in there through the window. *Fuck, I feel sick.* I force myself to walk up to the door and open it.

Abbie is standing there in a pair of pale blue pyjama shorts which show the flawless skin on her legs and matching vest top with lacy trim. *She is so damn beautiful.* Her hair is flowing over her shoulders and she smiles a full smile at me as I come through the door. She immediately comes over and drapes her arms around my neck, kissing my cheek. *She smells so good. I breathe her in so I never forget the way she smells.* She starts to trail kisses down my neck and presses up against me. I feel nauseous. *I don't know how to say goodbye to her. I love her more than anything.*

I gently take her wrists and try to unwrap her arms from around my shoulders. "Abbie, we need to talk," I say gently into her hair.

"I don't want to talk. I missed you today." She runs her hands across my chest and they start to head south. I take her hands and remove them from me, instantly missing her touch. *I can't believe I'm putting a stop to this.*

"Not now," I say a bit firmer this time. She stops and looks at me confused.

"Jake, what's wrong? You're acting weird." She looks at me with those big blue eyes and I swallow hard, trying to find the right thing to say. *This is the hardest thing I've ever had to do.*

I stroke the back of her hands with my thumbs as I talk. "So, you know I told you that me and Dad move around a lot and we would probably be moving away somewhere at the end of the summer?" I pause, trying to find some balls to say what's coming next.

"Yes," she says hesitantly. Her eyes are frantically searching mine, trying to find answers about what I'm going to say.

"But it's ok, we've talked about this. Wherever you move to we have a plan, remember?" She pauses, searching my face for some clue as to what I'm thinking.

"I know and I wish to God that could still happen, but there is no plan for this." I drop my head and look at the floor. I can't bear to look at her worried face any more.

"No plan for what, Jake? Please, just tell me what's going on? What's changed?" I can hear in her voice she's starting to panic and when I manage to look at her again, there are tears in her eyes.

"Abbie, I'm so sorry, we are going to the States... tomorrow." I can barely get the last word out. It catches in my throat and comes out as barely a whisper. I'm still holding her hands in front of me and I try to pull her closer so I can hold her, but she drops my hands and steps back like I burned her.

"What?" The tears have spilled over now and are running down her cheeks. *This is torture.*

"When I got back, Dad was waiting for me. He had been trying to get hold of me while we were away. He said we're moving to the States because of some business opportunity he is pursuing." I look anywhere but at Abbie as I talk. I can see she is wiping away tears as she listens.

"But you said you wouldn't be going far and that you'd be able to visit all the time." She's trying so hard not to cry. I just want to hold her but when I step towards her, she takes a step back. *I can't believe how much this hurts. Watching her in pain and knowing I'm the cause.*

"You promised Jake," she whispers as she wipes away more silent tears. The pain in my chest is unbearable. I have no idea how to make any of this any better for either of us.

"Abbie, I'm so sorry. If there was anything I could do to change this, you know I would." I start to choke on the words as they come out and my voice cracks, letting on just how much this hurts me too.

"I love you so much and I'm going to find a way to get back to you no matter how long it takes me." I wipe my own tears away with the arm of my t-shirt. "I promise." I add in barely a whisper.

I look up at her and her eyes are all red and puffy and her shoulders are heaving with the sobs she is still desperately trying to hold back.

"Like you promised before, Jake? Your promises mean nothing!" She lashes out at me with her words. If she had slapped me across the face, it would have hurt less than what she just said.

"Abbie, please, I'm so sorry, please believe me, I will come back. I love you and I've meant every word I've said to you." I try again to close the distance between us, but she pushes me away this time. She's angry and hurt. *This is killing me.*

"Just go." She sobs as she starts to lose control of her emotions altogether.

"Abbie..."

"GET OUT!" she yells at me and opens the door for me to leave.

*This can't be how we end. I can't leave like this.* I hear movement upstairs and I know Abbie's parents have woken from Abbie shouting. I can't deal with them as well; this is bad enough. I take one last look at Abbie through my own tears, pleading with her not to leave things like this, but she doesn't meet my eyes. She looks at the floor as she holds the door open, waiting for me to leave. She is shaking with the effort of holding it all together until I've gone. I don't prolong the torture for either of us any longer. I do what she asks. I walk past her through the open door and commit everything about her to memory, but the look on her face in this moment will haunt me forever.

"I will come back for you," I say quietly, more to myself as I step out into the garden and make a run for my car. I don't look back, I can't. I've just shattered two hearts into a million pieces tonight and I don't know if either of us will ever recover.

# Chapter 11

## Abbie

It's been ten days since Jake left. Ten hollow days of nothing but numbing pain. I've barely left my room. I can't remember the last time I ate. I ran out of tears several days ago. I can't even cry anymore. Now there's just nothing. I spend hours staring at the walls, clutching my chest, hoping I can fix the gaping hole in it. Louisa has messaged a thousand times but I just can't bring myself to talk to anyone.

My parents held me as I sobbed in the beginning, then backed off and gave me space to deal with my heartbreak. Eventually Mum just started leaving cups of tea outside my door and knocking so I knew they were there. I don't think she knows how to help me. Maybe I can't be helped. Dad avoids my room altogether; I think he's fresh out of ideas. Crying women make him uncomfortable.

I lay on my bed staring at the patterns on my artexed ceiling. When I was little, I used to be able to see pictures in the swirling pattern of the plaster. Now everything looks like Jake, or his guitar, or his gorgeous smile, or his muscular physique. *Ugh! This is actual hell! When will the pain ever stop?* My phone vibrates on the bed next to me. I glance at it to see who it is. I've long since stopped dashing to grab it in case it's him. It's never him. He's gone.

**You doing okay today hun? Please let me come see you. You can't hide in there forever. Louisa X**

*Yes, I can.* I turn my phone over and sigh. I just can't deal with any of this. I fiddle with the paper wristband that's still there from the music festival. The best days of my life, swiftly followed by the worst. I think about that weekend and then stop. *Don't torture yourself.* I've been talking to myself in my head a lot lately. I think I might actually be going crazy. I twist the paper wristband around between my fingers. The writing has worn off and the edges have gone all soft, but I still can't bring myself to take it off. *How could he just leave like that? I know I got angry, but I was hurt. He hasn't even called or text.* I have been going over and over this in my head. When I think back to the way he looked and sounded that night, he seemed just as upset as me. *So why hasn't he called?* I text and apologised. I even tried to ring, but it went straight to answerphone.

I know I can't carry on like this forever, moping and hiding in my room, but I have no interest in anything anymore. It's only a matter of days before school starts again. Normally I'd be busy buying new stationery and reading up on the coming syllabus to get a head start, but I haven't even picked up my planner to see what I need. I don't even care.

The sound of voices from downstairs brings me out of my relentless, inner torture. I concentrate on the voices to see if I can work out who's here. I have no interest in seeing anyone, but it's nice to know who I'm ignoring. Before I can figure out who it is, there's a knock at my bedroom door and it swings open. Louisa is standing in the doorway with her arms folded across her chest, looking as if she just swallowed something nasty.

Without moving from my foetal position on the bed, I mumble sarcastically. "Ever heard of waiting to be let in after you knock?"

"Ever heard of showering?" she throws right back at me. "Jesus Abbie, have you been in here this whole time? As in, literally in your bed not moving? You look like shit and it smells like death in here!" She still has her face screwed up as she glances around the chaos of my room.

"If you've come to cheer me up, you're doing a crappy job," I say to her without bothering to look at her. She takes a big sigh, and makes her way over to my window to throw it open, careful to step over all the clothes and cups I haven't bothered to pick up off the carpet over the last ten days. After she's taken a big lungful of fresh

114

air, she comes to sit by me on the edge of the bed.

"What are you doing here, Lou? You only text me like fifteen minutes ago." *That fresh air is nice.* I reluctantly admit to myself. I hadn't noticed just how stuffy it had gotten in here.

"Yes, and yet again you didn't reply. This nonsense has to stop now. It's gone on long enough," she says in a tone usually reserved for mothers scolding their children.

"Nonsense?" I'm getting annoyed and irritated now, so I lean up on my elbows and look at her. "He broke my fucking heart, Lou! It's not nonsense!" *How can she be so insensitive? She's meant to be my best friend!*

"There we go, you said it out loud." She's smiling at me with a mixture of sympathy and smugness as I realise she deliberately pushed my buttons to make me talk. "I know he did hun. Let's talk about it."

Over the next hour and a half, I finally say all the things that have been going around in my head since Jake left. I cry and talk and cry some more. I thought I'd run out of tears, but apparently not. As soon as I started talking to Louisa, the floodgates reopened and out poured a tsunami of my inner most thoughts and feelings. I know I can talk to Louisa, I can tell her anything, but it took me a while to get there this time. It was almost like all the while I hid in my room and didn't say it out loud it might not be real. I wouldn't go as far as to say I feel better, but I certainly feel lighter now that we've talked. All this time Louisa has hardly said a word. She has just listened and hugged me and passed me tissues when necessary. When I finally stop crying and have finished pouring my heart out, my eyes are all red and puffy and my nose is blocked up. My ribs ache from all the sobbing and I have a headache.

"So, how about that shower?" Louisa nudges my arm with hers and smiles at me.

I let out the first hint of a laugh in ten days. "Yea, maybe you're right," I say as I look over at myself in the mirror on my dresser. "Geez, I look like an extra from a horror film," I groan as I take in my mascara-streaked appearance.

For the rest of the afternoon Louisa forces me to look after myself. After I shower and dry my hair and put clothes on other than my pyjamas, I must admit I do feel much better. We spend the afternoon doing some of my favourite things. Some of my favourite *girl* things. Nothing that will remind me of Jake, or rather nothing that will remind me more than the constant ache in my chest already does. Louisa paints my nails and we watch silly movies together; strictly comedy only. By the time she leaves that evening, I'm glad she came and forced me to finally return to the land of the living.

She hugs me on the way out. "You know where I am if you need me. No more hiding, ok?"

I nod and squeeze her back tightly. I take a

deep breath and head back into the house where my parents are waiting in the kitchen. I can tell by their faces they are treading carefully, trying to gauge my mood and state of mind.

"Feeling a bit better, angel?" Mum asks tentatively.

I nod and give her a small smile and I can see them both visibly relax and drop their shoulders slightly. I must have really worried them being shut up there for so long refusing to talk and eat.

"Cuppa?" Dad offers as he gets out of the armchair.

"Yes please, that sounds nice," I say and I realise I actually mean it. On his way past Dad puts his hand on my head and strokes my hair like he did when I was little.

"You're going to be ok, kiddo. You'll see." He gives me one last pat on the head as he leaves to make the tea. *I really want to believe that's true.*

\*\*\*

The new school year has been back in full swing for a few days now and I have forced myself to play an active part in daily life, at least on the outside. Louisa and I don't have a lot of classes together this year, which means I can mostly get through the days without saying much to anyone.

I've been hoping to run into Harry so I can ask him if he's heard from Jake. I don't know if I really want to know the answer. *What if he's been in touch with Harry and not me? No, he wouldn't do that, would he?* I keep looking for Harry in the corridors between lessons, hoping to catch sight of him, but there's been no sign of him so far.

Today is the only day in my timetable where Louisa and I have a free study period together, so we decide to go sit in the library. I try to look busy in my notebook, so Louisa won't want to talk too much. I don't know what else to say to her. I'm doing my best, but nothing has any purpose or meaning anymore. I just go through the motions for everyone else's sake.

Eventually she calls me out on my fake reading, probably because I haven't turned the page in quite some time. "You doing ok, hun?" She has to whisper because talking is not strictly allowed in the library.

I look up from the same page I've been staring at for probably almost ten minutes and nod. As I look up at Louisa, I notice a group of girls come and sit down at the small table behind her. Not only are they talking and laughing, but they are also messing about on their phones, all of which are against the library rules. I give it all of five minutes before they are kicked out by the overbearing librarian who runs a tight ship here.

As I try to go back to my pretend reading. I

can't help but overhear what the girls are talking about; they're not exactly being quiet. They are scrolling through photos on their phone when I hear one of them mention Harry.

"Oh my God, look at this one from Harry's party last year," one of them says as she passes a photo around on her phone. All the girls giggle at whatever image is on the screen. Louisa has heard too and has straightened in her chair, trying to eavesdrop.

"Oh and this one, look at him, he's so hot." Another girl passes around a different photo on her phone. The girls are all swooning and practically drooling over the photos.

"He's alright, got nothing on that guitar player guy who was there though. Do you remember him?" one of them says. I instantly stiffen and freeze in my seat. *She's talking about Jake.* Louisa looks at me with sympathy as we continue to listen. The girl doesn't stop there.

"He was the hottest guy I think I've ever seen. Did you see his muscles in that black t-shirt? Damn, if he hadn't disappeared halfway through, I would've been all over that," she says as she flicks her hair over her shoulder and pouts. I can feel tears start to sting the back of my eyes. *I need to get out of here.* I hurriedly pack up my books and try to block out the rest of their conversation.

"I think he was a friend of Harry's," one of the others adds. I can't help but still hear them as I rush to gather my stuff up.

"He was definitely older than us, I reckon he's got plenty of experience." All the girls giggle at the that last comment.

*For the love of God, please stop! I can't listen to this.* I shove the last book into my bag and stand up in such a hurry that my chair tips over causing a loud bang and everyone turns to look at me, including the group of girls who were talking about Jake. *My Jake. Except he isn't mine anymore.* Now I'm upset and embarrassed and can't get out of here quick enough.

The further we walk away from the library and the group of girls the more I start to calm down. The threatening tears have subsided and I can breathe again. *How could they talk about Jake like that? Like he's some prize to be handed around. They just assume because he's older than us and insanely good-looking that he must have been with loads of girls. People are such arseholes!*

As we round the corner to the next corridor, we catch sight of Harry up ahead. Louisa spots him the same time I do and calls him.

"Harry!" she yells.

Harry turns to look for who called his name. When he sees it's Louisa he instantly grins and gestures for her to follow him into an empty classroom. *Oh geez, he thinks this is a quick hook up!* I don't think he saw me standing there too. *Awkward.* Louisa tugs on my arm and pushes us through the sea of people in the corridor until we get to the classroom Harry went in. As we go through the door Harry is sat on one of the tables with his bag casually slung over one shoulder. He is still grinning like the cat that got the cream until he spots me trail in next to Louisa. His face instantly drops.

"Fuck, Abbie, are you alright? You look really ill!" Harry blurts out when he sees me. *Great, I knew I must still look like shit but it sure as hell hurts to hear it out loud.*

Louisa shoots a glare at him and nudges his leg.

"Harry! That is not helpful! She's fine. Aren't you Abz?" She waits for me to reply but I just nod and give Harry a weak smile.

"Ooook, if you say so. So, what's this about? I thought you were dragging me in here to have your wicked way with me," he teases Louisa, although I don't think he's actually joking. Maybe they've hooked up at school before.

"No Harry, that was a summer thing. We both knew that. Time to move on," she says matter-of-factly. Harry laughs and holds his hands up defensively.

"Can't blame a guy for trying." He grins and shakes his head at Louisa's complete lack of interest.

"So anyway, Abz wants to know if you've heard from Jake." Louisa gets straight to business and I feel uncomfortable all of a sudden. *Harry must think I'm such a loser.* Harry's face instantly changes, all traces of humour gone now.

"No, I haven't," he says as he looks at the floor. I must admit a slight feeling of relief washes over me that it's not just me he's ditched.

"What happened, Harry? You must know, he lived with you." I finally find my voice realising how much I need the answers to these questions. He shifts uncomfortably on the table but doesn't speak, so I go on.

"We had the best weekend together and then he turns up at my house in the middle of the night and tells me he's leaving for America the next day. Just like that! He just left!" I realise I'm getting louder and faster the more I talk about that night.

"We argued because I was upset, but he hasn't called. Why hasn't he called?" By the end of my rant, I'm practically shouting, and I angrily wipe away a tear that has escaped down my cheek. Harry looks genuinely terrified by my outburst of emotion, but he swallows and attempts to reply.

"I don't know what to tell you, Abbie," he says quietly. "I'm as angry about it all as you are."

"I doubt that!" Louisa scoffs. "You weren't in love with him!" I glare at Louisa to shut up. Harry doesn't need to know that. I gesture to Harry for him to continue.

"His dad is a real prick. Always moving him around. We knew they would go again after the summer, but it's not normally far. All I know is we heard shouting that night when we were all in bed. It was Jake and his dad downstairs. Then Jake left, which I take it now was to go see you. In the morning when I got up Mum and Dad said they had gone. There was a note on the kitchen table from Harry's dad saying there was a business deal in the US and they had to go." Harry does look genuinely upset as he relays the story.

"I tried phoning him loads of times but his number says out of service and all his social media profiles are gone." The same thing happened when I tried to call. It never occurred to me to look for him on social media though. I don't use it.

"Why would he do that? Cut all ties from everyone like that?" I ask quietly. *None of this makes sense.*

"I honestly don't know Abbie, but you can bet your life his dickhead dad is the reason. He's involved in some shady shit and now it looks like he's got Jake all mixed up in it too." Harry pauses and rubs the back of his neck.

"You need to leave it alone and move on, Abbie," he says, gently. *As if that's even possible.*

"I need to get to class, you girls going to be ok? I really am sorry, Abbie," he says as he gets up to leave. I've never seen the sensitive side of Harry before. I'm glad Jake has a friend like him.

When I get home, I think back on my earlier conversation with Harry. It has been replaying in my head all day. I have come to the sad realisation that this really is where mine and Jake's story ends. He's gone and never coming back. I pick up the music festival wristband that has been laying on my dresser since the day Louisa came around and I run my thumb over the faded print. I reach around and take off the plectrum necklace Jake gave me for my birthday and place them both in my top drawer carefully. *It's time to pack Jake away.* I take one last look at the items and commit them to memory before I slowly close the drawer. All I have left now is the Jake sized hole in my life and the constant ache in my chest to remind me he ever existed. *Bye Jake.*

*- 8 years later -*

# Chapter 12

## Abbie

Today has been a long day. I love my teaching job, but it is tiring. I've been teaching for three years and have just started at a new school this term. These new kids are wild! I know I've got my work cut out. The staff at the new school are great though. Much more supportive than my old job which was one of my reasons for leaving.

It's the end of the week and I'm walking home through the high street. It doesn't take long, it's about a fifteen-minute walk and it does me good. It gives me a chance to clear my head before I go home. My bags are heavy with marking tonight though and all I want to do is go home, run a hot bath and have a glass of wine. *That's about as exciting as my Friday nights get.* It's late September, so the air is getting damp and chilly and my walks home are becoming darker. I pull my scarf tighter around my neck and quicken my pace.

I arrive home to be greeted by Maisy. Her scruffy little face and waggy tail always make me smile. No one is ever as pleased to see me as she is. My parents bought her for me to keep me company when I moved out and got my own house. Not that I've moved far, I'm still in the same town and I'm pretty certain if I shouted from my garden Mum and Dad could hear me from theirs. I don't live an exciting life by any means, but I'm content. *I guess.*

I throw my keys down on the counter and kick my shoes off, heading straight for the fridge. I pour myself a glass of wine and set the bath running. *Heaven.* Once it's run deep enough, I step in and slide under the bubbles. *That feels so good.* I take a sip of my wine and put it back on the side. Checking my phone for the first time all day, I find there's a missed call from my mum and a text message from Louisa.

### Hi hun, you haven't forgotten about tomorrow night have you? X

*Oh shit!* I groan out loud to myself. I had forgotten that Louisa was dragging me out on yet another double date tomorrow. I sink back in the bubbles and sigh. She does this all the time. She meets a guy and tries to hook me up with one of his idiot friends. I think back to the last one a few months back. *What a disaster that was! He was such a sexist pig I made my excuses and left before dessert!* You'd think Louisa would have given up by now. None of them ever interest me, but it's like finding me a man is her life's mission. I don't understand why. She should put her efforts into making her own relationships last longer. Louisa is a serial dater and has been for years. She still enjoys the thrill of the chase and quickly gets bored with them. *Poor guys.*

I message her back.

**I'm not feeling well. I think it's serious, maybe the plague? X**

She texts straight back in shouty capitals. *She's so easy to wind up.*

**YOU DO NOT HAVE THE PLAGUE! I think you will like this one. X**

*I highly doubt that.* I've never liked any of them in the four years we have both been back from Uni. Louisa and I were apart for three years while we attended different universities. She studied journalism while I qualified as a teacher.

**You say that every time. Don't worry I'll be there x**

I take a few more sips of wine and try to forget about tomorrow as I sink down into the hot water.

***

I hate this date already and it hasn't even started yet. I reluctantly had to agree to meet them all outside the pub because Louisa is coming straight from work. Otherwise, I would have gone with her. I still don't like arriving at places on my own, that has never changed. I go to tap the name of the pub into my sat nav as I start the car on the drive, but realise I can't remember what she said. I hunt around in my handbag for the scrap of paper I wrote it down on the other day. *The Rose* I read out loud to myself and type it in. As the map starts to load a sudden realisation hits me hard. *That's the same pub I went to with Jake. The one where we had our first kiss! Shit! Now I definitely don't want to go.*

For years it was a full-time job trying *not* to think about Jake. He consumed my every waking thought for a long time after he left. Slowly, but surely, though, I managed to put my memories and thoughts away in the same box where I keep his necklace and lock them away. That's usually where they stay, but every now and then something will make me think of him and it's always like a sledge hammer straight to the chest when it happens. In the beginning when I thought of him it would be with sadness and love, but over time those feelings got replaced by anger. Anger at how he could just leave and never look back, not even a phone call.

I'm certain he is the reason I never enjoy any

of Louisa's double dates. They've not all been bad guys, many of them have even been pretty good-looking, but they all have one fatal flaw, *they're not Jake.* The irony isn't lost on me that the one man whose memory makes my blood boil is also the only man I dream about. *Ironic, huh?* Just because I've managed to teach my conscious mind not to think of him much anymore doesn't mean my subconscious has followed suit. Unfortunately, in my dreams Jake is very much present and in high-definition hotness on a regular basis.

I take a deep breath and set off to the pub. When I pull up in the car park, I can see that Louisa is already standing outside with two men. They seem nice and normal looking. *That's a start, I guess.* As I get out of the car and walk up to them, I realise they are more than just nice and normal looking, these two are off the charts gorgeous. *Where does Louisa find these men?* They all turn to greet me with a smile and Abbie introduces me to her date, whose name is Mike, and the other man shakes my hand and kisses me on the cheek as he tells me his name is Scott. The gesture is purely platonic and friendly, but it makes my shoulders tense up. It would seem being back here already has my senses on hyper-alert. *It's going to be a long evening.*

When we go through to find our table, I can see that things have changed inside from when I was last here, but not enough. It's the smell that hits me first, it smells exactly the way it did that night when I came to watch Jake play for the first time. The tables have been re-arranged a little and the place has clearly had a lick of paint, but it's essentially the same. To further add to my discomfort, we are seated by a table that is in direct view of the small stage area. It's not as big as I remember it. I rub my hands on my coat discreetly before taking it off and hanging it over the back of my chair. *I'm sure my palms are sweating.*

"So, Abbie," Scott says as we take our seats. "What is it you do?"

He is good looking. I notice when he smiles, he has dimples in his cheeks. It also didn't escape my attention when he took his coat off that he is built like a rugby player.

"I'm a primary school teacher," I say, trying to look as relaxed and comfortable as possible. "What about you?"

"That's awesome, you must love all the time off." I roll my eyes internally. *Here we go again, why does everyone think teachers only teach for the holidays?* I try not to let my irritation show as he continues.

"I'm a fireman," he says quietly, as if he's used to it drawing a lot of attention. *Explains why he's built like a tank,* I think to myself. He's actually quite sweet. I really should make more of an effort to give him a chance rather than being so preoccupied with my surroundings.

Over the course of the evening, Scott and I are pretty much left to talk amongst ourselves as Louisa and Mike barely take their eyes off each other. He's been the perfect gentleman, topping up my wine glass regularly and making a point of listening to the answer when he asks me a question. It's amazing how many dates I've been on where that wasn't the case. Often too busy trying to look down my top or checking out someone else walking past. At least Scott has the decency not to do either of those things.

I'm trying so hard to give Scott my full attention the way he is me. He does have a lot of interesting things to say, but I just can't stop my mind from wandering back to the night I was last here. I can almost hear Jake singing and see him up on the stage in all his sweaty gloriousness from that night. It's a night I never let myself think about, along with so many others, but being back here I can't help it. It's like my mind is showing a re-run of the entire thing on a loop.

Suddenly, I realise I must have been staring at the stage and not heard what Scott said because he turns to look at what I'm staring at before turning back to me.

"Abbie? You ok?" As he asks me, he reaches across the table and puts his hand over mine. I'm immediately snapped back to the present and without thinking I pull my hand out from under his and put it back in my lap. I don't miss the confused look on his face at my bizarre behaviour. *Geez, I'm such an idiot. Get it together.* I also realise that Louisa and Mike have stopped talking to see what's going on.

"Sorry, please excuse me a minute. I need to use the bathroom." I get up as quick as I can and scurry off the toilets where I won't have so many eyes on me while I compose myself. Not that I get much of a reprieve before I hear the door open and Louisa stomp in after me.

"What on earth is wrong with you?" she asks as she glares at me with her hands on her hips.
I don't turn around; I just look at her in the mirror and shrug.

"In case you haven't noticed, there is a smoking hot fireman out there who hasn't taken his eyes off you all night and you can't even hold a half decent conversation with him because you keep staring off into space. What's going on?"

I give a big sigh as I take my lipstick out of my bag and start to reapply it in the mirror.

"I don't know Lou, I'm just not feeling it. He's really nice and all that, but…"

"But what, Abz? There's always a but!" She hesitates, as if deciding whether to say the next thing she wants to say. "Is this about Jake Greyson?"

Just the very mention of his name makes the hairs on the back of my neck stand up. We haven't talked about Jake for years, he's always the elephant in the room. *Why would she bring him up now? I don't think she even knows we ever came here.*

"Why would you say that?" I ask her trying not to look affected by the question, but failing miserably.

"I didn't know whether to tell you when I saw the article, but I guess you've already seen it. So, what if he's coming back, Abz? You can't keep letting someone you spent one summer with affect you for the rest of your life. Do you think I don't know what's been going on all these years?" Louisa is rambling out of annoyance; she's clearly wanted to say these things to me for a long time.

"Hold on, go back the first thing you said. What article?"

"Jake and his band are coming to the UK on tour," she says. "I assumed that's what you've got your knickers in a knot about."

I shake my head at her. "How would I know that?"

"It's big news, Abz, you know how famous he is now... world famous. It's been all over social media, which I know you don't do, but it made the front page of Rolling Stone magazine."

I had heard several years back that Jake had made it to the big time and his band had gone global. I remember stopping dead in the street one day when I saw his face on the front cover of another magazine. I purchased a copy and read it countless times before tucking it away in the box where I keep all my Jake memories.

I carry on shaking my head. "No, I didn't know that." *This is a lot to process.* He's never come back to the UK since the day he left. I wonder if he even remembers me? *Of course not you idiot. He's a world-famous rock star and you're just a girl he spent one summer with years ago.*

"Then what is wrong with you tonight if it's not that? Scott is clearly into you and he's a nice guy." Louisa doesn't really get it, but I can't say I blame her; neither do I and I'm the one living it!

I let out another sigh "I know, I'm sorry. I'll do better. Come on let's have pudding." I kiss Louisa on the cheek and link arms with her to walk back into the restaurant. *I can put this to the back of my mind for one evening, can't I?*

I do my best to enjoy the rest of the evening and it passes quick. Scott and Mike are nice guys. The chocolate fudge cake here turned out to be heavenly, so that certainly helped things. As we all head out of the restaurant to our cars, it's clear that Louisa has every intention of going home with Mike. *Well, this is awkward.* Scott says goodbye and starts to lean in for a goodnight kiss. *Oh God! Oh no!* I start to panic inside. I don't want him to kiss me, and especially not here. This is where Jake kissed me for the first time, I can't have Scott taint that memory. I turn my head at the last minute so he can't reach my lips and peck him on the cheek instead. *What the fuck is wrong with me?* This guy is like a pin-up, but I feel absolutely nothing when I look at him.

*Maybe I'm dead inside.*

Scott remains a perfect gentleman and respects the distance I swiftly put between us. He smiles awkwardly at me but doesn't comment on my blatant rejection of his advances.

"It was lovely to meet you, Abbie. I hope I'll see you again sometime." I smile and nod slightly in return. *Thank goodness he didn't ask for my number.*

And there we have it, I have managed once again to sabotage another perfectly good date with a perfectly nice man. The only crime these poor men are ever guilty of is not being Jake Greyson. *I need to sort my shit out before I end up alone forever with my dog.*

# Chapter 13

## Jake

As soon as the plane touches down at Heathrow, I think I'm going to throw up. I'm finally home. Everything that's happened over the past eight years has been about getting me to this point. I can't fuck this up, not now. Thank God the guys and I were on a private flight so no one could see 'The one and only Jake Greyson' shitting himself for the entire journey. This was how a recent magazine headline referred to me back in the US. I have no idea what the article was actually about. I never read the shit that gets printed about me. I dread to think what's out there about me in the media over the years. I've not exactly handled fame well.

The airport is filled with paparazzi. The, all too familiar flash of cameras starts up the minute we walk into the terminal. *Fucking leeches, I don't have time for this shit today.* Our security team walk ahead of us to clear the way. Once we have made our way through the scrum of press, I go with the guys to check into the hotel. I've booked us in for one night close to the airport so we can sleep off the jetlag, and then we have two weeks off to go our separate ways before we start the tour. *Two weeks to find her.*

I look in the mirror of the hotel bathroom. I look like shit. All I want to do is go start my search for Abbie. I've waited so long and been through so much to get back here, but I need to sleep first. It's just after ten in the evening now. I'll feel better after a shower, a shave, and some shut-eye.

*** 

Twelve hours later, I'm feeling refreshed. I've said goodbye to the lads for a couple of weeks and now I'm standing on Harry's parents' doorstep. It's been a long time, I've missed them. I ring the doorbell and wait. I have absolutely no idea if they even still live here, but not much has changed looking at the outside, so I'm hopeful. I ring again, but no one answers. *Damn it.* I turn back towards my car and run my hands through my hair in agitation. *Now what? How will I find Harry and Abbie?*

"Jake?" I hear a female voice behind me from the house. I'd know that voice anywhere. *Julie.*

"Oh my god, Jake, is that really you?" I turn to see a teary-eyed Julie. She sees that it's me and throws her arms around me in a hug. "I've been so worried about you." She takes my face in her hands and looks me over in that way mothers do, as if checking for signs of injury or distress.

"Come in, darling." She ushers me inside the house and calls up the stairs. "Mac! Mac! You have to come down here!" I take a seat at the kitchen counter while Julie fusses around me, waiting for Mac to come down the stairs. Everything is exactly as I remember it. It's strangely comforting.

Mac comes into view, and he actually smiles. I'm not sure I've ever seen him smile.

"Well, blow me down, if it isn't Jake Greyson! How are you, son?" *Son*. The sentiment catches me off guard and I feel a lump form in my throat. I clear my throat and swallow the emotion that's bubbling up.

"I'm doing ok thank you, Mac. It's good to see you both." There's so much I want to say and ask, but I don't know where to start. Julie sets a cup of tea down in front of me. She's remembered how I like it.

"Harry will be coming over shortly, dear. He'll be so pleased to see you." Julie gives my arm a squeeze just like she used to and takes a seat next to me.

"How is Harry? What's he doing with himself these days?" I ask as I drink my tea.

Julie goes to speak, but Mac jumps in. "He's doing well. He's taken over the law firm now and is very successful at it. It's meant I can retire and take a back seat. I just help out in an advisory role a couple of days a week." I can see how proud Mac is that Harry has made something of himself.

"That's great news. Good for him." I'm so glad Harry and his family are happy and well.

Julie adds. "He lives in the city as he doesn't like the commute, but he spends a lot of time here still when he's not working." Just then I hear the front door open and shut.

"Speak of the devil," says Mac. "Morning Son, look who dropped by," he shouts to Harry who is still in the hall somewhere.

Harry comes into the kitchen in a full suit and tie, looking every bit the hot shot lawyer.

"Jake fucking Greyson!" He breaks into a huge smile as he walks over to me. "How the hell are you, man?"

"Harry! Language!" Julie scolds, but she's smiling at our interaction. Harry slaps me on the back and pulls me in for a bear hug.

"I'm good, bro. Look at you, doing well for yourself, I hear." I gesture to his designer suit.

"Can't complain my friend. The ladies love it." *Same Harry I remember.* He has the same stupid grin it's just on a more manly face. "So how's fame treating you?"

"It's absolutely mental." Harry and his parents sit and listen intently over the next couple of hours as I tell them all about the band and our rise to fame. I explain how tours work and recording contracts, what New York's like and what life is like now. We talk for hours and I ask them what's been happening back home while

I've been away. The whole conversation flows naturally and feels so comfortable. It's good to be here. We laugh and talk, Julie makes lunch and still the conversation doesn't run out. There's so much to talk about.

Eventually the conversation comes to the inevitable topic of my sudden departure all those years ago. Julie is the one who's brave enough to bring it up. We've talked around it this whole time.

"How's your dad darling?" she asks gently. I've never known how much they knew about the circumstances around us leaving. "We know why you had to leave. We tried to make him see sense, but he was in over his head. There was nothing we could do to stop him," Julie says sadly.

"I'm so sorry that he involved you all in any way and I'm even more sorry that I haven't been able to get in touch with you all these years." I stare into my tea cup unable to look any of them in the eye. I feel so sad and embarrassed about what happened. "I promise I will explain everything," I add quietly.

Julie gives me one of her reassuring arm squeezes. "There will be plenty of time for that later darling. You don't owe us any sort of explanation. None of it was your fault. We are just so relieved you are alive and well."

I look up at the three of them and the warm smiles on their faces tells me that they all feel the same way. For the first time in a long time, I start to relax knowing I still have their acceptance. It's like a huge weight has been lifted off my shoulders.

"Anyway, we have some things to attend to don't we, Mac? Let's leave the boys to catch up." From the look on Mac's face I can tell that's not true at all, but that Julie just wants to give us some time and space to talk.

Once they've left the room Harry puts down his mug and looks at me like he's really studying me.

"It's so good to see you man, but how are you really?" *Damn lawyers and their inbuilt lie detectors.*

"Honestly? I'm a mess." It feels good to finally admit that to someone. I run my hands through my hair, a sure sign of my stress. "The fame is hardcore, man. It sounds awful to moan about something most people dream about, but it's true. I get followed and photographed everywhere I go, and then slated on social media for every bad decision I make... of which there have been plenty."

Harry chuckles. "Yeah, I've seen a few headlines over the years, you've certainly had an eventful time. Although I know more than anyone not to believe everything I hear and read, I wouldn't do well in the court room if I did."

I nod in agreement. "Some of it's total bullshit, but unfortunately some of it is true. I've got into more fights than I'd like to admit." I shake my head as I think about some of my past misdemeanours.

"So, if it's as rough as you say it is, man, why don't you give it up? You must be able to afford to by now. Fuck, I'm surprised you didn't land a private helicopter in the garden."

I laugh out loud at Harry's ridiculous suggestion. It feels good to laugh, it's been a while.

"It's a long and complicated story. Why don't we go out for a beer tonight and I'll fill you in?"

"Yea, that sounds really good man." Harry gets the same cheeky glint in his eye I remember. The one he saves for when he thinks there's fun to be had.

"I'll have my driver come pick you up. We'll need to go somewhere with exclusive booking areas, obviously," I say a bit more casually than I meant to. This shit is my normal life now. I can't just go out in public for a quiet drink.

"*Obviously*, Mr Famous Fucking Rockstar." He laughs sarcastically. Just like that we slide back into our old routine of brotherly banter. It's like I've never been away. *Almost.*

***

Harry and I have been at the bar for several hours now. We've got a private booth in an exclusive club where only the rich and famous hang out. It's more discreet that way. We can enjoy our night out without being hounded by fans and photographers.

Over the course of the evening, I have explained the whole story to Harry. Every fucked-up detail since the night I left. For the first time ever he's speechless, just listening. When I'm finally done, he blows out a breath before downing a mouthful of beer.

"Fuck me man, that's a hell of an eight years you've had." He goes to speak a couple of times, but I don't think he can decide what question to ask first. Eventually he settles on; "So where is your old man now?"

"I left him over there with enough money to get his shit together and told him to stay the fuck out of my life for good." Harry nods at my answer and rubs his hand across his chin in thought.

"I take it your legal team for the band knows nothing about any of this?" he asks.

"No man, course not. The other guys don't even know. I've managed to keep it quiet the whole time, which was no easy task when my whole life is played out under a microscope."

One of the bar staff saunters up to our table with a flirtatious smile on her face and a sway in her hips that I'm sure is exaggerated for our benefit as she walks over.

"I hope you're enjoying your evening, Mr Greyson. Is there anything I can get for you and your guest?" She flutters her eyelashes and leans over the table to collect our glasses. She leans over more than is necessary to make sure we get a full view of what's spilling out of her dress. The less than subtle gesture has definitely caught Harry's attention.

"Hi, I'm Harry, Mr Greyson's friend and lawyer. I'll have another beer please, Miss..." He takes her hand and kisses the back of it as he waits for her to offer her name.

"You can call me, Ava." She smiles sweetly at him as she takes our empty glasses and disappears back to the bar. Harry has to rearrange himself in his jeans as she walks away.

"You have no shame man." I laugh and shake my head at him. He's a supposedly respectable lawyer but still behaves like a horny teenager. "Anyway, since when did you become my lawyer?"

"Since now. I know you seem pretty certain that your past problems with these people are dealt with and over, but you never know so it doesn't hurt to have someone in your corner who knows the score. Plus, I'm the best, I never lose. Those fuckers won't stand a chance if I come after them." Harry smiles cockily at me.

Ava then reappears with our beers and places them on the table.

"Is there anything else I can get for you gentleman?" I shake my head politely and look at my beer. It's hard to look a woman in the face when she's deliberately putting her goods out on display. Being famous I get this all the time.

Women who think if they dangle themselves in front of me, I won't be able to resist. The irony is that couldn't be further from the truth. There's nothing I find more attractive than a woman who has no idea how beautiful she is. *Someone like Abbie.* Harry on the other hand seems to love it. He leans closer to Ava and whispers in her ear. I can't hear what he's saying, but it makes her blush and giggle so I imagine he's not asked her for a packet of crisps.

As Ava heads back to the bar, Harry gives me a wicked grin. "Well, I know where I'm getting my kicks tonight. Now let's get to the real crux of the story. You've danced around it all night my friend. Don't think I haven't noticed. You want to find her, don't you?"

For all his endless pratting around Harry still gets me. "Yeah man, I need to find her. Since the day I left everything I've done has been so I can come back for her." I run my hands through my hair starting to feel tense. *What if Harry has no idea where she is?*

"Eight years is a hell of a long-time man. What makes you think she would have waited for you?"

"Hope, I guess. All I could do was hope that if she felt even a fraction of what I feel for her then she'd trust I'd make my way back to her."

"That's some deep Jane Austen shit you're hitting me with. I had no idea you had it this bad, man." Harry chuckles at his own joke to try and lighten the mood.

"I hate to piss on your bonfire but last I heard Abbie was married to some high-flying doctor with a couple of sprogs running around."

*Shit no! This can't be happening.* "Fuck!" I say much louder than I meant to and launch my beer mat across the table onto the floor.

"I'm shitting you man, she's single." Harry ducks as I launch another beer mat, but this time I aim directly for his head.

"You're such a dick! Tell me what you know. Where is she?" *I can't believe he's messing with me right now!*

"Calm down, lover boy. I don't know exactly where she lives, but I still hook up with Louisa from time to time. I swear that woman gives the best head in all of England." I'm glaring at Harry now willing him to get to the point. "Anyway, she tells me all the time how she takes Abbie on double dates with her, but she never likes any of them. She's convinced it's because of you."

My mind is spinning with this new information. On the one hand I'm so fucking relieved that she's not met someone else and I still have a chance. On the other hand, I feel like shit if it's true that I hurt her so bad she's never given anyone else a chance.

"I hate to say it bro, but I think she could be right. I haven't seen Abbie since we left school, but when she came back for final year after you left, she was a mess. She looked really ill for ages and I never saw her at another party. Louisa said she didn't get out of bed for days. Sorry, man."

I don't even know what to say. I feel like I did that night all over again, as if I've had all the air knocked out of me. The thought of being the cause of her pain makes me feel sick. I need to make this right.

Harry fills the silence. He can see my mind has gone into overdrive. "Listen man, Louisa is never going to give me her address, especially if she suspects it's for you. She still blames you for everything, but I do know where they like to eat out *a lot* so you could try that."

Finally, a small ray of hope that I have a chance to fix things. *I'm coming baby.*

# Chapter 14

## *Abbie*

It's just after seven when I arrive at the new Italian restaurant in town to have dinner with my work friends. I've been here lots of times now and it's fast becoming my new favourite place to eat. They do the most divine tiramisu. I spot my friends sitting at a table in the far corner and wave as I head over and sit down. Shelly has already ordered me a glass of wine, which I am very appreciative of.

"Ugh, how long was today's staff meeting?" she asks the group as she swirls her own glass around in her hand. Everyone nods and rolls their eyes in agreement.

Steve puts down his menu and adds. "The boss man does like to go on a bit." Steve is quite good looking in an older, distinguished sort of way. He's rocking the silver fox vibe and I guess for most women he would be considered quite a catch. *I'm just not feeling it though*. I never like anyone enough to want to make a go of anything. Steve has hinted a couple of times at the idea of going on a date, but so far, I've managed to deflect his advances without too much of an issue. I feel bad though, there's absolutely nothing wrong with him. *It's me.*

We are all catching up on the day's events and have chosen what we want to eat when the waitress comes over to take our order. She starts to go around the table asking each of us in turn, but she doesn't get far when there is suddenly a lot of noise and commotion at the front door. The atmosphere in the restaurant instantly changes to one of excitement. *What is going on?* Shelley is having a hard time hearing the waitress over the noise.

I lean in to Steve so he can hear me. "What's all the excitement about?"

"I don't know, but I think I heard someone on the table behind say it's someone famous." he shrugs, seeming rather unimpressed by the whole thing. "It must be the Queen judging by all the fuss!" He laughs at his own joke as I crane my neck to try and see who it is, but there's too many people in the way.

The waitress comes to me and I just about hear her ask me what I would like over the noise. I glance down at the menu to check the Italian again. I hate mispronouncing and sounding like an idiot. When I look up at the waitress a gap has appeared in the crowd of people at the entrance and now, I can see exactly who all the fuss is about.

*Holy. Fucking. Shit.* I'd know those eyes anywhere. They haunt my dreams. *Jake.* His eyes are focussed on me through the crowded restaurant like a laser beam. I freeze on the spot, unable to do anything other than stare right back at him. My mouth goes dry and my heart rate soars. I can't even think straight. *How is he here?* We must have only locked eyes for a few seconds, but it feels like time has stood still. All I can hear is my pulse thumping in my ears.

"Ma'am, what can I get you?" The waitress repeats for maybe the second or third time. I just continue to look past her at the man who has occupied my subconscious for the past eight years. I feel like I can't breathe. Then all too soon, our gaze is broken as Jake is ushered from the door by a member of staff around to a quieter part of the restaurant.

"Are you alright Abbie?" Shelley asks. "You look like you've seen a ghost."

I shake my head, still unable to process what is happening. *I need to get out of here. I can't breathe. I can't deal with this.*

"I'm sorry everyone, I'm not feeling well. Rain check?" I stand up in a rush almost knocking over my wine.

"I'll walk you home," Steve says as he starts to stand. "You look ever so pale."

"No!" I say a little too abruptly. *I need to be on my own.* "No, thank you Steve, honestly I'll be fine." I try to sound a little less rude. I grab my bag and head to the door as quick as I can. I almost run through the restaurant in my desper-

151

ation to get outside.

I reach the door and step out into the fresh air, gasping lungful's of air as if I were being suffocated. It's started raining while I was inside and the cold drops on my skin are just what I need to calm myself down. My brain is running at a hundred miles an hour along with my pulse. *What is he doing here?* I knew he was coming back to the UK, but what is he doing *here*? In this exact town and restaurant. I always wondered how I would feel if I ever saw him again, now I know: *a shitty mess!*

I head down the street towards home, walking at a fast pace. It's raining hard and I didn't bring a coat. I can feel the droplets soaking into my jumper as I half walk, half run to get home.

"Abbie!" I hear my name shouted from somewhere behind me. *Surely not? Please tell me he hasn't followed me.* I keep my head down and quicken my steps even further. The panic beginning to rise again.

"Abbie, wait!" His voice is louder, so I know he's catching me up. *Shit I don't know what to do or say to him. I never expected to see him again.* My head is a swirling mess of emotions and confusion.

He closes the gap between us and gently pulls my arm.

"Abbie. Where are you going?" He sounds as distraught as I feel.

I spin around to face him, my fear and hurt

turning to anger. "Home," I say angrily before trying to continue walking. I don't want him to see the affect he has on me and how much pain he caused. *I just want to get home.* He blocks my path though so I can't get past and his expression softens.

"Please just talk to me, Abbie." I can't look him in the eye for fear of crumbling completely. I give into my anger instead.

"Talk about what, Jake? I have nothing to say to you!" I raise my voice more than I meant to, taking us both by surprise. I focus on the puddles gathering on the floor still not able to look at his beautiful face.

His frustration is rising to match my anger. "You at least owe me an explanation!" he practically shouts.

*Of all the nerve! What an entitled, jumped up arsehole! I imagine now he's famous everyone just bows to his every whim! Well not me!*

"For what?" I yell back. "You left me remember?" I make the fatal mistake of looking at him. He's standing there in the pouring rain, water dripping from his hair into his gorgeous brown eyes. His anger is palpable, almost rippling over his body as he watches me and yet he has never looked sexier.

"You know I had no choice! I never gave up on us Abbie, that's on you!" He looks genuinely hurt as he continues to yell at me in the rain.

"What the hell are you talking about Jake?"

We've started to attract some stares and a few people have taken out their phones to film us. Great. That's just what I need! To be plastered on social media as the crazy woman yelling at a famous rock star in the street! Jake notices too and regains some composure. I can see behind him his security guys are getting twitchy at Jake's unexpected exit and the scene we are causing.

"Abbie, please just come with me so we can talk in private. You have no idea what I've gone through to get here." He glances over at the gathering onlookers then back at me.

"Please Abbie, the papers will be all over this. I just want to talk." He runs his hand through his dripping wet hair the way he always used to and I feel a little of my resolve weaken. I can't let him back in, it hurts too much.

"I'm sorry, Jake. I can't." It comes out as barely a whisper and I'm not sure if the wetness on my face is solely down to the rain anymore. He takes a step closer to me and I realise that he is even broader than he used to be. His muscles more defined and a five o'clock shadow adorns his square jawline. He still smells the same. I feel my knees start to tremble at his proximity and my breathing speeds up.

He picks up my hand and puts a key card in my palm. "If you change your mind this is where to find me." He says quietly as he looks deep into my eyes. Then he turns and jogs back to the restaurant as the onlookers are left wondering what they just witnessed. Hell. I'm not even sure myself. I scurry home as quick as I can before any of them try to talk to me.

Several hours later I keep staring at the key card. I've tried to ignore it, but it's taunting me, daring me to use it. I'm sitting curled up on the sofa still trying to dry out from earlier. I've been too dazed to do anything about my soaking wet clothes. The TV is on, but I'm not watching it, I'm lost in my own thoughts staring at the damn key card. *What did he mean by 'I never gave up on us Abbie, that's on you'? He left for America and never contacted me again. What part of that is my fault?* Maybe there's more to it than that. What if there's something I don't know? I think back to the hurt on his face today. It did seem genuine. Maybe I should just hear him out. *It can't hurt, can it?* I remember the weeks I spent crying my heart out after he left. The aching pain in my chest. *Yes, it really could hurt.*

I sit like this for another hour arguing with myself, driving myself crazy. *Oh, fuck it.* This is my one chance to find out why he never called. I don't know how long he's in the country for. It's now or never.

I brush my hair and apply simple make-up. I throw on jeans and a tight-fitting jumper. I want to look nice, but not like I'm trying hard. I search the hotel's address and head out the door before I change my mind again.

It's gone midnight when I arrive outside Jake's hotel room. One of the security men from earlier is stationed outside his room, but he doesn't question me, he just nods politely. Jake must have told them I was coming... *presumptuous*. I swallow hard and take a deep breath. *Should I knock or use the key card?* I opt for both. I give a gentle knock as I push the door open. It's really quiet inside.

"Jake?" I call out. No answer. I slowly wander further into the suite and look around. This place is next level luxury. I round the corner and see Jake sprawled across the enormous bed, fast asleep on his back. He's shirtless, wearing only a pair of light grey pyjama bottoms. He's absolutely gorgeous. I stand in the doorway watching him sleep. He looks so peaceful. I let my eyes roam over his physique and allow myself to enjoy the view for a minute or two. I notice he has had more tattoos since the last time I saw him, but he is otherwise just like I remember him, only even hotter and manlier somehow.

He stirs and opens his eyes. When he sees me standing there, he smiles a slow, sexy grin.

"You came." He props himself up on his elbows and smiles wider. "Have you come to talk or yell at me some more?" This is the cheeky Jake I remember so well. I can't help but smile back.

"Talk," I say to him. "Maybe you could put some clothes on first?"

He chuckles as he reaches for a t-shirt. "Sorry,

is this distracting?" He gestures to his six-pack with a flirtatious smile.

"A little," I reply, trying to hide my own smile. *How does this feel so comfortable already? Why do I instantly feel calm when I've spent the last eight years feeling angry and hurt, trying to convince myself I hate him?*

We head out into the living area and take a seat on the sofa.

"Can I get you anything to drink?" he asks. I shake my head.

"No thanks, I'm fine. Listen, Jake, I'm sorry about before. To say you took me by surprise would be an understatement." I look down at my lap embarrassed by my earlier behaviour.

"No, I'm sorry, I shouldn't have put you on the spot like that." He pauses, as if choosing his next words carefully. "It's good to see you."

His eyes roam over my face and we just look at each other in silence for a moment. There's so much to say, I don't really know where to start.

"What did you mean earlier? When you said you never gave up on us, that was on me?" I don't know why I just blurted that straight out. I study his face, watching a myriad of emotions pass over it as he considers his answer.

"I want to tell you everything that happened right from the moment I left you that night." He looks at me with genuine sadness. He reaches out to touch my face, but then something stops him and he puts his hands back in his lap. Maybe this is just as hard for him as it is for me.

I nod for him to go on. I decide to just listen without interrupting him. I never thought I'd get to see him again and hear things from his side. Now that I'm here, I realise how badly I need to hear what he has to say. I've spent such a long-time pushing thoughts and feelings of Jake as far down as they could go and my head and heart are telling me I need this.

"I've waited so long to see you again. I've gone over this day in my head hundreds of times and what I would say to you. Never did it play out with you and I shouting at each other in the street though. That I did not see coming." He gives me a lopsided smile. I don't know whether he's trying to make light of things to calm my nerves or his. I smile back, but I still don't say anything. I need to hear this from him in his own words.

"When I left your parent's house that night I went straight home to pack. Dad and I had a huge row about everything before I came to see you, so we were staying out of each other's way. As soon as I was packed, he left a note for Harry's parents and we left. I was so angry and confused. We didn't speak a word to one another during the flight. When we got there, he hired a car to take us to our new place. It was a tiny apartment in a really rough town not far from New York. It was awful, I hated it. None of it made any sense."

I listen in silence to his story. All these years

I've spent angry with him, thinking only about my own heartbreak. Never once did I think about whether he had actually been happy or not.

"I started unpacking to look for my phone so I could let you know I was there and realised my phone had been broken on the flight. In my rush I had slung it in the front pocket of my suitcase and I assumed that during all the loading and unloading in baggage it got knocked and the screen was smashed. It wouldn't work at all. I found out later that wasn't strictly true, but I'll get to that."

He pauses and picks up my hand. My whole body tingles from his touch. The effect he has on me has not changed at all.

"I was devastated, Abbie. All my contacts were on that phone. I took it to a repair shop and they said there was nothing that could be done. The phone had been damaged beyond repair on purpose. Life was making less and less sense. Harry's number was on there too, I didn't see or speak to him until I got back to the UK last week."Jake takes a deep breath.

"I wrote you a letter saying I was sorry and that I was going to do everything I could to get back to you, but I didn't know if it got to you. You never replied." His thumbs are tracing circles on the backs of my hands as he talks. I have so many questions for him, but I don't want to interrupt him. I just shake my head to let him know I never got them.

"I tried asking Dad if he could get in touch with Mac so I could get to you through Harry, but he said we had to cut all ties with our life in the UK. He admitted to breaking my phone so I wouldn't be able to contact anyone. Nothing was making any sense."

Then a few nights after we arrived there, dad was out, and some guys came to the apartment looking for him. Big ugly fuckers. I told them I didn't know where he was, but they beat me black and blue anyway. That's when I knew Dad had got himself in some real deep shit. I had a black eye, fractured jaw and two broken ribs."

I put my hand over my mouth in shock. "Oh, Jake!" It's the first time I've spoken this whole time. I can't stop a few stray tears from spilling over and down my cheeks.

"I'm so sorry these things happened to you." I move closer to him on the sofa and run my fingers through his hair and down across his stubble. All the anger and pain from the last eight years starts to melt away. I don't even know the rest of the story yet, I'm not even sure if it matters. *I still have so much love for this man.*

Jake leans into my touch and carries on. "I forced Dad to explain what the hell was going on. Turns out he had got himself mixed up with some nasty mother fuckers back in London. He owed them a ton of money that he didn't have a hope in hell of ever paying back. He had been involved in drug running for them and a batch went missing. So, he moved us across the other side of the world, thinking he could run from it. Like I said, it only took them three days to find us." He wipes away my fresh tears that won't stop falling with his thumbs.

"Please don't cry, baby. I'm here now," he whispers. *I haven't heard him call me that in so long.* I'm not even sure what exactly is making me cry, the whole thing is so overwhelming.

"Carry on," I whisper back through my tears. "Then what happened?"

"I made a decision that night that I was going to do whatever it took to pay those scumbags off and be able to come home to you. I knew all the time my dad owed a debt we would never be safe and if I came back it would put you at risk. I didn't write to you again to keep you safe. I started playing at small venues around New York to try and bring in some cash and started to build a gig circuit. Music is all I know, so I had to give it a shot. I met some guys doing a similar thing, and we formed a band. I booked us into every small venue that would take us to try and build a name for ourselves, and we sent demo discs to every record label I could find on the internet in hopes of landing us a deal and breaking through to the big time. We tried for almost two years, but we just couldn't get our break. I'd almost given up and was considering taking an internship instead when a scout saw us play one night and we got signed."

I smile that the story had finally taken a happier turn for him.

"Things moved really fast from then on, all of a sudden we had recording deadlines and big venue gigs and we became famous in America almost overnight. It was insane. I now had some serious money to play with so I followed Dad one night when he left the house, hoping he would lead me straight to the meatheads. Dad had been paying them small bits here and there, enough to keep them off our back for the most part, but I wanted them gone for good. They took me through to one of the guys in charge, and I asked him how much the debt was. It was a lot and they had doubled it for Dad trying to run. He said if I could bring him the full amount in one lump sum cash then they would leave us alone for good, but of course they were slapping on hefty interest every month. I think he said it for fun at first, he never believed for a second I'd be able to come up with the money and he admired the balls I had for confronting him. From that night on it took me five years to gather together enough to clear Dad's debt. It wasn't until we went global that I could afford it."

"Jesus Jake, how much did you have to give them?"

He swallows hard and looks at our entwined hands. "Ten million."

I audibly gasp. "Shit." I don't even know what

to say. *That's such a lot of money.*

"It's only money, Abbie, I earned it for that purpose. I've lost more important things in my life." He smiles at me sadly. I want so badly to reach up and kiss him, but I want him to finish his story. We both need this.

"To their complete surprise I paid them off and then I stayed away for another year to make sure they were true to their word. I couldn't risk coming back here and putting you in danger. I was touring all over the world by then, but they never came back for me or Dad again. I thought for sure once we got really famous, they would come for me again, but they were true to their word. Once I knew it was safe, I set up a UK tour so we could come back and I went straight to Harry's to apologise and see if he knew where you were." He pauses and reaches up to run his fingers across my cheekbone.

"And here we are. Everything I've done has led me to this moment. It was all for you. I never stopped loving you, Abbie. I'm so sorry about everything."

I climb onto his lap with tears still running down my face and wrap my arms around his neck. I kiss him on the lips with so much force that he topples back against the sofa cushions. I can't control myself, it's like every emotion I've felt over the last eight years is pouring out from me to him in this one kiss. It's frantic and beautiful all at the same time. *God, I've missed this man.*

I break away for a second to look at him.

"I love you too." I pant breathlessly before returning to our kiss full force.

We stay like this, tangled up in each other until I notice the sun start to rise from the gap in the curtains.

We have talked and kissed and talked some more. We talked about everything, he wanted to know what has been happening for me while we were apart, he told me all about his music and what it's like to be famous. I don't think there's anything we haven't talked about. At some point we must have fallen asleep because I wake up on his chest and check the time. *It's almost midday, we've been asleep for hours.*

I carefully lean up and get off the sofa without waking Jake. He must be exhausted. Somehow, I feel emotionally drained and yet lighter all at the same time. I look at his gorgeous face. I still can't believe he's actually here. Not only that, but he's here and never stopped wanting to be here. I'm still trying to get my head round everything.

I tiptoe to the bathroom to freshen up a little. *Holy cow, the size of that bath!* The bathroom is incredible, it's bigger than my lounge! The whole room has floor to ceiling marble tiles and in the centre is the biggest roll top bath I have ever seen. I walk over to the enormous mirror and try to do something with my smudged makeup and messed up hair.

"Abbie?" I hear Jake call from the other room.

"Just in the bathroom," I shout back. I give up with the attempt at making myself more pre-sentable. This will have to do. I walk back out into the main room to see Jake leaning against the wall waiting for me. As soon as he sees me, he walks over and wraps his arms around me.

"I thought you'd snuck out," he says into my hair as he holds me tight.

"Of course not." I trail small kisses along his jaw from his ear to his lips and he lets out a deep sexy groan.

"Last night was a lot to process," I tell him gently between kisses.

"I know, baby," he says as he takes my face on his hands. "But we've got loads of time. We'll fig-ure everything out. This time we're going to do this right."

I nod and smile as he pulls me in for another kiss, this time becoming more urgent. His hands fist in my hair and he walks me back until I hit the wall. I become breathless as my arousal grows. *I really do want this... so much, but not now.* "Jake," I breathe. "Let's do this right, like you said."

He lets me go and smiles the most wickedly handsome smile

"You're right." His breathing is still erratic as he steps back a little. He takes my hands and grins at me. "Abbie Daniels, will you have dinner with me?" *How could anyone resist those eyes?*

I smile back at him "Yes, Jake Greyson, I will."

# Chapter 15

## Jake

Tonight, might just be the most important night of my life. My reunion with Abbie didn't exactly go to plan, so tonight sure as hell must. I don't think I'll ever forget the look on her face when she saw me at the restaurant. It completely crushed me. It was the same look she gave me all those years ago. The one that gave me a glimpse inside at all the pieces of her broken heart.

When I left her standing there in the pouring rain looking more beautiful than she ever has, I thought I had blown my chance. I had paced my hotel room for hours wondering if she would come and how to make things right. I eventually gave up and fell asleep on the bed only to wake and find her standing there. I wasn't convinced I was actually awake to start with.

The important thing is Abbie knows what happened now, and she's prepared to give me another chance. Tonight has to be perfect. My biggest problem is how to achieve the perfect date when I get recognised wherever I go. Abbie doesn't need all that on our first date. I want to be able to give us time and space to talk without all the cameras and pressure. That's a lot for anyone to deal with.

I take my phone out and dial Harry's number. He answers after a few short rings.

"Jake, how's it hanging my friend?" I laugh at his ridiculous greeting. *How is this man a lawyer?*

"I have big news, Harry. I fucking found her!" I know I'm grinning like a lovesick idiot. Luckily, I'm calling from my hotel room so no one can see me.

"Well fuck me, it actually worked! How many nights did you have to eat at the same restaurant?"

"Five. It was worth every God damn pizza just to see her again." We both laugh at the ridiculous situation I find myself in.

"And? Come on man, spill! How did she react?"

"She panicked and ran at first. There was a lot of yelling at each other in the rain."

"Damn, sounds like the start of a great porno." Harry interrupts.

"Shut up man, it wasn't like that. She calmed down and came back to my hotel in the middle of the night." I'm trying to give him the edited highlights, but the damn joker keeps interrupting me.

"Definitely steering into porno territory now." He laughs down the phone.

"Fuck off Harry, this is serious. I'm going to

do it right this time, no fuck ups."

"I'm only messing with you. Seriously bro, I'm happy for you. I'm glad it's all working out. It does beg the question though, why you're on the phone to me and not locking lips with your lady right now?"

"I need your help with tonight. I need to take Abbie somewhere on a date where we won't become tomorrow's front-page headline." I'm hoping Harry has some ideas up his sleeve because it's been so long since I've been home and a lot has changed.

"Say no more."

***

I take a deep breath as I knock on Abbie's front door to pick her up. I don't think I've ever been this nervous before. Performing in front of a crowd of thousands has nothing on this. *I'm a grown man for fuck sake, but right now I feel like I'm nineteen all over again.*

I swallow hard when she opens the door, she literally takes my breath away. She is wearing a black lace dress that hugs her every curve and a pair of black shiny heels. Her hair is down and loose, her full lips are red and shiny, but in the classiest way. *Holy mother of God. How am I meant to control myself when she looks like this?* A memory flashes through my mind of the night we lost our virginity. The vision of her standing at the end of my bed in her black bra and leather trousers. This woman has always brought me to my knees.

"Hi," she says shyly. I can see how nervous she is, the tension rolling off of her is palpable.

"Hey baby." I take a step towards her and take her in my arms, pulling her in for a kiss. I intended for it to be a romantic kiss to put her at ease, but once our lips meet and our bodies touch, the atmosphere instantly shifts.

She gently moans into my mouth as she runs her hands down my chest and my hands wrap around her waist.

I reluctantly break away and step back. "Geez woman, if you carry on like that, we won't make it to our date. You look incredible." I swear she gets more beautiful every time I see her. I let my eyes roam over her body, drinking her in.

Her cheeks are flushed now from our kiss and her eyes are twinkling. "Thank you. You scrub up alright yourself," she teases.

"Let's go before I keep you here all to myself." I warn. *Now there's a thought.*

When we arrive at the restaurant, I'm blown away. *Harry really has delivered.* Knowing my need for privacy and discretion, Harry called in a favour from a client. He owns a restaurant out in the countryside called The Lake House. Harry specifically requested that we have a private dining area all to ourselves.

I take Abbie's hand as we walk up the steps to the entrance. I hear her gasp as she takes in her surroundings.

"Jake, this place is amazing!" The building itself is a beautiful rustic barn that has been converted and modernised in places. Huge floor to ceiling windows wrap around two sides of the building with a view overlooking the lake.

We are personally greeted at the door by the owner, Nathan, with a warm smile and a friendly handshake.

"Good evening, Mr Greyson, we are really honoured to have you here. You must be Abbie," he says as he takes her coat. Abbie nods as she continues to look around in amazement. We follow Nathan through the restaurant to a side doorway and he gestures for us to go through. We have our own private seating area that is closed off from the rest of the restaurant. It's cosy and romantic, lit only by candles and a roaring open fire in the corner. *It's perfect. I really owe Harry one.*

Nathan puts wine and champagne on the table before leaving us to look at the menu. In all honesty I'm having a hard time thinking about food. The way Abbie looks in that dress in the flickering candlelight is making me want to lay her across the table and make love to her right here.

I decide to put the menu down and pick up the bottle of champagne.

"I think we should celebrate," I say as I pop the cork.

"What are we celebrating?" she asks. If I'm not mistaken, she's feeling just as turned on as I am right now. *I've seen that look before.*

"Starting over, second chances, finding each other again... love." I don't miss the way her pupils dilate at the last word. "The reasons we have to celebrate right now are endless."

"I'll drink to that, Jake Greyson," she says with a smile as we clink glasses and take a sip of the bubbles.

Our waiter for the evening comes in to take our order so I'm forced to take my eyes off Abbie and look at the menu. It's hard to concentrate on food when the only hunger I have is for her. All I can think about is how much I want to lay Abbie across this table and do unspeakable things to her. From the look on her face, I think she's imagining the very same thing.

We have so much to talk about and my God I want to hear about everything I've missed, I really do, but the way she looks tonight is making all coherent thoughts impossible. I have eight years of worshipping this gorgeous goddess to catch up on and I can't wait to get started.

The waiter makes sure our wine glasses are full and we are enjoying our evening before leaving us to it. As the door closes Abbie is the first to break the silence.

"It's lovely here, Jake. How did you know about this place?" she asks before taking a sip from her wine glass.

"The owner is a client of Harry's. I asked him to find us somewhere private. The cameras take some getting used to, I didn't want to frighten you away already."

"I'm so glad you're back in touch with Harry. Under all the bullshit he's a good guy." Abbie pauses before asking her next question.

"What's it like, being famous?" I know I need to be honest with her but I'm worried that the answer will intimidate her. This life is not for everyone.

"It's not easy. In all honesty I struggle with all the attention and it is hard having the whole world know your business all the time." Until I came home, I never voiced how hard it is before. The waiter interrupts my train of thought bringing our meals in. Despite me being a different kind of hungry I can't deny this food looks and smells amazing.

"You managed to keep the business with your dad out of the media, how did you do it?" Abbie asks as she admires the plates of food.

"With great difficulty." I reach over and take her hand. "Anyway, that chapter of my life is over now. I want to focus on this one, the one with you in it." I trace little circles over the back of her hand with my thumb. I suddenly remember how I used to do this when we were together before. It's like we instantly fit back together as one piece.

"So, tell me, what does this chapter have in store for us, Jake?" She naturally leans in closer waiting for me to reply.

"A whole lot of hot and heavy sex I'm hoping."

Abbie bursts out laughing and slaps my arm. "Jake! And there was me thinking you were going to say something romantic and try to woo me!"

I give her my best cheeky grin. "Baby, you know my heart has always belonged to you. I want to show you how much the rest of me has missed you too."

Abbie raises an eyebrow and bites her bottom lip. *Fuck! I'd forgotten how much it affects me when she does that.*

"And what parts might those be?" she asks seductively.

"Baby if you want dessert, I suggest you stop being so damn sexy. Otherwise, it will be you on the menu. I would love nothing more than to bend you over this table right now and show you just how much I've missed you."

Abbie's eyes widen and she smiles at me with those full pouty lips of hers. "We've waited this long, Jake. I'm sure you can wait through one piece of chocolate cake." She tries to feign indifference. She knows exactly what she's doing to me. *Two can play that game princess.*

I nod at her as I finish the last of my meal.

"Very well, dessert first then."

I call the waiter over and ask him for two pieces of chocolate cake and he refills our glasses. I gesture for Abbie to come round and sit next to me instead of opposite while we wait for dessert. *Let's see how she fares now she's in touching distance.*

I tuck a piece of hair behind her ear and run my fingers down her neck to her collarbone as I lean in and kiss just below her ear. *That spot has always been her Achilles heel.* I hear a slight moan escape from her as my lips brush up and down her neck. I rest my hand on her bare thigh and start to run my fingertips up and down her leg as I continue kissing her neck. She parts her legs slightly under the table letting me know in no uncertain terms where she wants me to be. *Oh, baby don't tempt me.* As I start the ascent again with my fingertips up the inside of her leg, I can feel her breathing growing more rapid in anticipation. My fingers reach the top of her leg and brush along her lace underwear with the lightest of touches. She shivers all over, but I don't linger. Instead trailing my fingers back down the other thigh away from where she craves.

"Jake," she whispers needily, as she turns to kiss me on the lips this time.

"Yea, baby?" I know exactly what she wants, but I need to hear her say it.

"Touch me."

I grin as I start the slow, torturous trail back

up her thigh. This time I pause when I get to the top with my fingers hovering just over her lacy underwear.

"Here?" I whisper through our kiss as I press lightly between her legs. She nods and starts to breathe more heavily. In one swift movement I pull her underwear to the side and sink my fingers deep inside her.

"Fuck, Jake!" She hisses as she pulls me closer to her body and deepens our kiss even further. I slowly circle my fingers round inside her as I pull away to look in her eyes. I know exactly what's about to happen, but Abbie is so lost in the moment that she's completely forgotten we will be interrupted. I hear the waiter coming around the corner with our dessert so I slide my fingers out of Abbie and smooth her dress back down. She looks at me completely flustered and with so much need and desire. I can see she is desperately trying to get her breathing back under control as the waiter puts down our deserts and leaves again. I lean into her and whisper in her ear.

"We've waited this long Abbie, I'm sure you can wait through one piece of chocolate cake." Echoing her words from before. She opens her mouth in shock and then giggles.

"Well played, Jake Greyson." She picks up her fork and breaks off a small piece of chocolate cake. As she puts the fork in her mouth, she sucks the fork clean slowly as she pulls it from her lips.

"Eat that fucking cake fast because I'm taking you home," I growl at her.

\*\*\*

The sexual tension in the car on the drive back to Abbie's was like nothing else on earth. Neither of us dared to move or speak for fear of losing control. I can see Abbie's hand shaking as she puts the key in the door. I'm pressed up against her back kissing the back of her neck as she fumbles to open the door. She steps through the door and turns to look at me with a mischievous grin on her face.

"Oh, would you like to come in for coffee?" She once again feigns innocence as she smiles at me.

"Quite the funny one tonight aren't we, Miss Daniels? I'm hoping for a whole lot more than coffee." I kick the door shut behind me as my lips crash into hers. Neither of us able to wait a second longer.

"Only naughty school boys call me that," she whispers against my lips before fisting her hands in my hair. I can't help but moan in pleasure. Having Abbie back in my arms again is all I've thought about for a very long time.

"What about naughty guitarists who want to see what's under that dress?" Our hands are everywhere now and our kisses are frantic.

"That works too, let's go." She grabs me by the hand and leads me up the stairs giving me a sexy view of her gorgeous arse swaying in that little dress as she walks. It's then I realise we are being followed by a bundle of scruffy fluff who is trying to jump at my legs.

Abbie laughs. "This is Maisy, my ferocious guard dog." The dog sits at my feet and cocks her head to one side hoping for a fuss.

"Nice to meet you, Maisy, but there's only one woman I'll be fussing tonight." I give her a quick pat on the head before stepping around her to give Abbie my full attention. She is standing next to the bed biting her lip nervously, but with a twinkle in her eye which lets me know she's as ready for this as I am. I grab Abbie and swiftly pull her back into my arms, eager to continue what we started downstairs. I reach around and slowly undo the zipper on the back of her dress and let it fall to the floor. I thought Abbie was the most beautiful thing I'd ever seen when we were young, but she has only improved with age. She stands in front of me now a confident woman in her black lace lingerie and she is sexy as hell. Every fantasy I've ever had about her over the years we were apart have just been blown out of the water by the real thing. She starts to slowly undo the buttons on my shirt whilst my hands roam over her almost naked body sending goose bumps scattering across her skin as I go. She traces the outline of my abs with her fingertips before reaching for my zipper. She strips me out of my trousers and boxers. The level of my arousal is more than apparent now. Without warning Abbie drops to her knees in front of me and slowly licks the length of my shaft as she looks up at me through her eyelashes. *Fuck, if I don't take control of this situation soon then this will be over before it's started.*

"Abbie, stop, I won't be able to last. I need to be inside you. Get up on the bed, baby." She eagerly does as she's told and crawls on to the bed with me.

Once she's laying on the bed I kneel up and remove her lacy lingerie.

"Now it's just you and me baby, nothing is between us anymore." *I thought this day would never come.* I lie on top of her enjoying the feel of her naked body against mine and she starts to rotate her hips trying to build the friction. I reach over to my wallet for a condom, but she puts her hand on my arm to stop me.

"I'm on the pill and I've never not used one before. Have you?" she asks almost shyly.

"No, I'm clean," I reassure her.

"Then let's not," she whispers in my ear and nibbles on my earlobe. "Let's keep it with nothing between us."

"Baby, are you sure that's what you want?" *God, I love this woman.*

"More than anything." Neither of us wastes any more time with foreplay. It's the intimacy and closeness of being completely one that we both need. I slowly spread Abbie's legs apart with my knees and lower myself so I'm hovering over her.

"Jake," she says, hesitating suddenly and looking deep into my eyes. "Be gentle with me."

"Abbie, I'd never hurt you. If I do anything you don't like you tell me straight away and I'll stop." *How could she even think that?*

"I don't mean physically. Be gentle with my heart, Jake. It's not a tough as it used to be." I can't bear to think of the pain I've caused her. My own was bad enough, I can't even begin to understand hers.

"Abbie, your heart is the most precious thing I've ever been given. I'll look after it always, I promise." I slide inside her and she holds me tight. We cling to each other so there is no space at all between us and even that isn't close enough. For all the light-hearted joking we've done this evening we both knew this moment, when it came, would be bigger than the both of us. I start to build a steady rhythm inside her and I press my forehead to hers trying to ground myself. As our momentum builds so do the emotions we have kept in us all these years. I'm scared when the dam breaks it will overwhelm the both of us. Abbie grips hard on my shoulders and I feel her nails bite into my skin. Her hips rise to meet me with each thrust of mine as we start to climb. I pull back up onto my forearms so I can see her beautiful face.

Despite the tsunami of emotions, we find ourselves caught up in, Abbie starts to relax and lets the pleasure and desire win over the rest. She wraps her legs round my waist pushing me deeper and arches her head back. Her beautiful breasts bounce with every thrust as she tangles her fingers in my hair.

"Baby, I'm getting close." I tell her as I push into her even deeper. Abbie cries out in pleasure as I thrust into her for the final time and we both find our release. She tips her head back as she climaxes and screams my name.

I collapse on top of her physically and emotionally drained. I roll us both over so she is laying on my chest and I don't crush her. I stay inside her as we manoeuvre, neither of us ready for the separation yet. Her head moves up and down with my chest as we both start to slow our breathing. I lay there stroking her hair, just thinking about how happy I am in this moment. I'm exactly where I'm supposed to be. I feel something wet on my chest so I lift her chin up to face me. Tears are rolling slowly down her cheeks onto my chest. I can't explain it but somehow, I know exactly what she's thinking and feeling without the need for words.

"I know baby, I know," I say as I wipe away her tears. She lays her head back down and snuggles into my chest. Within minutes I can tell she is completely relaxed and has fallen asleep in my arms. *This makes everything that happened to get me here worthwhile. I'm home.*

# Chapter 16

## *Abbie*

I wake to the smell of breakfast cooking downstairs and I instantly smile remembering who's down there cooking it and what happened last night. I still can't believe he's really here, and this is really happening. Last night was more incredible than any reunion I had ever imagined between us.

Before going downstairs, I take the opportunity to brush my teeth and check I don't have make-up smeared down my face. I scoop my hair up in a messy bun on top of my head and throw Jake's shirt on that he wore last night. It smells of him and I love it. As I head for the bedroom door Maisy lifts her head to look at me and cocks her head to the side.

"Don't look at me like that," I say to her. She starts to wag her tail.

"You would have done the same thing. Who could resist a man like that?" Maisy lays back down realising walkies are not on the agenda yet.

I head downstairs to find Jake in the kitchen wearing just his boxers. He has his back to me frying bacon and is singing along to the radio. He hasn't heard me come down yet so it gives me a few seconds to stand back and admire the view. *How the hell did I get this lucky?* I didn't think it was possible to improve on perfection, but he is even more delicious than when we were younger. I can't even work out exactly what's changed about him, he's just so manly now.

He turns to see me leaning on the doorframe watching him. "Good morning, beautiful." He gives me his signature heart stopping smile and I feel my insides clench. *I don't think he will ever not trigger a physical response in me.*

"Hungry this morning?" I ask him as he comes over with the spatula in his hand to kiss me on the lips.

"Hmmm." He groans. "I worked up quite an appetite last night." He looks me up and down in his shirt and licks his bottom lip. "I like this way better on you." He reaches around and gives my bum a cheeky squeeze before returning to the hob.

"Bacon sandwich and tea ok?"

"Sounds amazing, thanks." I take a seat at my little table and scroll through my phone to check for messages. There's one from Louisa. *Shit, I really need to tell her about Jake. So much has happened since Friday night.* I make a mental note to call her later. I'm not going to waste a minute with Jake, I don't know long he can stay for. We haven't had that conversation yet, neither of us wants to burst the bubble we're in.

Jake's voice brings me out of my thoughts as he places two mugs of tea and bacon sandwiches on the table in front of me.

"You have no idea how much I've missed tea," he says as he drinks from his steaming hot mug. "Tea just isn't the same in the States."

"More than you missed me?"

"Not even close, baby. I didn't miss anything as much as I missed you." I smile at his response and start eating my breakfast. Maisy has come to sit at our feet in hope of us sharing our bacon sandwiches. *Not a chance missy.*

"So, what's your plan for the rest of the day?" I don't want to assume it will include me but I'm secretly hoping it will.

"Well firstly I'm planning on taking you for a long hot shower." He raises his eyebrows flirtatiously. "And then I thought we could go out for the day, get some fresh air. How does that sound?"

I get up from my seat and go sit on his lap, wrapping my arms around his neck. "Sounds perfect." I tell him before taking a huge bite out of his bacon sandwich.

He looks at me in mock horror. "Right, that's it. Shower. Now!" He growls at me as I squeal and jump off his lap running for the stairs.

Jake has us both naked and under the running water in record time. He pushes me up against the shower wall. The cold tiles on my back in contrast to Jake's hot skin against my front makes me tingle all over. The water is pouring over our faces and into our mouths as we kiss each other fiercely. I fist Jake's hair in my hands and tug hard. His hair is sexy as hell anyway, but when it's wet it's even hotter. I can feel every firm ripple of his muscular chest pressed up against me and I let my hands wander up and down his biceps.

Jake moans into my mouth as his hands cup my wet breasts.

"You're so fucking beautiful," he groans. He lifts me up so I wrap my legs around his waist and he drives into me hard and fast. This Jake is different to the gentle, loving one from last night. This Jake is intense and dominant and I think I love him even more. There's so much steam in my tiny shower cubicle that I can't see through the glass anymore. Jake isn't making love to me today; he's fucking me hard. Without warning he pulls out from inside me and spins me around roughly so my back is against his front. Somehow in the tiny space he manages to bend me over and drive back into me from behind. He slams into me over and over again and I cry out with pleasure. My hands are gripping the tiled wall as best I can while his roam over my breasts. It's as if no amount of closeness will ever be enough.

"Fuck, Abbie!" he shouts as our bodies shudder through our orgasm and he empties himself inside me.

***

Since our epic shower sex this morning I have been floating around on cloud nine. After we got ourselves cleaned up and dressed, Jake suggested we take Maisy for a walk through the park to get out in the fresh air.

It's a chilly Autumn day so we take thick jackets. Jake has his collar pulled up around his neck, a baseball cap on and dark sunglasses in the hopes he won't get recognised too much and we can enjoy our walk in peace.

Jake holds my hand as we stroll through the park. Such a simple, normal way to spend a Sunday, but it feels so right. I can't help but think about how far removed this must be from his usual life. I shake the thought away though and instead focus on enjoying the day. I'm not ready to think about what happens next; here and now is too perfect.

Maisy loves every minute of our time in the park, running about in the sunshine. Jake can throw sticks a lot further than I can so I think he's Maisy's new best friend. *I thought dogs were supposed to be loyal?*

Neither of us speak much on our walk, both of us just enjoying the quiet and the bright, cold air but Jake does stop on several occasions to pull me in for a kiss. Not just a kiss actually, more like a grope filled make-out session. He takes my breath away every single time. *I hope to God this feeling never goes away.*

As we are about to head home, a group of teenage girls arrive at the park. It's obvious they recognise Jake despite his attempt to disguise himself, as they keep looking over and whispering. Eventually one of them plucks up the courage to come over.

"Excuse me, are you Jake Greyson?" She giggles nervously.

Jake smiles at her; the poor girl doesn't stand a chance. No one is immune to that smile. "Yes, I am."

The girl turns back to her friends and flaps her hands in the air. "Oh my God, it is him!" She squeals as her group of friends all run over to us.

"Can we have a picture with you, please?" one of the others asks, her face turning a bright shade of scarlet as she speaks to Jake.

"Well, you'll have to ask my girlfriend if it's ok with her," he says looking at me in a way that makes my stomach flip. That's the first time he's called me that since this whirlwind began three days ago.

"Be my guest," I say. "Here, pass me the phone and I'll take it for you." One of the girls hands me her phone as they all huddle around Jake getting as close to him as they can. One of them rests her hand on his arm as they all smile or make kissing faces at the camera.

"Thanks so much." The first girl says as they all start to disperse. "You're a really lucky lady," she says before her and her friends all head off into the park.

"Yes I am," I mumble to myself as I look at Jake. His sunglasses are now propped up on his head and I can get lost in his deep chocolate eyes. I wrap my arms around his neck and ask him;

"You do realise the effect you have on poor girls like that, don't you? In fact, every woman ever?"

His hands snake around my waist as he unleashes that deadly smile on me again.

"I only care what effect I have on you," he says in a low, rumbly voice that makes me feel the need to squeeze my thighs together.

"I'd love to spend the evening showing you, but I have work to do." Although I can't for the life of me remember what work I need to do while Jake is trailing kisses up and down my neck.

"Well, let's go and get your work and take it back to my hotel room. I can order us food while you work." He hasn't stopped kissing my neck whilst he speaks and I can feel him hardening against my thigh.

I let out a little giggle. "Something tells me you'll be a distraction, Jake Greyson."

He pulls back slightly to look at me with a cheeky grin. "Scouts honour, I'll be on my best behaviour." He laughs and does a boy scout salute.

An hour and a half later Jake pulls into the hotel car park. I have packed a bag with all my work in it, but not my overnight stuff, much to his disapproval. As much as my world starts and ends with Jake, I can't afford to let it affect my teaching. The kids deserve better than that and I'm nothing if not professional.

As we walk towards the front entrance of the hotel, a group of photographers appear from nowhere and start flashing cameras in our faces. The ambush takes me by surprise and I don't know how to handle a situation like this. Jake tucks me behind him in an attempt to keep me out of their way but there's so many of them his efforts are futile.

"Jake Greyson, who's your latest love interest?" One of them asks as they thrust a microphone in his face. Jake ignores them, swatting the microphone away like an irritating fly. More flashes of cameras go off and there are so many of them firing questions at us I can't think straight.

"Miss! Miss!" I hear one of them yell as they try to get me on camera as Jake marches us towards the hotel doors through the swarm. "Miss, where did you meet Jake?" I hear one of them ask.

Just as we almost reach the doors one of the photographers pulls me by the arm away from Jake in a desperate attempt to get a photo.

"I take it you know Jake never beds the same woman twice. He'll throw you out with the trash in the morning like all the rest."

As much as the words sting, I see it for what it is. A desperate attempt to get a reaction from one of us. I won't stoop so low as to give him what he wants. Jake on the other hand turns like lightning with a murderous look on his face and punches the photographer square in the jaw sending him tumbling down the steps. The sea of photographers parts and goes silent momentarily as they all step away from Jake. It only lasts a second before they start filming the unfolding carnage, lapping up the new turn of events for their story.

"Touch my girl again and you'll have more than a broken jaw, you scumbag!" Jake growls at the crumpled man at the bottom of the steps.

He turns to take me by the hand and I realise I've frozen to the spot like a deer in headlights. Jake bundles me into the hotel foyer before they can snap any more pictures and we ride the elevator up to his suite in silence. He's still breathing hard and fast from the adrenaline. I can see his shoulders rising and falling in my periphery, but I don't look directly at him.

Once we get inside his room, Jake turns to me and reaches out to stroke my face.

"I'm so sorry, baby..." he starts but he stops when I take a step back out of his reach. He gives me a confused look and tries again to reach out for me.

"I'm sorry he scared you, the bastard."

"It wasn't him that scared me, Jake, it was you!" I yell angrily at him.

"What?" He looks hurt and confused all at the same time. "I was trying to protect you, Abbie, they don't get to harass you like that and they certainly don't get to touch you!"

"Right, and swinging your fists around is the answer is it? You could have killed him, Jake!"

This time when Jake steps towards me and put his arms around my waist I let him. I can feel my initial anger subsiding now I've said what I needed to say.

"I know. I'm sorry. That's not the way to handle it. I'm not exactly known for handling my fame well." He looks at the floor ashamed of himself like some sort of adorable puppy. Just like that I know the fight is over, I can't even stay cross with him for more than five minutes. *What is wrong with me?*

When his eyes return to me, they are twinkling with mischief. "Besides, I seem to remember the last time I threw a punch for you, you said it was kind of sexy." He makes quotation marks in the air with his fingers as he grins at me.

"Hmm, maybe that's true, but we're not teenagers anymore, Jake. You're a big boy now and you have to act like one." I give him my best teacher line and pretend not to notice the innuendo in my statement.

"Indeed, I am Miss Daniels." He brushes his lips against my neck and nuzzles just below my ear where he knows it drives me wild. "Why don't you go wait for me in the bedroom while I do some damage control for my bad behaviour? Then I'll come show you how big boys really act." He winks at me and swats my behind with his hand as I scurry off to the bedroom with a smile on my face.

The last thing I hear before I leave the room is Jake pick up the phone.

"Harry, I need you to make something go away for me, bro."

# Chapter 17

## Jake

It's raining hard outside. I'm in my hotel room watching the droplets drum against the windows. I'd forgotten how much it rains in England. The sky is a really murky grey colour so you can't really tell where one thing ends and another begins on the horizon.

I'm trying to write a new song while Abbie has to work, but I can't concentrate. I just keep looking at the clock counting down the hours until I can see her. We only have four days left together before I have to start the tour, and I want to make the most of it. I arranged to pick her up tonight from her house, but the more I sit here thinking about it, the more I want to surprise her and pick her up from work. I decide to take my phone out and message her.

**How's your day baby? Missing you already. Jx**

I have no idea what time her lunch break is so I could be in for a wait. I've given up on song writing for the day and instead put my brain to more practical tasks like phoning the guys about the arrangements for the first part of the tour. We travel to Manchester on Friday morning for our opening show, so I want to make sure all the travel and hotel arrangements are organised. Also, it will give me something to distract myself from thinking about how I'm going to have to leave Abbie again while we are on tour.

Once I get off the phone from all my calls, I see Abbie has replied to my message.

**It's nowhere near as incredible as the last 3 days but it's ok. What are you doing today all alone in that big hotel? X**

I can't help but smile at her message. Just knowing I'm going to see her later is enough to get me through the day.

**Mostly thinking about all the things I want to do to you later. What time do you finish? Jx**

She must still be on her break as my phone pings again straight away.

**I'll leave at 5 then I'll have enough time to have a bath and get ready for my hot date at 7pm. Got to go now, See you tonight x**

*That's what you think. I have other ideas.* I start searching on my phone for a local florist so I can surprise her with a bunch of flowers at the school gate. I know she leaves much later than all the children so she won't get too embarrassed by me being there. Although, I can't deny how much I love it when that sexy pink blush creeps across her cheeks. Especially when I know I'm the one that put it there.

At five o'clock I park outside the school gate and lean against the railings to wait for Abbie. I've got a huge bunch of red roses (bit of a cliché I know, but they are her favourites) and I'm wearing a black leather jacket over my dark t-shirt with the collar pulled up. I figured I'd go with all the things she likes best after my cock-up last night. I'm still trying to earn back some brownie points.

It was an idiot move. I didn't think, I just saw red when he pulled Abbie's arm like that and tried to make her feel like she wasn't worth anything. Thank god Harry is able to sort shit like this out for me now.

The sound of footsteps pulls me out of my thoughts and I lean off the railings to see Abbie coming down the path. She's wearing a long, fitted black coat that covers her skirt and her legs are bare with black pumps. She looks stunning. I doubt she will ever stop taking my breath away. *Thank goodness she only teaches infants so they have no idea how hot their teacher is.* As she gets close enough to see me standing there her eyes widen in surprise. *There it is, that beautiful pink blush she gets.*

"What are you doing here?" She smiles as she reaches me and plants a kiss on my cheek. Her eyes quickly scan the area to see if we've been noticed.

"Well, I wanted to surprise you and give you these."

"They're beautiful, thank you. I thought you were picking me up at seven? I'm not ready."

Abbie takes the flowers and looks down at her work clothes.

"Well, there's been a change of plan. We're going out with Harry and Louisa later for a few drinks. They wanted to grab the opportunity to catch up like old times. So, I thought I needed to cram in my alone time with you first. We only have four days left."

A brief look of sadness passes over Abbie's face at the last part. The fact our days together are so limited before I start the tour is a topic we have both danced around and mostly avoided all week.

"Oh shit! Louisa! I haven't even told her I've seen you! So much has happened and I haven't gotten around to texting!"

I chuckle at her. "Yea she's not very pleased with you. Harry told her when he decided he wanted us all to go out, so she's had the Harry version of events which I can only imagine will require some heavy editing."

"Damn it, this isn't funny." Abbie hits me on the chest as she laughs. "She's going to roast me later!"

"Well, then I best enjoy that cute arse of yours before it gets burnt."

***

Back at the hotel I've run Abbie a bubble bath in the ridiculously oversized bathtub. She looks like some sort of Greek Goddess up to her shoulders in bubbles with her hair piled up on top of her head. I stand in the bathroom doorway admiring the view when she flashes me a gorgeous smile.

"Are you just going to stand there ogling, or are you getting in?"

*You don't need to ask me twice.* In one swift movement I pull my t-shirt over my head and drop my jeans. Abbie bites her bottom lip as she watches me strip. If I wasn't hard before, I definitely am now. I slide in the bath behind her so she's sitting between my legs and I lay her back to rest her head against my chest. We lay together in silence for a few minutes enjoying the hot water and the closeness of each other. I slowly rub her stomach and breasts with a soapy sponge and Abbie quietly moans in appreciation. As much as I want to bury myself deep inside her right here in the tub, I think it's time one of us addressed the topic we have both been so expertly avoiding.

"Abbie?" I mumble gently in her ear. "You

know I have to leave to start the tour on Thursday, right?"

She nods against my chest, but doesn't say anything. "I don't want to leave you again, baby when I only just got you back, but I have no choice. I have to do this."

"I know." Her voice is so quiet it's barely audible. "You're the infamous Jake Greyson, you have to do your thing."

She finally looks up at me with a forced smile but it doesn't reach her eyes. "I'd never hold you back from what you love."

"Baby, you are what I love. The rest was just a means to get back to you. We will figure out a more permanent way for this to work."

She looks down at the bubbles. I'm having a hard time reading her emotions.

"I love you too, Jake. It's just that none of this makes any sense. When you say it out loud it's absurd!"

"What is?" *I'm really not sure where she's going with this.*

"The fact that you love me like you do. I mean look at you. You're *you* and I'm just me. You're off the charts smoking hot and I'm distinctly average. You're famous, I'm a nobody. You're a rock star and I'm a school teacher. Need I go on? This sort of thing doesn't happen in real life, hell it doesn't even happen in the movies! No one wrote that plot line because no one would believe it!"

Abbie goes back to staring at the bubbles waiting for my reaction. I can feel the familiar pang of anger rising in the pit of my stomach. Not at Abbie but at myself, knowing that everything that has happened between us is probably one of the biggest contributors to her lack of self-confidence.

I tilt her chin up so she's forced to look at me. "Don't ever say those things again. You hear me?" I say as calmly as I can manage.

"Don't ever doubt my feelings for you Abbie. I love you more than life itself. My entire life's purpose has been getting back to you and I will spend forever making the last eight years up to you. This separation is only temporary, I will be back as soon as it's over and then we can make plans. Ok?"

"Ok." She nods as tears start to build in her eyes.

"Abbie, you are so far above average it's ridiculous. You are most definitely not a nobody and what you do makes a difference. I wish you could see yourself the way I do." I lean down and gently sweep my tongue through her lips pulling her in for a kiss.

Abbie's phone rings bringing us both out of the moment. I lean over to grab it for her.

"It's Louisa." I grin, knowing that she's ringing to give Abbie hell for not telling her about us yet. "Want to take it?" I hand Abbie the phone.

Abbie rolls her eyes. "I've got to face the

music sometime, might as well be now." *This is going to take a while.*

"Hey, Lou!" Abbie answers the phone as I run a trail of kisses down her neck. She silently smiles at me as she tries to push me away.

"I was totally going to tell you. We've just been err... busy." Abbie giggles down the phone. I can hear Louisa ranting on the other end of the phone, but I can't make out what she's saying.

I bend down into the water and take Abbie's nipple into my mouth and gently bite down making her squeal and scoot backwards in the bath sending water sloshing over the side onto the floor. Louisa's voice gets several octaves louder over the phone and Abbie glares at me as she tries to compose herself. I flash her my sexiest smile as I stand and step out the bath. I'm going to leave her to it, but not before giving her something to think about while she's on the phone. I make a deliberately slow show out of drying myself and flashing her all my best bits.

"Uh-uh, yea totally. I'm really sorry. I will tell you the whole story right from the beginning. I promise." Abbie tries to pacify Louisa as she watches my little performance. I turn around and rub the towel across my back giving her a view of my arse before turning to face her again and drying my dick with unnecessarily slow strokes of the towel. Abbie doesn't take her eyes off me and almost drops the phone in the bath.

Content I've had the effect I wanted to. I wink at her as I turn and walk out the bathroom naked.

"Yes, I'm still here." I hear Abbie say as I head into the bedroom to get dressed.

\*\*\*

When we arrive at the bar it's packed with people. I've arranged for a couple of security guys to come with us tonight, but follow at a discreet distance, just in case. In my experience being out in a busy bar and club where people are drunk when you're famous normally leads to a troublesome night. People just don't know when to back the fuck off.

I hold Abbie's hand as we weave our way through the mass of people in search of Louisa and Harry. Abbie looks stunning as always in a figure hugging little black dress and heels. *She is one hot fucking teacher.* I spot Harry at the bar and head in his direction. A few people have already started to recognise me, the tell-tale elbow nudging and whispering going on as we pass by.

Harry lifts his chin at me in greeting when he spots us and we clap each other on the back. Louisa pulls Abbie in for a hug even though she's glaring at her and smiling at the same time. *Women are weird.* She then turns her attention to me and narrows her eyes.

"Well look who's back. The famous Jake Greyson," she spits through gritted teeth.

"Lou, you said you'd be nice!" Abbie looks embarrassed as she swats her friend on the arm.

"I am being nice. Not being nice would be cutting his balls off and wearing them as earrings. Which is exactly what I'll do to you if you hurt her again." She pauses for dramatic effect, still glaring at me. "We clear?"

I try not to let the amusement dancing at the edges of my lips show. I should be glad really that Abbie has such a good friend looking out for her.

"Crystal." I say as straight-faced as I can manage. Harry looks highly entertained by the whole exchange and Abbie rolls her eyes as Louisa leads us all to the dance floor.

"She's such a firecracker. Going to get me some of that tonight. It's been a while." Harry shouts in my ear over the music as we follow the girls to the dance floor.

The music is so loud it's making my chest vibrate. Loud music is no stranger to me in my line of work. Hell, I've even been told if I don't stop in the next few years, I'll likely start to lose my hearing but this shit isn't music. I know Abbie hates this type of thing too. We are both only here to make up for being shitty best friends.

We take our place on the dancefloor and Abbie wraps her arms around my neck. Harry and Louisa are already grinding against each other like a pair of horny teenagers.

"I wish those two would just get together already," Abbie laughs in my ear.

"Nah, they're both too busy pretending to enjoy sowing their wild oats." I joke back.

"They must have sown enough to open a cereal factory by now." I smile at Abbie.

I like this version of Abbie, the funny one who isn't worrying about anything or feeling self-conscious. The one who just enjoys the moment. I bring her in for a long, deep kiss. We missed out on far too many of these, I need to make up for lost time.

Despite the shitty music the evening is good fun. Although I can't help the twang of resentment that hovers in the back of my mind knowing that the four us could have been having nights out like this for years, but that kind of thinking isn't going to do me any good. I have to get past it and move on, otherwise it'll eat me alive. On the whole, the evening has been low key where fans are concerned. Security are doing their job and I think it's helped that most of the night my face has been attached to Abbie's in the dark, so it's no wonder I've not been recognised much. There's been the odd starry-eyed girl, but nothing compared to clubs back in New York.

Abbie and Louisa are dancing together while me and Harry excuse ourselves to the bar to get another round in. I'm not entirely sure it's a good idea as Abbie is already way more tipsy than I've ever seen her, but she's having a good time and I want to enjoy every minute of the time we have left. Harry orders a round of shots, two more beers for us and cocktails for the girls. Harry and I are chatting when I feel a hand sexily creep up and over my shoulder.

"Hey baby," I turn to talk to Abbie only to discover the hand does not belong to her. Instead, there is a woman with long dark hair, a ton of botox and a dress that leaves little to the imagination. Next to her is another woman who I assume is her friend.

I clear my throat. "Sorry, I thought you were my girlfriend." I look at the hand which I can't help but notice is still on my arm.

"I could be," she purrs as she leans closer to me. *Is this chick for real? Who says that?* "You're the guitarist, aren't you? Jake Greyson?"

I nod and sip my beer. I really don't want to get into conversation with this over confident blow up doll.

"And I'm his lawyer, Harry. Nice to meet you Miss..." Harry extends his hand and waits for her to give her name.

"Sabrina. And this is Melanie." She gestures to her silent friend who is clearly the less confident of the two.

In a bold move Sabrina leans across me, still with her hand on my arm and takes one of the shots from the bar throwing her head back and swallowing. She grins seductively at me and edges even closer. *Fuck I need to shut this down, this woman is freakin' nuts.*

"I think you'll find that's mine." Sabrina turns to where the voice came from. Abbie is standing there with her hands on her hips and fire in her eyes.

"Geez, it was just a shot, bitch. I'll get you another one." Sabrina says dripping in attitude.

"I'm not talking about the drink. I'm talking about my boyfriend. The one you still have your hands on... *bitch*."

Abbie marking her territory has to be the hottest fucking thing I've ever seen. I want to throw her over my shoulder and carry her out of here caveman style, but I also want to see this play out. *It's sexy as fuck.*

Sabrina laughs in Abbie's face. "Oh please. As if he'd even look twice at someone like you."

*This has gone far enough.* I pull Abbie in closer to me and wrap my arms around her waist protectively making it quite clear that we are together but Abbie puts a hand on my chest to stop me.

"It's ok, Jake. I can handle this," she says before turning back to Sabrina. "Listen *Missy*, not that I need to defend myself to *you*, but Jake has most definitely looked at me twice. In fact, he's never stopped looking. So how about you take your fake boobs and your trout pout and get your grubby hands off my boyfriend?"

Before Sabrina even has a chance to respond Abbie picks up her cocktail and pours it over Sabrina just as my security guy comes to escort her outside. I'm not sure who's more shocked, Abbie or Sabrina.

Abbie turns to the three of us who are still in the process of picking our jaws up off the floor. Even Louisa is speechless.

"Oh my God!" Abbie squeals as she covers her face with her hands. "I can't believe I just did that!" She goes bright red with embarrassment. I can't even hide how proud and turned on I am right now.

I lean in to her and whisper darkly in her ear. "We're going home. Now."

# Chapter 18

## *Abbie*

"I think I'm going to die," I grumble into my coffee cup as I sit on the sofa in Jake's hotel room, nursing the hangover from hell. I can hear Jake's smug chuckle from across the room, but I can't lift my head to look at him. It hurts too much. I think there is an army of elves inside my head with tiny sledgehammers.

Jake comes and sits next to me on the sofa and takes my head in his lap, stroking my hair.

"At least you were drunk enough to fall into a deep sleep. I had to listen to those two most of the night!" He gestures to the other bedroom in his suite where Louisa and Harry stayed over for the night. "If I wasn't so grossed out by listening to my best friend going at it through the wall I'd be impressed. The guy's got stamina." Jake laughs.

"Hmmm. Glad I missed it. Although I bet we weren't exactly quiet ourselves." I raise an eyebrow at him which is about all I can manage right now.

Jake bends down and kisses me in his lap. "It was fucking hot... until you passed out."

I giggle and shake my head at him. "I did not pass out."

"Whatever you say, gorgeous." He slides his hand inside my pyjama bottoms and runs his fingers up and down the inside of my thigh. He's just about to touch me where I crave when we hear the door to the other bedroom open. A very tired looking Harry and Louisa emerge wrapped in big fluffy white hotel robes.

"Put her down, man, I haven't even had breakfast yet," Harry grumbles as he and Louisa take a seat on the opposite sofa.

"Sounded a lot like you had Louisa for breakfast to me," Jake shoots back.

Harry just grins and Louisa doesn't look at all embarrassed. She just pours herself a coffee and gets comfortable. Nothing ever phases her. I on the other hand am still mortified by my own behaviour last night. I would never normally do something like that, but I had way too much to drink and was fed up of every woman in that club thinking they could try their luck with my boyfriend. Not that that's an excuse. Jake said last night was nothing compared to the attention he gets back in America. The thought makes my stomach churn.

Jake orders us all full English breakfasts on room service and the four of us spend the morning eating and catching up. It feels so easy and comfortable, like it's always been this way. After her initial warning to Jake, Louisa has been perfectly nice to him since and everyone is getting on fine. I even start to feel vaguely human again after several cups of coffee and a greasy breakfast.

"So, what's everyone's plans for the rest of the day?" Harry's asks us all as we laze around the hotel room too stuffed to move.

"I have an article to finish writing this afternoon. The deadline is tomorrow morning, so I need to get my arse in gear." Louisa complains.

I remember my brief conversation with my mum the day before. "Actually, my parents were hoping to drop by later to see you Jake before you go on tour. They're excited to hear all about your life in the States. Is that ok?"

Jake looks genuinely pleased. "Yea of course. Why don't we cook for them at your place? It'll be great to see them again."

"Well, I for one am going to hit the gym for the afternoon and try and work off some of this breakfast. Can't have it compromising this God like figure, can I?" Harry gestures to his chest through his robe and Louisa rolls her eyes.

"Didn't hear any complaints from you last night, princess." He winks at Louisa who acts like she's gone deaf. *It's so obvious they like each other. I don't know why they both still insist on messing around with other people.*

After Louisa and Harry leave, we head back to my house to prepare for the evening. Maisy is over the moon to see her new best friend come through the door behind me.

"I thought dogs were meant to be loyal," I mutter under my breath as she launches herself at Jake. He laughs and ruffles her fur before scooping me up and sitting me on the edge of the worktop standing between my legs.

"Is that more jealousy from you I detect, Miss Daniels?" He arches one eyebrow. "You're so damn sexy when you're jealous." Jake starts peppering my neck with kisses and grabs a fistful of my hair.

"Well, I wouldn't need to get so jealous if I didn't have to compete with every female in the vicinity for your attention. Not just humans either apparently!"

Jake barely lifts his lips from my neck. "There is no competition." His lips brush my skin as he speaks. "You have my undivided attention, always." He stops what he's doing and holds my face in his hands so I'm forced to look straight into his beautiful eyes.

"When are you going to realise that the sun rises and sets with you? There is nothing else Abbie, only you."

"I love you," I tell him, still lost in his intense gaze.

"I love you too, baby. More than you'll ever know."

The rest of the afternoon passes in a blur of food prep for dinner with my parents intertwined with a lot of hot and heavy making out. The time we have together is racing by far quicker than either one of us would like and we can't keep our hands off each other. There's an unspoken need between us to make up for lost time and save it to memory before Jake has to leave again. All be it temporarily, but leave all the same.

The doorbell chimes just as we get the chicken in the oven. Maisy sprints down the hallway with excitement and beats me to the door.

"Hi Mum. Hi Dad." I kiss them both on the cheek in greeting.

"Hello angel. Lovely to see you." Mum is already looking down the hallway for Jake. She was so excited when I told her he was back and we were making a go of things. That's what's great about my parents, they don't bear a grudge. I told them on the phone all about what happened when Jake left and now all my mum wants to do is mother him and love him to death.

When I take them through to the kitchen Jake is stirring gravy. I gave him strict instructions to not stop stirring under any circumstances. It was pretty clear early on in the afternoon that Jake has absolutely no clue what he is doing in the kitchen. *He may be the sexiest God damn creature to ever wear a cooking apron but chef extraordinaire he is not.* He turns to greet my parents with that smile of his that could melt chocolate.

"Mr and Mrs Daniels, so lovely to see you again," he says, still stirring the gravy with one hand. I can't help but giggle at the sight of him. He looks so out of his comfort zone in the kitchen.

I let Jake off of cooking duty, which he is only too relieved about and instead takes the opportunity to catch up with my parents and share a beer with Dad. Watching him so effortlessly chat with my parents makes me feel all warm inside. I don't know how I survived so long without this man in my life. He's like the missing piece that makes me complete.

My parents listen with intrigue as Jake tells them all about his rise to fame over the past eight years. Thankfully he leaves out his tendency to punch photographers. When I call everyone to the table, conversation flows easily and everyone seems to be enjoying their food.

"This is delicious, angel," Mum says as she takes another mouthful of her chicken. "Your skills have vastly improved from when you first moved out and you used to invite us over for beans on toast."

Jake laughs at my mum's love of embarrassing me. "Well, she's doing much better than me. I spend so much time in hotels that my skills are still sadly at the toast and Pot Noodle stage."

Dad chuckles into his wine glass and sits back in his seat.

"So, Jake, what's the grand plan now you're

back?"

"Well, the UK tour starts on Thursday. We open in Manchester for three nights then move on. In total we have sixteen dates in four locations. It's intense. Then we return to New York to start recording the new album. So, as soon as I get back to the States we can start looking at how soon Abbie can move out there with me."

Jake looks at me with the most intense expression and I freeze. We've never explicitly discussed what will happen after the tour and now he decides to announce it so matter-of-factly over dinner in front of my parents. *What the hell?*

"What? I can't just move to New York, Jake." I fidget awkwardly in my chair. My eyes flitting between him and my parents.

"No, I know, we'll obviously make plans first." He shrugs and smiles casually.

I can feel the panic starting to rise inside me that he's putting me on the spot like this in front of my parents. *Why is he just assuming that I'll move half way around the world? We haven't even discussed this!*

"I'm not moving to New York. My life is here; my job, my parents, my friends."

"They have schools in New York, Abbie, and we can move your parents out there with us if they like. Money isn't an issue, baby."

It's not just panic I can feel now, its anger simmering away, threatening to burst out of me. *How can he be so blasé about this like it's no big deal?*

"My parents do not want to live in New York. *I* don't want to live in New York!" I grip the edge of the table trying to keep my voice calm. My mum pats my knee under the table in an attempt to pacify me and my dad clears his throat awkwardly.

"What are you saying? You know I came back for you, we talked about this." Jake's expression turns serious, finally realising that I'm not ok with this.

"No Jake, you said you came back *for* me. I assumed that meant you were moving back so we could be together." Jake looks at me in silence for a moment. There's so much we clearly want to say to each other, but don't want to air our dirty laundry in front of my parents.

After a while Jake says, "But Abbie the guys live in New York, the *label* is there. I can't just leave." He holds my gaze waiting for my response.

"Well, I can't just uproot my life either Jake so where does that leave us?" I raise my voice more than I mean to as angry tears start to threaten. I stand up and glare at him causing my chair to scrape along the floor.

"Listen angel, I think you and Jake have a lot to talk about," Mum says gently. "We'll head home now and give you two some space." I reluctantly break eye contact with Jake and nod at mum. I walk my parents out and say my goodbyes on the doorstep. I apologise to them both, but they won't hear of it.

Once I've waved my parents off, I take a deep breath and head back inside. Jake is stood leaning against the table with his arms folded across his chest staring at the floor. I stand and watch him from the other side of the room, waiting for him to say something, but he doesn't. Jake runs his hands through his hair and continues to stare at the floor. He looks so sad and lost that I can't even be angry with him anymore. I have so much love for this man it's ridiculous.

"Jake…," I say gently. "Don't you think we should talk about this?"

"What do you want me to say?" he says sadly. "For years all I've thought about is coming back to find you. I never once thought about what to do if I got here and you didn't want to be with me."

"Wait, that is not what I said!" I cross the room and wrap my arms around his waist forcing him to look at me.

"Being with you is all I've ever wanted, but I'm not ready to just up and move to the other side of the world away from everything and everyone I know. You must remember how scary that is?"

Jake nods as he runs his thumb across my cheekbone. "I guess I never thought of it like that." He leans forward and gently kisses me on the lips. "I'm sorry."

We stand there for a while with our foreheads

pressed together just holding each other.

"So, what happens now?" I eventually ask him.

"Well, firstly I think let's just take it one day at a time. When your term finishes you can come up and stay with me on tour for a few nights. That's not that long and then we'll go from there. How does that sound?"

"Sounds perfect." I smile. "And secondly?"

"Secondly, we technically just had our first fight so I think some make up sex is in order." He sexily raises one eyebrow and flashes me his best smile. *How is any woman meant to resist that face?*

"Another great suggestion, Jake Greyson... let's go."

# Chapter 19

## *Jake*

I don't claim to know much about women, but I do know that usually when they say something is 'fine' it's absolutely fucking anything but fine. Abbie used the word 'fine' when I tried to talk to her about our fight during dinner with her parents. Not good.

Everything was great when we had make-up sex and then again... and again. This morning when I tried to talk to her about it though, Abbie just said everything was fine and brushed it off, so now, I don't know what to think.

I leave tonight. I get picked up at nine to drive to our first venue and check in. We prefer to check in late at night when we are less likely to be hounded. I need to know everything is ok before I go, I can't leave with any bad feeling or doubt. Abbie is on her way over now so she can see me off. I plan on making sure she doesn't forget just how great we are together and giving her something to think about while I'm away.

I strip naked and sit on the edge of the bed with my guitar strategically placed on my lap. I sit and wait for the sound of the key card clicking in the door. While I wait, I look at all my bags packed and piled up in the corner. I can't really remember what it's like to call somewhere home. I've travelled from hotel to hotel for so long now that I wonder what it would be like to settle somewhere. A sudden moment of realisation dawns on me. *Even if I moved Abbie out to New York, how much would I actually be there? I'm barely ever there really. Just brief spells between tours.* I really need to think about how I can make this work for us both. Without realising it I start to play a new riff and lyrics start to come to me. I haven't written anything new in ages. *Maybe I should play naked more often.*

I get so lost in the new song I'm playing that I don't hear Abbie come in. I have no idea how long she's been standing there watching me when she clears her throat. I stop playing and look up at her. I grin from ear to ear when I see her standing there looking hot as fuck in a tight grey dress and heels.

"You literally packed all your clothes I see," she jokes as her eyes roam up and down my body.

"Well, I remember you telling me once that I rock your world, so I thought I'd remind you just how much before I go." I slowly run my hand up and down the fretboard of my guitar and I can hear Abbie's breathing quicken as she walks towards me.

"Hmm, funny how you remember it that way." She smirks as she reaches me. I lift the guitar off my lap as Abbie straddles my lap and runs her fingers through my hair. "I'm fairly certain those were your words, not mine," she whispers in my ear before nipping at my earlobe.

"So, it's not true?" I run my nose up and down her neck and Abbie tips her head back and moans.

"I never said that." I slide the zipper down on the back of her dress and watch as it falls off her shoulders revealing her perfect breasts. I lift her up so the dress falls to the floor and flip us over so she's laying underneath me on the bed. I plan on savouring every inch of her and imprinting every detail on my memory for while I'm away. I pull her legs apart with my hands and she gasps.

"Baby I'm going to rock your world so hard, the only name you're going to remember while I'm away is mine." I growl before positioning myself at her entrance and slamming in deep.

\*\*\*

Two and a half hours later I get a text to say the van is waiting downstairs. Abbie is sprawled across my bed asleep on her front. Her hair splayed out across the pillow and her bottom half covered by satin sheets. *God she's so fucking beautiful.* I run my fingertips up and down her spine to gently wake her.

"Abbie baby, I've got to go. The guys are here,"

I tell her gently.

She stirs and rolls over to look at me as she processes what I've just said. She sits up and throws her arms around me.

"I've told the hotel you're still here and you can check out whenever you're ready. No rush." I smile at her and brush strands of her crazy, just fucked hair out of her face. "I love you."

"I love you, too." She tries to smile back but it doesn't reach her eyes.

I lift her chin up so her eyes are forced to meet mine. "I'll see you soon." I kiss her on the lips with everything that I have before turning to pick up my bags. Without looking back, I leave the hotel room and head for the elevator. I can't look back at her or I might never leave.

I try to clear my head and regain my composure as I head down to the underground car park. Our black minibus with the tinted windows is parked up along with the two other cars that our team travel in.

"Greyson. Enjoy your time off?" Vince is leaning against the minibus finishing a cigarette that he is clearly not allowed to be smoking inside the car park. He claps me on the back and slings his arm around my shoulders. "Been getting plenty of British pussy I hope."

The guys have no idea about Abbie. I never told them about her or my reasons for seeking fame. *This will be a fucking awkward conversation when it happens.* I just laugh at him and throw my

221

bags in the back before climbing in. The rest of the guys are inside, along with Ralph, our manager.

The journey passes reasonably quick with the guys all sharing their conquest stories from the past two weeks and Ralph barking out orders for the opening show. It's gone midnight when we arrive at the hotel. We manage to get checked in without being spotted which is nice. Once I'm in my room I flop onto the bed noting that it's not as comfy as the previous one. *Maybe that's just because Abbie's not in it.* I take my phone out and message her to let her know I'm here before falling asleep.

***

The opening nights of the tour in Manchester go off without a hitch. Each night is a sell out and the crowds are electric. I love it when a crowd is responsive and interactive, it gives me an extra buzz on top of the adrenaline of performing. We sound really tight each show and it seems like everyone's really got their head in the game. Even Ralph is happy for once. Not even the slightest hint of constructive criticism so far, which is a first as he's usually riding our arses.

I've spoken to Abbie every day since I left in one way or another. We text every day because timings don't always work out to call her. Our tour schedule is gruelling. I sleep most of the way on the drive from Manchester to Leeds. I can't ring Abbie because, for one thing there is zero fucking privacy on tour and for another she'll be teaching now. It's the middle of the day. So, I decide the best use of my time is to sleep. I've never been known in the band for being social. The others like to party and talk shit, I've always kept myself to myself. It's nothing against the guys, just habit, I guess.

The nights in Leeds go pretty smoothly too although it's me who's losing focus and I know it's not gone unnoticed. The others have made a few comments about my sloppy playing at times and I know I need to get my shit together. It's just the longer I'm away from Abbie, the less sense all of this makes. I did pitch the new song I wrote to them as a peace offering and it went down really well. For reasons they will never know I decided to call the song, 'The Naked Truth'.

After the last gig in Leeds, we get invited to a party at some reality TV stars' house. I'd rather pluck my eyelashes out one by one, but Ralph gives me no choice with the 'It's good for the band image' speech. *Fuck that.* So here I am at this twat's house with all these wannabe celebrities all trying too hard. I've had a few more pints than is necessary, but it's the only thing making this Godforsaken night bearable. Everywhere I turn there are women pawing at me and thrusting their fake tits in my face like I'm some sort of raffle prize they can win over. The other guys love it, they're in their element. In fact, I'm pretty sure I just saw Luke heading up the stairs with two women, undoubtedly for a threesome.

My phone buzzes in my pocket and a picture message comes through from Abbie. She's leaning over her desk at home with a tight black skirt on and a white blouse unbuttoned to the bra. She's put on secretary glasses and tied her hair up. Underneath she's written;

**I hope you're being a good boy. Miss me? ;) X**

*Fuck baby, like you wouldn't believe.* I hit dial and she picks up on the first ring. I make my way out on to the balcony where it's quiet.

"What the hell are you trying to do to me? Sending me pictures like that when I'm all the way over here. Do you have any idea how blue my balls are?" I try to sound pissed off but she knows me better than that. I hear her giggle on the other end of the phone.

"I just didn't want you to forget about me." She tries to sound confident and not at all insecure about our situation, but I also know *her* better than that.

"Not a chance in hell baby. In fact, you're all I *ever* think about. You're quite the distraction." She doesn't say anything, but I know she's smiling down the phone.

"We're flying to Edinburgh tomorrow and

once those nights are done, you'll be coming to meet me in Newcastle. Not long now." I'm trying to sound upbeat and convincing for her sake but it does feel like a fucking eternity away.

"I know. I can't wait to come and see you." I hear her stifle a yawn.

"It's very late, Miss Daniels, I suggest you get your sexy little self off to bed now."

She laughs, but doesn't argue. "Ok. Love you."

"I love you, too." I hang up the phone and head back into the party. I'm going to find the guys and tell them I'm done for the night. *I've shown my face, what more do they want?*

I wander down the hallway towards the stairs when I hear Vince's voice coming from one of the rooms. *Bingo! I'll tell him I'm heading back to the hotel.* The door is open so I walk straight in only to find Vince bent over a coffee table with a group of people snorting a line of cocaine.

"What the fuck are you doing?" I roar at him. Vince looks up slowly to see where the voice is coming from. His eyes are bloodshot and his gaze is hazy.

"Oh, hey man. You having a good night?" he asks almost in slow motion. *Fuck.*

I storm over and yank him up by the arm. "Why in the hell would you snort that shit up your nose?"

I'm absolutely furious. Drugs are a sore subject for me. I've seen how that industry fucks people over and ruins their lives whether they're a user or a supplier or just a prick caught up somewhere in the chain like my dad.

"Calm down man, I'm a rock star remember? We're supposed to do hard core shit like this." He laughs and the group of people all laugh along with him.

"You're a fucking idiot is what you are! Do you have any idea how bad this makes us look?"

Vince smirks and runs a hand through his hair as his eyes roll in his head. "Oh, come on man, let's be honest. It's not like anyone really gives a fuck what the rest of us do. It's all about Jake-Fucking-Rock-God-Greyson!" He pokes me hard in the chest as he continues. "The rest of us are invisible and insignificant. It's you every-one loves. We're only here because despite how fucking awesome you are, no one can play guitar, bass and drums all at the same time!"

It takes every ounce of self-control I have not to punch him square in the face. *I can't believe he just said that shit! I really hope it's the drugs and alcohol talking and that's not how the band really feels, otherwise we have a serious fucking problem.* I ball my fists at my sides and swallow my anger.

"See you in the morning." I growl before I turn and leave the room. *Fuck this shit.*

# Chapter 20

## *Abbie*

Newcastle is cold, like, really cold. I hug my coffee cup close to warm my hands as we watch the snow fall from the coffee shop window. Louisa and I have been shopping all day since we arrived this morning. Jake got a second backstage pass and ticket as he knows I hate going to things on my own and he will be busy all day up until the show.

Louisa jumped at the chance to come with me and enjoy some much-needed girl time. We rarely get the opportunity these days, so today has been wonderful, despite the biting cold.

"I still think you should go back for that top and bag." Louisa licks a huge lump of cream off the top of her hot chocolate.

"Maybe. I don't know." They were really nice but really expensive.

"Well, what else are you going to wear tonight? You need to start showing him what he'd be missing if you don't sort yourselves out." Louisa is so matter-of-fact. Everything is black and white in her world. I wonder what it's like not to get bogged down by all the complicated shades of grey?

"It's not that simple, Lou. It's complicated." I take a bite of my cookie and sip my coffee.

"Except it's not though is it? Are you honestly telling me that you love your job so much that you'll be content teaching snot covered little kids and marking pictures of rainbows for the rest of your life while you miss out on being with Jake and all that goes with him? All because you wouldn't up and leave your job to go with him?" She raises her eyebrows at me waiting for an answer. *She has a point.*

"It's not just work, though. What about my parents? And you?" Louisa rolls her eyes, clearly unimpressed with my counter argument.

"Your parents want you to be happy Abz, wherever that may be and I'm a big girl who can look after herself. I'm also a big girl who will very much enjoy the benefits of being best friends with a rock star's wife." She winks and giggles as she scoops more cream with her spoon.

"Let's not get ahead of ourselves eh?" I laugh at her ridiculousness. Jake and I can't even agree on which continent to live on so we are a long way off marriage being on the cards!

"Anyway, about that top and bag..."

*\*\*\**

At six thirty a limo with blacked out windows arrives to pick us up. *Jake really has pulled out all the stops.* Part of me wonders whether this is just the way it is or if he's trying to show me the lifestyle I could have if I moved with him. I doubt it's the latter, he knows the money and the fame are not part of the appeal for me. I loved him long before he had any of that.

Louisa squeals like a school girl when we climb inside the limo. There's champagne on ice and luxurious leather massage seats.

"Wow!" she yelps as she excitedly pours two glasses of bubbles and takes a seat. I sit next to her and smooth my new top down. Louisa won, unsurprisingly and we went back for the top and bag. It is lovely. It's a rich purple corset shape with a lace up back and no straps. The bag matches and I finished the look with black ripped jeans and heels.

By the time we get to the venue Louisa and I are a little tipsy from all the bubbles. We fall out of the limo door in a fit of giggles and Louisa falls right into the arms of one of Jake's security team. I recognise him from Jake's hotel. Louisa grabs both his biceps to stop her fall as she hurtles into his chest.

"I'm so sorry!" she says, as she looks up and realises what's happened.

The security guard sets Louisa on her feet without making a single facial expression.

"That's quite alright ma'am. Are you ok?" Louisa reluctantly let's go of his arms and steps away without taking her eyes off him. I stifle a giggle at the unfolding scene.

"Please call me Louisa. I'm fine, thank you." The security guard nods and turns indicating for us to follow him. Louisa looks at me with wide eyes and mouths,

"Holy shit he's hot!" as we scurry after him in our heels.

We learn the security guy's name is Liam and he sorts us out with our backstage passes. Louisa is thrilled to discover that he will be personally accompanying us for the evening at Jake's request to make sure we are looked after.

The next hour and half before the show is spent behind the scenes watching what goes on. It's incredible how many people are involved in a show this size. I had no idea the work that goes into it. To think it all starts with one man and his guitar and ends in a sell-out world tour involving teams of hundreds of people. It dawns on me just what a big deal Jake is. I've always known he's a big deal but I never *really* thought about just how successful and talented he is. A sudden surge of pride washes over me swiftly followed by a pang of guilt. *How could I ever ask him to give all this up for me? I don't want to live without him, and he shouldn't have to live without this. I guess that makes the solution pretty clear.*

I'm suddenly pulled from my thoughts as

Louisa tugs my arm and we are lead down a corridor towards the VIP lounge. Liam gets the barman to mix us a cocktail each and goes to stand by the door so we can enjoy ourselves. Louisa instantly strikes up conversation with some people at the bar leaving me to quietly stand and sip my drink. I feel something light hit the back of my head. I spin around about to give someone an earful when I see Jake through a gap in a side door beckoning me to go to him with his finger. I slip away through the door after him hoping no one has seen me go.

As soon as I'm through the door Jake pulls me into a storage cupboard and shuts the door behind us. He pushes me back against the door and invades my mouth with his tongue. *God, I've missed him.* My senses are overwhelmed by all things Jake. His smell, his taste, the way he feels pressed up against me. He moans into my mouth with a deep rumbling sound and it makes my knees go weak.

"We're not meant to see anyone before a gig. Ralph's kind of a dick that way," Jake tells me as he kisses along my jaw and down my neck. "But I couldn't stand knowing you were here somewhere and not come find you." His lips return to mine and he kisses me again with such urgency that I forget to breathe.

"Are you ok? How has your day been?" Jake stops kissing me and looks at me as if checking for signs of injury or distress. "Have they been looking after you?"

I giggle at his overprotective fussing. "Jake, I've had a brilliant day... and it's only just getting to the best bit."

"Oh yea? And what's the best bit?" he raises a sexy eyebrow and smiles.

"I'm about to see my legendary boyfriend do what he does best in front of thousands of people."

"Well, it's not what I do *best.* That's not for public viewing." He flashes me a wicked grin and all the muscles south of my waistband clench.

"I've got to go baby before Ralph loses his shit. I'll see you soon." He kisses my forehead and turns to leave.

"Stay with Liam, I mean it. Shit gets wild out there sometimes."

I return to the VIP bar and slide in next to Louisa.

"Where have you been?" she eyes me suspiciously.

"Toilet." I drain the remainder of my cocktail knowing we will be going through soon.

"Uh-uh. That's why your lipstick is all smudged right?"

I swear I see the corner of Liam's mouth twitch in amusement. He must've known where I was otherwise, he wouldn't have let me out of his sight.

***

From our viewpoint at the side of the stage, Louisa and I have been able to see everything perfectly. We're so close to the band that my ears are ringing and I swear I can smell Jake. The air is buzzing with sweat, adrenaline and testosterone, it's incredible.

I haven't seen Jake perform in person since we were teenagers and it was never like this. This is a whole different league. I've watched him countless times on YouTube over the years but being here experiencing it for myself is mesmerising.

The whole experience is an assault on the senses, but in the best way. The roar from the crowd is deafening as they eat out of the palm of Jake's hand. The stage lighting is so bright it's blinding and it hurts my eyes to peek out at the crowd. Not that I'm interested in looking anywhere other than at Jake. His black t-shirt is wet with perspiration and clinging to the outline of his muscular chest. The muscles in his arms strain and bulge with the force of his guitar playing. His messy brown hair is waxed up at the front and his forehead is dripping with sweat. *Why do I find sweaty Jake so sexy?*

Some of the songs I recognise tonight, but a few of them are new. When the current song ends the crowd are screaming, they can't get enough. *I know how they feel!* Jake picks up a bottle of water and takes a big swig from it before pouring it all over his head and shaking his wet hair.

"This song is something brand new for you. We've never played it publicly before. It's called 'The Naked Truth.' I wrote it during a recent moment of inspiration." Jake looks sideways to me for the first time and winks.

As the song starts to play, I recognise that it's the song he was playing the day I came home to find him waiting naked for me with his guitar. I smile to myself realising the significance of the title. An inside secret that only he and I share.

*Could I do this? Could I give everything up and live this life for him?* I watch him from the side lines knowing that's exactly where I would always remain; on the side lines. *Would that really be so bad?* He's the star. I've never enjoyed a lot of attention and I don't want it so I'd happily take a back seat and support him following his dream. It wouldn't be easy. Today has shown me just what a commitment this is for Jake and how much of a demand on his time it is. Not that it should be a surprise. *What was I expecting? You don't become a world-famous rock star by working part-time hours.*

As I stand there watching him, I realise that the answer is clear. There was never really any question was there? It was just fear that was stopping me see from seeing what is glaringly obvious. I would follow this man anywhere. I need him more than air.

At the end of the show the chants for 'more' are deafening. Jake waves at the crowd and drops the mic causing the feedback to echo through the stadium. He lifts his guitar strap over his head and jogs straight off the stage towards me. He picks me up in his arms and swings me around before leaning in for a kiss. I can feel his heart beating a hundred miles an hour and he's out of breath. The physical exertion of the show is clear to see, he's dripping with sweat. *No wonder he's so fit when he's doing this multiple times a week.*

The sound of Louisa clearing her throat brings us out of our kiss.

"I can't deny Greyson that was pretty impressive," she says, trying to keep her poker face, but failing miserably. There's no way anyone could *not* feed off the energy in this room.

"Was that a compliment?" He nudges her elbow and she smiles.

"Don't get used to it. I don't give them often." She rolls her eyes. "So, when you two manage to untangle yourselves from each other, what's the plan?"

"A shower is first job on my list." Jake wipes his forehead with the hem of his t-shirt showing a lovely line of abs above his waistband.

"I'll meet you at the backstage entrance when I've finished up here so we can head back to the hotel."

Jake leaves with the other band members and

Liam reappears from out of nowhere making me jump.

"Seriously, you're like a ninja!" I say to him. "How can someone your size be so damn quiet?"

"He can sneak up on me any time. That's one seriously hot ninja," Louisa whispers in my ear.

"Security guards need certain skills ma'am. Like being light on your feet and having excellent hearing." He gives Louisa a sideways glance letting her know he heard her comment.

"Busted." I giggle and loop my arm through hers. "Let's get some more of those cocktails."

# Chapter 21

## Jake

The past week since Abbie came to see me has been hell. My heart's just not in this anymore, it's wherever she is.

The situation with the guys is certainly not helping things. I did my best to make out that everything was fine whilst Abbie was here so she didn't worry, but that couldn't be further from the truth. *The band is a fucking shit show.* Vince's drinking and drug use is spiralling out of control. He's only lucid half the time. Tensions are running high among us and the cracks are starting to appear. Ralph continues to pile on the pressure and the guys can sense I'm off my game.

To top it all off over the last three days, rehearsals have ended in heated rows between us that would have led to a punch up had the security team not stepped in. Tonight, I reached my limit. Vince turned up forty-five minutes late for the pre-show sound check so off-his-face that he couldn't even walk straight let alone play bass. *I'm done. This isn't the life I choose anymore. I choose Abbie.*

As soon as we finish the show, I race backstage to grab my phone. I know she'll be asleep and it'll go to voicemail but that's fine. At least she will know.

"Hey Abbie, I know it's late and you're probably asleep, but these last few days have got me thinking. Things are not working for me the way they are. I'm going to come home. We need to talk."

I finish the voicemail with, "I love you so much, I don't want to be away from you for a second longer." But the phone makes a weird beeping noise in my ear. *Damn it.* I don't know at what point my message stopped recording properly. It doesn't matter. I'm going straight there.

I'll drive through the night and tell her in person. *I'm coming, Abbie.*

I don't know why it's taken me so long to see what's been staring me in the face. The whole reason I even pushed so hard to make the band a success was to pay off Dad's dirty fucking debt and get back to Abbie. It's always been about her. If it comes down to a simple choice between music or Abbie, she wins every time. I'll give it all up in a heartbeat to be with her.

I grab my guitar and start to pack my stuff up as quick as I can.

"What the fuck man?" I hear Robbie come in the dressing room behind me. "Where are you going?"

"You'll have to finish the last few shows without me. I'm done." It's all the explanation I offer in my haste to get out of there.

"You can't be done, it's your band!" He folds his arms across his chest and blocks the doorway. "Too good for us now Greyson, is that it?" He looks furious as he tries to stop me leaving, but I can't think about this right now. I need to go.

"No man, it's nothing like that, I've got some shit I need to deal with." I grab the last of my things and head for the door, but he doesn't move.

"Get out of my fucking way, Robbie or I swear to God..." I'm starting to lose my temper now in my desperation to get back to her.

"Or what? You'll hit me like the damn photographer? What has happened to you? Ever since we got to the UK you've been off your game and acting like a total dick."

I look at the floor and run my hands through my hair. I've never been honest with any of them about my reasons for coming to the UK.

"Step aside Robbie, I've left a note for Ralph explaining everything." I push past him with my shoulder and stride a few steps down the corridor before turning back to him.

"For what it's worth, I am sorry." I mumble before getting out of there as fast as I can. I don't even look back.

***

As I drive down the motorway in the car I 'borrowed' from the band entourage, I'm lost in my own thoughts. For the first time in a while, I'm thinking clearly and I know what I need to do. I'm even having a hard time sitting still in my seat as I'm buzzing with excited energy. *I'm going to see my girl.* I know why I've been so het up the last few weeks, it's because we've been apart. I've missed her so much. I know all too well what life without her is like and I never want to go back to it. When I get home, I'm going to tell her I've quit the band so we can be together properly. I'm going to ask her to marry me too. It's been a long road getting to this point, so this can't just be *any* proposal. *I need to sweep her off her feet.* I've got a three hour drive ahead of me so that should give me plenty of time to think of the ultimate romantic proposal.

I try to relax and settle into the journey. I turn the radio on and flick through the stations looking for a ballad in the hope it might provide some inspiration. Madonna comes on, *nope.* The BeeGees, *definitely not.* Then one of my own songs comes through with the next flick of the button. *Hell no!* I never listen to my own songs. I keep flicking, but to no avail so I give up and turn it off instead, deciding to just be alone with my thoughts in the quiet.

I've always liked driving at night. There's

something captivating about all the headlights moving about in the darkness. I used to love watching New York from my apartment window at night. I was on the 24th floor so I could see for miles across the city. All you could see were thousands of tiny lights moving around in the city that never sleeps. I momentarily wonder where Dad is and what he's doing. I try not to think of him often, but I know one day I will need to address my feelings around my relationship with him, or lack of to be more accurate. I think back to the day I cleared the debt and set us both free. I didn't feel much of anything except the overwhelming need to finally set the wheels in motion to come back to the UK. To come find Abbie. I shook his hand and went to walk away when he called after me.

"Thank you, son. What can I ever do to repay this?" That is the one and only time in my life he has ever called me son and I remember tensing at the sound of it coming from his mouth. I turned back to him and said;

"You can stay the fuck out of my life from now on. You've done enough." They were the last words I spoke to him. I had also transferred him enough money to live off of for quite some time, but he didn't know that then. I'm assuming he does now.

I know Abbie thinks I was too harsh, but that fucking man has brought nothing good to my life and he was the sole reason Abbie and I lost eight precious years. Abbie is a better person than I am, she has such a big heart, it's one of the many reasons I love her so damn much. Her ability to see the good in people and put others before herself is exactly the reason why she deserves the life she wants. If she doesn't want to move to New York then she doesn't have to. If she doesn't want to spend countless weeks waiting for me to come back from gruelling tours then she doesn't have to. From here on in, Abbie doesn't have to do anything that doesn't make her happy. That is going to be my promise to her.

I realise I've been so lost in my thoughts about Abbie and our new life together that I've driven a surprisingly long way. I'm making good time so I'll be home before I know it. I need to stop for fuel though so I decide to pull into the next service station. Before getting out the car I put my baseball cap on and wrap my scarf high around my chin. It's late at night and I have no security with me so this is a bit of a risk. *Fans can do some crazy shit sometimes.*

Once I've filled up the car I step inside to pay and pick up some food. I hadn't realised how hungry I am. Whilst standing in the queue I check my phone to see I have seven missed calls and a voicemail from Ralph. *I better call him back; I owe him that much.*

I dial his number and I don't have to wait long for him to pick up.

"What the fuck Jake?" he yells down the

phone.

"Ralph listen..." I try to explain calmly, but Ralph isn't done yelling.

"What the hell are you thinking? Have you lost your fucking mind? You are a multi-million-aire, world famous rock star in the middle of a sell-out tour and you write me a note telling me you're walking away for some woman? What the fuck is wrong with you Jake?" He doesn't pause for breath at all as he continues to shout down the phone at me.

"She's not just some woman Ralph... she's *the* woman," I say quietly and calmly.

"Well, that's just great, Jake, I'm real fucking pleased for you." He spits sarcastically down the phone. "Why can't you bring her on tour with you so you can get your kicks in between shows like every other normal son of a bitch?"

"Because that won't make her happy and making her happy is all I've ever really cared about, to be honest." I realise as I say this just how true it is.

"Jake, I don't know where you've left your fucking balls, but I suggest you use this little road trip you're taking to find them! This isn't over, we are not done! Go fuck this out of your system while I handle the absolute shit-ting chaos you've left here and I will call you to-morrow!" The line goes dead as Ralph slams the phone down in anger.

I probably should care more that I'm about

to walk away from the only life I've ever really known and more wealth and success than I could have ever dreamed about, but I don't. I've never been more sure of anything.

I grab my order of burger and chips and get back in the car. I decide to give the radio another go and actually find a song I like this time. I pull back out into the motorway traffic and start to sing along at the top of my lungs. *I'm so fucking happy right now!* I take a bite of burger and a swig of my coke while I start to mentally plan what kind of proposal I'm going to go for. Abbie isn't one for a lot of attention so no grand public gestures. Also, the army of Jake loving teeny-boppers who stalk my every move will make her top of their hit list so probably best to keep Abbie as under the radar as possible. *It's got to be romantic. Come on Jake, think man, think!*

I reach for my coke again, but knock my bag of chips off of the central ledge where I had balanced them and they fall into the footwell.

"Shit." I try to lean forward and reach down to pick them up, but I'm too big to fold myself up like a fucking pretzel in the gap. I feel around as best I can, but can't find them so I peer down into the darkness. Total waste of fucking time as I can't see a thing in a dark car on a dark motorway.

As I sit back up my eyes return to the windscreen in time to see the brake lights of the car in front glaring angry red at me. The car is way too close, there's no way I can stop in time. I slam on the break, but I brace for impact knowing I have no chance of stopping. It all happens so fast, but the car smashes into the back of the one in front, sending me into a tail spin at such high speed that I'm flung off the motorway and the car rolls several times at high speed. It comes to a halt on its roof and the last thing I remember is a cracking sound as searing pain runs through my head and neck. Then it all goes black.

# Chapter 22

## *Abbie*

By the time I get out of work tonight it's really late. I had so many reports to write and paperwork to complete that I'm here later than usual. Walking across the car park to my car I'm trying to rummage around in my bag to find my phone. I haven't had a chance to look at it since lunchtime and I keep hoping there will be a message from Jake. His voicemail from last night keeps playing over and over in my mind. I hope to God I'm wrong but I'm worried he's going to come back and break up with me. Nothing good ever comes from 'we need to talk'. All day I've felt sick to my stomach. I can't go through it again. How can he come back into my life and say all those things and then break my heart all over again? There has to be some mistake. Hopefully once he comes home, we can talk things through and work it out. I know our lives couldn't be more different, but surely after everything we can find a way to be together?

I laid awake most of the night last night after hearing Jake's voicemail and I've definitely made up my mind that I'll move to New York with him if that's what it takes. I see now how unfair I was being. Despite what he says, music is

Jake's life and I can't see him doing anything else. He's world famous for God's sake so he must be doing something right! I can't expect him to give all that up for my boring life in England. I'll do whatever it takes to keep us together this time. When he gets here, I'm going to tell him I'll quit teaching and go with him. I can always teach over there if I decide to, there are schools wherever we choose to live.

I finally find my phone in the bottom of my bag and see I have twelve missed calls. *What the hell?* Most of them from a number I don't recognise, two from Harry and three from Louisa. *Seriously what can be so urgent?*

I decide to ring Louisa back first and hit dial on the hands free as I get in the car. She answers on the first ring.

"Abz, where the hell have you been? Why don't you answer your God damn phone?" she screams in my ear.

"Err hi. I've been at work, just like every other day. What's up your arse?" I'm really not in the mood for her drama today.

"Abbie it's Jake... there's been an accident." Instantly my blood runs cold and I hit the brake as I'm reversing out of my space.

"What?" I can barely get the word out.

"Harry and the hospital have been trying to reach you all day, that's why he phoned me. Jake was in a car accident last night. You need to get to the hospital."

All at once my thoughts are racing and my head is spinning. I can't think straight, I think I'm going to throw up.

"Abbie are you there? Did you hear me?" I know Louisa is talking on the other end of the phone, but I can't make any words come out to answer her.

"Abbie!" she yells. "Get your shit together! You can fall apart later all you want, but right now he needs you, so get your arse to the hospital and I'll meet you there. I'll text you the hospital details."

"How bad is it, Lou?" I manage to whisper as tears start to fall.

"He's been in surgery for several hours. It doesn't look good, hun. Please just get there and we can talk then," she says more gently

I nod, not really thinking about the fact she can't see me.

"Drive safely," she adds quietly before hanging up.

I try my best to stay calm on the drive to the hospital, but it's no use. I can't get my breathing under control and my vision is blurry from the tears. I need to calm down so I can drive safely. I'm no use to Jake if I crash my own car. *What was he even doing in the car? The band stay together when they're on tour so there would've been no need for him to be in his car. None of this makes any sense.* I can't even begin to start worrying about the severity of his injuries. If I let myself start thinking about it, I know I'll spiral into a complete panic. *I just need to get there and see him, then we can deal with whatever happens together.*

After what feels like an eternity I park at the hospital and make my way to the main entrance. I have no idea where the ICU is or if that is even where to find him if he's still in surgery. Thankfully, as I rush through the double doors, I see Louisa and Harry waiting for me. Louisa grabs me and pulls me in for a hug. She doesn't say anything, what would be the right thing to say in this situation anyway?

Harry nods at me in greeting. I can tell by his face the seriousness of the situation. Harry is always smiling and joking, I've never seen him look like this. His eyes are sad and empty.

"He's this way," Harry says quietly as he turns and heads up the corridor towards wherever Jake is. Louisa and I have to hurry to keep up with him as he strides through the hospital. We arrive at a waiting area with a coffee machine and a few chairs. Harry gestures for us to take a seat, but I refuse, instead pacing the room knowing I wouldn't be able to sit still at a time like this.

"Where is he? I need to see him. When can I see him?" I ask them both, frantically.

"Abbie, I know you're worried, we all are. I need you to sit down and listen to me." Harry is really calm and assertive. This must be what he's like when he's in lawyer mode. I quietly do as he asks this time and take a seat next to him. Louisa sits the other side of me and holds my hand. *Shit, I can't take any more bad news. How much worse can it get?*

"As you know Jake was in a car crash sometime during the night and was rushed here. The hospital rang me because Jake has no contactable family and, as his lawyer, they contacted me to find out who his next of kin is. Abbie it's you." For the first time since Harry started talking, I look up from the floor and straight at Harry.

"What?" *What is he talking about?*

"A few weeks ago, Jake asked me to draw up some legal documents that make you responsible for everything. You're the only person he trusts to make decisions for him if he can't. That means you will need to make decisions about his medical care, Abbie."

I can't process what he's saying. *What the fuck is happening? Why didn't I know about any of this?*

"He's also written you in his will, Abbie, he wants you to have everything."

I can't help it, but hearing these words makes my anger and emotions boil over. I stand up in a rush and shout louder than necessary for such a small space.

"I don't fucking want it! I don't want any of his money! I just want him!" I drop to the floor on my knees and sob. I sob so hard it makes my chest and throat hurt. Louisa crouches down next to me and wraps her arms around me just letting me cry.

"Is he going to die?" I ask them between sobs. I feel Harry's hand on my shoulder.

"We don't know anything yet. He's been in surgery since early this morning, but that's all I know. I'm sure they'll update us as soon as they can. I'm going to get you a coffee. You're going to need your strength and energy." Harry gives my shoulder a reassuring squeeze before walking over to the coffee machine. Louisa strokes my hair and helps me up off the floor and back into a seat.

After a few deep breaths and some sips of industrial strength coffee I manage to think a little clearer.

"What was he doing in the car? Do the rest of the band know what's happened?" I realise I have so many unanswered questions.

"I spoke to their manager, Ralph on the phone early this morning. They are aware of the accident and are in the process of cancelling the rest of the tour. In answer to your other question..." Harry pauses and I look at him urging him to go on.

"Jake was on his way to you." I look at him puzzled, but don't interrupt him. "When I spoke to Ralph, he said Jake was on his way home to tell you he wanted to quit the band and start a life here with you."

The tears silently slide down my face again.

I don't know what to say, what to do or what to think.

"You mustn't blame yourself, Abbie," Louisa says gently. "It was just an accident."

Suddenly I feel like I'm going to be sick, I rush to the nearest toilets and just make it into one of the stalls before throwing up. *I need to get a handle on my emotions. I'm no use to Jake like this. He needs me to be strong.* Sitting back against the toilet door with my head in my hands, my mind starts to race once more. *What if he doesn't make it? I can't lose him again. What if he does but he blames me for what happened?* I can't even begin to process everything yet.

"Abbie," I hear Louisa through the toilet door. "The doctor's here."

When I emerge from the toilets I'm greeted by a middle-aged man in scrubs, his surgical mask pulled down below his chin. I search his kind face trying to gauge any sort of clue as to what he's going to say. He looks tired, he's been in the operating theatre for hours working on Jake, from what Harry said.

"Hello, Miss Daniels, I'm Doctor Cartwright," he says shaking my hand. "I've been with Mr Greyson since he arrived in the ER. Would you like to come with me?" he asks softly. I nod and follow him down the corridor to a set of double doors. Dr Cartwright stops before going through and turns to me.

"He has responded well so far during surgery,

and is now stable, but critical. I must warn you he looks worse for wear and he is hooked up to a lot of machines. The injuries he sustained were life threatening, and he's not out of the woods yet."

The double doors swing open as a nurse comes out and I catch a glimpse of what must be Jake laying in the bed. I don't hear anything else the doctor says. I know he's still talking to me, but I don't understand all the medical jargon and all I can think about is how close I am to seeing Jake now. *He's alive.* I interrupt Dr Cartwright.

"Can I see him now?" I ask impatiently. I feel like it's been an eternity since I got the phone call. *I just want to see him.*

"Yes," he says kindly. "It's important to talk to him as much as you can so he knows you're here. It will hopefully help his recovery if he knows he has a reason to wake up."

I nod and take his hand in both of mine.

"Thank you so much doctor, for everything." I don't think I've ever been more grateful to anyone before in my life.

"It's my pleasure, Miss Daniels. Now go be with your man and I'll be back to check on him tomorrow."

I take a deep breath and push the double doors open quietly. The room on the other side is silent except for the sound of beeping monitors and the whirr of machines. Jake is in a private room of his own with his bed in the middle surrounded by terrifying looking medical equipment. I know it's Jake laying there, but I can't process it, it doesn't seem real. He doesn't look like Jake. He's so pale and is covered in bruises. His head is bandaged and he has wires and tubes coming out of him. My usually strong, charismatic man, who's so full of energy, is lying there lifeless and drained.

I go to the side of his bed and pick up one of his hands. I can't even stroke it like I want to because of the cannula he has in it. I put it back down gently on the bed and instead run my fingers up and down his bare arm.

"Jake, it's me, baby. It's Abbie. I'm here. You're going to be ok," I whisper to him, but my voice cracks on the last word, and the dam opens again. Tears run down my cheeks and fall on his arm. I lean over the bed and bury my face into his neck, sobbing. I wish to God he could put his arms around me or say something. He doesn't smell like Jake I realise as I try to stop my tears from soaking his bandages. He smells like hospitals.

"I love you so much, Jake, you have to make it through this." Even if he were conscious, I doubt he would be able to understand me through my sniffing and crying. I feel a hand on my shoulder and turn to see Louisa looking at us both with pain and sympathy.

"Abbie, Harry and I are going to take turns to stay with you. We aren't all allowed to be here at once. We're going to head home for tonight, but one of us will be back in the morning."

I nod at her and squeeze her hand on my shoulder.

"Thanks Lou," I whisper before she heads out the door again, leaving me alone with the relentless beeping and whirring.

\*\*\*

Sometime during the night, I must have fallen asleep. A nurse brought a bigger, slightly comfier chair in for me by Jake's bed because I refused to go home to sleep. I don't know what time it was I eventually gave up the fight and drifted off to sleep, but I woke up with a stiff neck. The sudden noise of a machine alarm snapped me awake in a panic.

"It's ok dear," one of the nurses says. "Nothing to worry about." She could see my fear that something was happening to Jake. The night had been a constant stream of nurses in and out tending to Jake. I have no idea what any of them were doing or what any of it meant. I just sat and watched them go about their business. I was too scared to ask questions in case I didn't like the answers.

I get out of the chair to stretch my back and legs. I quickly check my phone and see I have a ton of messages from various people. I know I need to reply to them all, but I don't know what to say to anyone. I can't think about anything other than Jake waking up.

I go to Jake's bedside and stroke his bandaged head. "Good morning, gorgeous." I lean over and kiss his cheek. He seems to have a little more colour in his face today, which I'm hoping is a good sign, but what do I know?

"You need to wake up today, baby. The world needs Jake Greyson back... I need you back." I decide then and there that I'm going to do my best not to cry today. Crying isn't going to help him. I need to be strong for the both of us while he can't be.

I hear someone clear their throat at the doorway. I turn to see an exhausted looking Harry standing there with two cups of coffee in his hands.

"I thought you could use a decent cup of coffee this morning. Not the shit from that machine." He hands me a takeaway cup and a bag with pastries inside. "I know you probably don't think you're hungry but you should try to eat."

I smile, appreciatively at him but put the bag of pastries on the chair. I'm not ready to face food yet.

"Did you get any sleep?" I ask him as I hug my coffee, trying to draw warmth from it. The hospital is far from cold, but I've felt cold to my core ever since I got the news.

"A little. Most of the night was spent fielding phone calls from the band and management team. It's a media frenzy outside the main hospital doors."

"Oh of course, I didn't even think about that. I bet those blood sucking leeches are all over this story." The thought angers and saddens me that while Jake lays here fighting for his life the media are all scrabbling for a photo or some gossip.

"We will need to take you out a different way when you want to come and go," Harry tells me as he walks over to stand by Jake.

"I won't be leaving," I snap.

Harry leans over and ruffles Jake's hair. "Morning man, you ever getting up today? Lazy bastard." I appreciate Harry's attempt at humour and normality, but I'm not ready for that yet. Nothing about this is normal.

"What have the media been told?" I ask Harry.

"Ralph has given a statement with minimal details about his condition. Just stating he was in a car accident and that he is stable, but in a serious condition. The photographers are not allowed past security into the hospital. Ralph is sending some of the security team down to be outside Jake's room as an extra precaution. They should be here by this afternoon."

I nod as I take in all of what Harry is telling me. I feel like I'm constantly being hit with a barrage of new information lately. My brain can't keep up.

"Thanks Harry, for taking care of all this. You're a good friend."

Harry smiles and gives Jake's arm a rough squeeze. "It's ok, Jake's going to thank me in beers and pizza when he wakes up, aren't you man?" I can see that deep down Harry is just as scared as I am that Jake might not wake up. I can see it in the way the humour doesn't reach his eyes when he makes a joke.

"Harry, do you mind staying with Jake for a few minutes while I go and return some calls?"

"No, of course not. I'll come get you if anything changes."

As I walk down the corridor in search of a quiet spot to use the phone, I wonder how long this nightmarish alternate universe will be a reality for.

It's time to take the first step to facing the outside world again by returning all these calls and messages. The thought absolutely terrifies me. Somehow stepping out of this hell bubble would make it seem all the more real. *Fuck.*

# Chapter 23

## *Abbie*

T he next week falls into a torturous routine at the hospital. An endless cycle of machines, medication, observations and no change. Nothing changes at all. Jake still lies there on life support, but the rest of the world carries on without him as if he is frozen in time. The only sign that time is passing in the hospital room is Jake's stubble which grows longer and darker by the day. I've never seen him with so much facial hair and he looks even less like Jake. I run my fingers through his beard absent-mindedly as I give him his morning pep talk. This has become part of our new weird daily routine.

"Morning, handsome," I say to him, leaning forward to give him a kiss on the cheek.

"You're going to wake up for me today, right? I miss you so much, baby." Sometimes when I watch him, I think he moves his fingers slightly or twitch his cheek, but I know it's all in my head. It's all wishful thinking on my part. I need to hold on to whatever shreds of hope I can.

My parents have been to visit a few times and Harry and Abbie come regularly too. My mum and dad sat with us for a short while and bought me some fresh clothes and supplies. Jake's only meant to have two visitors at a time so they don't stay long. I don't think Mum could have lasted much longer anyway. I could see how desperately hard she was trying to hold back her tears and be strong for my sake. Mum has phoned the school for me and explained the situation, telling them I won't be in until further notice. There's no way I could go back to work with Jake in here. I haven't even left the hospital yet for a short time, let alone tried to concentrate on anything taxing like work.

Dr Cartwright comes into the room, breaking my train of thought.

"How's my star patient this morning?" He smiles at me as he grabs Jake's chart. It was Dr Cartwright's day off yesterday, so we had a different doctor doing the rounds.

"Still the same," I reply sadly.

"The same isn't worse my dear, so take comfort in small mercies," he mutters as he scans the charts and does his usual checks on Jake. When he's finished, he looks up at me and takes off his glasses giving me his full attention.

"Miss Daniels, I really think you should go home, just for a short while. The nurses told me you haven't left here since Jake was brought in. It'd do you good to go home, have a hot shower and grab some fresh clothes. Get some decent food inside you, not the ghastly stuff they pass off as food here and then you can come back feeling ten times better for Jake. What do you say?" he asks gently as I look at the floor.

"I can't leave him," I barely manage to whisper as my eyes fill with tears. "What if he wakes up? What if…he dies?" I wipe my eyes to catch the tears before they fall. I can't believe I even have any left.

"There are no guarantees I'm afraid, but if anything changes, we will phone you straight away. I have a meeting this morning with a specialist to discuss Jake's condition and so I will hopefully have more news for you this afternoon. Why don't you ask someone else to sit with him for a while so you can get out of here and clear your head? I promise it will help, you can trust me, I'm a doctor." He smiles warmly and pats me on the shoulder as he leaves.

*Maybe he's right. Maybe I should go home just for a little while. I really need to shower and wash my hair.* I haven't been home for almost ten days. I take my phone out and call Harry. He answers straight away. All of us are on such high alert.

"Abbie, is Jake alright?" Harry asks hurriedly.

"Yes, no change. I was just wondering if you're able to come and sit with him while I go home for a shower? The doctor has persuaded me I should get out of here for a short while and I've finally given in and accepted he might be right."

"Excellent, I'm glad. I think it's a great idea,

Abbie. Give me an hour to finish up here and get over to you." I can already hear him shuffling papers on the other end of the phone.

"Thanks Harry, see you soon." I hang up the phone and the sudden realisation that I'm about to leave him for the first time really hits me and I feel sick. I run to the bathroom down the corridor and throw up. *This is becoming a bit of a habit. I clearly don't cope well with trauma and stress,* I think to myself. I don't even understand how I have anything left to throw up. I've been sick so many times since I got the news and I've barely eaten a thing!

I wash my hands and rinse my mouth at the sink, studying myself in the mirror. *I look like utter shit.* I'm so pale and have really dark circles under my eyes where I've only had little bits of broken sleep in the armchair over the last week or so. I'm absolutely exhausted. I take a deep breath and stare at myself in the mirror. The only thought that I can focus on is the terrifying possibility that if I leave, I may never see him alive again. *What if he dies while I'm gone? I'll never forgive myself.* I'll just be as quick as I can so I come back and be near him and hear what the specialist has to say. *Everything will be fine,* I tell myself. *It has to be.*

Two hours later I arrive home. Poor little Maisy is so pleased to see me, she instantly launches at me licking my face and frantically wagging her tail. I know my parents have been coming in to feed and walk her, but she will still be missing the company.

"Hi, lovely girl. Sorry you've been all by yourself," I tell her as I bend down to give her a big fuss and a tummy tickle.

She follows me through to the kitchen where I put my things on the table and see the large pile of mounting post that has arrived in my absence. *Nope, can't even deal with that right now.* I put the kettle on so I can make myself a decent cup of tea while I'm here. I open the fridge and cupboards to see if anything takes my fancy, but the thought of all of it makes me nauseous, so I close them all again. I make my tea and head upstairs for a shower.

I can't deny the hot water feels good. My mind wanders back to the last time Jake was in here with me. What I wouldn't give to have his hot, naked body in here with me now. Feeling his perfect abs and running my hands through his wet hair. What I wouldn't give just to have him here at all. *Wake up Jake, please.*

Once I step out the shower, I hurry to throw on clean clothes and pack another bag so I can get back to the hospital as quickly as possible. I didn't want to leave him at all, but the doctor was right, I did need to come back and freshen up. Being away from him is making me anxious, but I have to believe he's going to be ok. *I just got him back, I can't lose him again, not like this.*

I drag a brush through my wet hair and grab

my toiletry bag from the bathroom cabinet. I throw in my toothbrush, toothpaste and various other items I may need. Buried in the mess of the cabinet I come across my contraceptive pills. I haven't taken them since the accident, I haven't even been home to think about it really. I go to toss them back on the shelf when I have a sudden realisation. *Shit!* My blood runs cold. *When did I last have a period?* I try to think back through the chaos of the last few weeks or so. I sit on the edge of the bath still wrapped in my towel trying to do the maths. *Shit! Shit! Shit!* It's been over six weeks since my last one. I've never been late before. *Maybe it's just the stress?*

I need to throw up again. I run to the toilet and dry wretch into it until my stomach hurts. There's nothing to bring up, I was already sick this morning and I've barely eaten while Jake's been in hospital. Now that I think about it, I've been throwing up for days but I assumed it was because I'm worrying about Jake. *How did I not see this before?* I sit on the bathroom floor with my head in my hands and sob. I really cry hard and let out all the pent-up emotions from the last ten days. I've tried to be strong at the hospital but the longer he stays unconscious, the harder it gets. And now this. *How can I have a baby? I can't do this without him. What if he doesn't wake up? What if he never meets his child?* I let the panic take me over for a while and swallow me whole. I let myself fall apart on the bathroom floor. My chest heaves with the sobs and my head aches.

Eventually my thoughts start to quieten and I begin to calm down. I take some deep breaths and try to stop crying. If I am pregnant, this isn't going to do the baby any good. First thing's first I need to take a test. *That's it, I just need to focus on one small step at a time. I can do that.* The whole picture is too much to cope with.

I finish getting dressed and pack my things. I don't want to delay getting back to Jake any longer than I need to. I've already been gone longer than planned. So, I decide to pick up a pregnancy test in the hospital pharmacy and take the test there. *I'll be closer to Jake.*

I text Harry to let him know I'm on my way back and apologise for the delay. Luckily the pharmacy is by the back entrance to the hospital which we have been using to avoid the press. There are less photographers and journalists out the front than there was in the beginning, but there is usually still the odd one hanging around according to Harry. Thank God we have had Harry to deal with all of that. There's no way I'd be able to deal with any of that of my own.

***

After I purchase the pregnancy test, I stuff it down to the bottom of my bag so no one sees it and make my way up to Jake's room. On the way I pass the newspaper stand and see there is a story about Jake's accident inside. *At least he's not on the front page anymore.*

When I get to Jake's room, I can hear Harry inside talking to Jake.

"I know we've always joked around, but I missed you when you were away, man. You're my best friend. You can't fucking die, Jake, do you hear me? You can't fucking die!"

I push the door open slowly to see Harry wipe a few stray tears from his cheeks as he stands and clears his throat.

"Alright Abbie? Feeling better?" He fidgets knowing I've caught him having an emotional moment. I decide not to say anything as I don't want to embarrass him.

"A little. Has the doctor been in yet?" I ask him. I'm hoping I didn't miss his update while I was at home dealing with today's possible revelation. *I honestly don't know how much more I can take.*

"No, not yet. Louisa stopped by, she said she'll call you later. She was pleased you'd gone home for a bit."

I nod and set my bag down on the chair giving Jake's arm a squeeze as I do.

"Right, I'm going to get going if you're alright here. I've got court tomorrow and I've got a lot of prep to do." Harry puts his jacket on and gathers his things. I think he needs to get out of here and deal with his emotional outburst from earlier.

"Yes of course, thanks so much Harry. I'll let you know what the doctor says."

***

When Dr Cartwright arrives several hours later, he finds me sat in the armchair in Jake's room staring into space. What he can't see is the positive pregnancy test I'm clutching in my hand inside my hoodie pocket. I don't know how long I've been sat there like this trying to process everything that has happened recently.

"Hello, Miss Daniels. I'm glad to hear you left the hospital this morning." Dr Cartwright smiles at me warmly. I nod and give him a feeble smile. I don't have an ounce of energy left. I'm physically and emotionally drained.

"Following on from our meeting this morning I need to talk to you about something." I can tell by his sombre tone that he isn't here with good news. *How much worse can this get? I sure hope Jake still has fight left in him because right now, I'm all out.*

"I met with a team of specialists this morning who are at the top of their field in neuroscience. We analysed Jake's condition and his response to treatment. We looked at his brain scans and his test results. We left no stone unturned, that I can assure you." I nod gesturing for him to go on.

"Unfortunately, while it's true Jake's condition has remained stable, he has shown little to no signs of improvement since he arrived. Therefore, it was agreed that it is looking increasingly likely that Jake may never wake up. He is potentially brain-dead, Miss Daniels." He pauses to let his last sentence sink in. I don't respond. I just continue to stare straight ahead.

"Which means in a day or so if there's still no change, we will be looking at making the decision to switch off life support." Dr Cartwright waits for a response, but I still can't muster one.

"Miss Daniels, do you understand what I'm saying to you?" He gently places his hand over mine and for the first time during our exchange I make eye contact. A single tear spills over and rolls slowly down my cheek dropping onto Dr Cartwright's hand over mine.

"Yes doctor," I whisper.

# Chapter 24

## *Abbie*

Time has stood still. It must have been hours since Dr Cartwright delivered the news, but I haven't moved. I haven't spoken. I haven't cried. I haven't done anything other than continue to sit here and stare into space. Sometime during my silent refusal to re-join the real world, Dr Cartwright left, unable to rouse any kind of verbal or emotional response from me. Something inside of me has broken. Something other than my heart, which needless to say is smashed into tiny pieces all over the hospital floor. Whatever it is inside of us that makes us think and feel and do, mine has broken seemingly beyond repair. I realise as I sit there that I haven't even been sick. It would seem even the baby is boycotting reality. I don't think I've had a coherent thought in my head the whole time I've sat here. Just endless white noise in my brain.

I feel a warm hand on my shoulder. I hadn't even heard the door open behind me.

"Angel, Dr Cartwright phoned to say he was worried about you. How are you holding up sweetie?"

*Mum.* I reach up and squeeze her hand on my shoulder. Mum pulls up the other chair and sits next to me. She doesn't press me for an answer. She doesn't fuss or flap or force me to talk. She just sits beside me so I know I'm not alone. Other than the whirring and beeping I've grown so used to, the room is silent. After an immeasurable amount of time spent in comfortable silence with my mum, I finally say something.

"They can't switch him off Mum," I say so quietly I wonder if she can even hear me. She looks straight at me so I know she did. "I can't lose him again."

"Abigail, listen to me. That man is a fighter. He spent eight years of his life fighting his way back to you, there's no way he's going to give up now... and neither can you."

I take a deep breath and try to swallow down the rising sob that's threatening. I slowly bring the pregnancy test out of my pocket. The one I've been clutching so hard for the past several hours that it's made my knuckles go white. I put it on my lap for mum to see as I give way to the tidal wave of tears that finally arrives after such a long, delayed reaction.

"Oh angel." She sighs as she scoops me into the biggest hug and holds me while I cry. I cry a whole river in my mum's arms. The irony isn't lost on me that despite facing motherhood myself, I still need my own mum; now more than ever. When I'm done, she takes my face in her hands and looks at me with tears in her eyes.

"You are stronger than you know, Abbie. I know you can do this," she says with way more conviction than I feel.

"Not without him I can't."

"You can, and you must. If the worst happens, then that little life inside of you is going to need you even more. The best way you can help Jake now is to be strong for him and his baby."

I nod at her knowing she's right, but absolutely terrified of trying to navigate the darkness on my own.

As if she can read my thoughts she says, "Whatever happens you will never be on your own. You are surrounded by people who love and care about you." Mum strokes my hair and manages to calm me down and soothe me in a way that only mothers can. I only hope I can be half as good at it for my own child one day.

\*\*\*

I wake up the next morning in the armchair snuggled into a blanket. Mum must have tucked me in after I fell asleep. I stretch and rub my aching neck. All these nights sleeping in a chair is not good for my posture. On the side I find a bottle of juice, a blueberry muffin, a box of pregnancy vitamins and a 'New Mum' magazine. There's a note beside it saying:

## Make sure you're looking after yourself, love Mum X

I smile for the first time in nearly two weeks and my hand instinctively settles on my stomach as if trying to draw the strength I need to make today better for all of us. I force myself to consume the breakfast Mum left, and surprisingly manage not throw it all back up. *So far so good.* I stand at Jake's bedside and run my fingers through his hair and beard.

"Good morning, gorgeous." It's the same greeting I give him every morning before gently kissing him on the cheek. "Today's a big day." I tell him. "I'm going to shave your beard for you." I laugh a little and squeeze his arm. I've decided that I need to do something positive and constructive to help give me focus. Returning Jake's face to his normal length of sexy stubble seems like a good place to start.

I dash down to the hospital pharmacy and grab a razor and shaving foam. I also grab some dry shampoo, hair gel and aftershave. *It can't hurt to spoil him a little can it?* I don't know why I didn't think to do this for him sooner. *Too busy wallowing in my own self-pity, I guess.* Well, that stops today. Jake has too much to live for to give up the fight. I just have to make him hear me.

An hour later and Jake smells like Jake again.

His hair is styled in that messy, just fucked way that he likes. One of the nurses kindly helped me work around the bandages and now his impressively chiselled jawline is visible once again.

"Looking good, Jake Greyson," I tell him as I run my fingers up and down his bare arms. I crave physical contact with him and this is as close as it gets. What I wouldn't give for him to be able to wrap me in his arms again. The longer he lays in this hospital, the further away that possibility gets.

When I'm done cleaning up, I kick off my shoes and climb onto the bed next to him. I'm not meant to sit on the bed, but if these are the last few days I ever get to spend with him, then I'll sit where I damn well like. I lay beside him squashed into the tiny space on the edge of the bed. My head tucked into the crook of his neck and my body pressed up tightly against his side. I take a deep breath and enjoy breathing in the familiar scent of him, now he smells like him again.

"Jake, your makeover wasn't the only reason today is such a big day. I actually have something really important to tell you so I need you to listen carefully, ok?"

The doctors are adamant that talking to him makes a positive difference. These are also the same doctors who are threatening to switch off his life support in a few days' time, so I honestly don't know what to think anymore. *It can't hurt to keep trying though, right? He needs to hear this.*

"It turns out that in between all the drama, we created something beautiful." I pick up his floppy lifeless hand and place it on my stomach.

"We're going to have a baby, Jake. You're going to be a daddy," I whisper against his ear.

I can feel Jake's pillow getting damp under my face as my tears slowly seep into it. "So now you have an even bigger reason to live because we need you, Jake. God knows I've always needed you, but now more than ever. I can't do this without you and I don't want to. So, you need to fight. You hear me? You need to wake up and live!" As I continue my one-sided rant at Jake my voice gets louder and angrier and I realise I'm gripping his arms, gently shaking him as if I can will him back to life.

Nothing. He doesn't twitch, he doesn't react, he doesn't flinch. There's just nothing. I put my hand on his chest and I can feel his heart beating. *How can his heart still beat when he's not really here anymore?* This is the cruellest hand fate could have dealt us. I rest my head on his shoulder with my hand still on his heart and his hand on my belly. "I love you more than anything." I whisper. "Come back to me."

\*\*\*

*The summer sun is warm on my face and it's so bright in the sky I have to screw my face up to see properly. Jake and I are laying side by side on a picnic blanket by the stream just like we did on my seventeenth birthday. I lean up on my elbow to look at him. He's wearing a tight white vest top and ripped jeans. Every outline of every muscle is visible through the fabric of his top and his arms are tucked up under his head as he lays with his eyes closed soaking up the sun's rays. He's so unbelievably beautiful, it feels as if my heart free falls from my chest. He is perfection personified and he looks so happy and at peace. I trace the outline of his features with my fingertips, across his eyebrows, down his nose to his lips which slowly bend into a sensual, sexy smile.*

*"See something you like?" he asks me. He's asked me that before, I'm sure of it. It's like I'm in some sort of weird montage of memories all blurred together. I want to open my mouth to answer him, but I'm scared this moment isn't real and if I speak, I'll break the magic. It's then I realise I'm wearing the plectrum necklace he gave me. It's hanging around my neck as if it's always been there, but in reality I haven't worn it since he left. It's been safely tucked away in my little box of Jake memories.*

*The sound of Jake's guitar playing somewhere in the background fills my head. The sound of it is so soothing, but I know it can't be Jake playing because he's right here... at least he was. The space next to me on the blanket where Jake was just laying is now cold and empty. Where did he go? This is so confusing.*

*A strange fluttering sensation starts in my belly, my extremely large pregnant belly. Wait, what? I reach down and touch my swollen bump which is wriggling and twitching beneath my hands. How is this happening? I can't be more than a few weeks pregnant, there's no way I can feel the baby kicking yet. And yet I can.*

Even as the beeping of the hospital machines start to infiltrate my mind, pulling me from my dream back to the harsh reality of our situation, I can still feel it, the gentle fluttering on my stomach. I open my eyes and look down at my belly trying to make sense of what's going on. Jake's hand is still there, resting against me. *It's him!* Jake's fingers are moving and twitching. The machines start making a different beeping noise and I jump off the bed in panic. I hit the emergency button and call out down the corridor.

"Nurse! He's waking up!" *He's waking up.*

# Chapter 25

## Jake

**W**hat the hell is happening? I feel like I've gone ten rounds with Mike Tyson, then been hit by a freight train. Why do I feel like shit? I try to open my eyes from what I can only assume is the worst hangover ever. Fuck, I don't even remember where I was last night, but it must have been a hell of an after-party. Everything is blurry and I can't focus on anything yet. My head is absolutely pounding with pain. I have never been this drunk before. *Maybe I was spiked?*

I don't even know where I am. Every time I try to open my eyes, I can't focus on anything but I'm aware of a lot of commotion and moving about in the room. *Maybe I'm still at a party. Did I pass out?* I try to speak to ask someone what's going on and where I am but my voice refuses to work. My mouth is as dry as the Sahara Desert. I can feel someone move against me. *Oh dear fucking God! Please don't tell me I've slept with someone. What the hell will I tell Abbie? I'd never knowingly cheat on her. Fuck! I'm so confused right now.*

"Jake?" *Hold on. That's Abbie's voice. How is she*

*here?* I try again to open my eyes and concentrate on my surroundings. It's hard to focus though with the blinding pain in my head. I can start to make out the outline of a person standing next to me looking over me. I blink a few times in an attempt to get my eyes and brain to start communicating. *It's Abbie.* I can tell by her voice and her smell, but now my eyes are adjusting and I can start to make out her features. Her beautiful face is etched with concern.

"Jake baby, take your time. You're in the hospital, but you're ok," Abbie tells me gently as she reaches up and strokes my face. "Everything's going to be ok," she repeats but under her breath as if trying to convince herself more than me. *Hospital?*

My senses are becoming more aware now and I can hear the beeping of machines next to my head. I realise I have a tube down my throat which would explain why I can't speak. I peer down at my body to check all my limbs are still intact which I'm grateful to see they are but I can see the full extent of the wires and the tubes coming out of me. *What the hell happened to me?*

I try really hard to remember how I ended up in hospital while Abbie speaks quietly with the nurses. The last thing I remember is walking out on the band after writing Ralph a note. *I was going home to Abbie. I was in a car accident.* The memory of the impact comes rushing back to me all at once and I know I'm lucky to be alive.

*How long have I been unconscious for?*

One of the nurses then comes to my bedside and starts doing things with the monitors and machines. The other one appears on the other side and smiles warmly at me.

"You gave us all quite the fright, Mr Greyson." She picks my hand up in hers. "Squeeze my hand if you understand what I'm saying to you."

I squeeze her hand as hard as I can, but my fingers barely move in comparison to the effort it took.

She smiles again. "Good, this is good," she says and looks across at Abbie. Abbie smiles, but looks absolutely terrified. *What have I put her through?*

I desperately want to tell her I'm ok, that I can hear her and I understand and that I'll be absolutely fine, but I can't. I can't get my voice to work, or my limbs to co-operate. It's frustrating as hell and I want to scream and shout!

"There's still a long way to go on the road to recovery, but this is an excellent start. You're going to need your rest, so what do you say we give you something to help with that and get this tube out so you can talk to your lovely lady here?"

I manage to nod my head at her, but I don't take my eyes off Abbie. I can see now how tired and pale she looks. I try to reach out for her, but I just don't have the strength.

Then just as quick as consciousness came, it

leaves me again as I surrender to the drugs the nurse gives me and drift back off to sleep.

*Six hours later*

I wake up in the hospital once again, only this time it's not so bad because I remember. I know what happened and how I got here. The pain in my head isn't as awful as the first time and I don't feel quite so groggy. The tube is no longer in my throat which is a vast improvement, but it feels as if a thousand razor blades have been left in its wake. I seem to be attached to a few less machines than last time too.

Looking around the room I can see I clearly have a private room to myself as I'm not on a ward. *That's comforting. I bet this gown I'm wearing has my arse hanging out of it.* I smile inwardly to myself, pleased that I seem to have maintained a sense of humour despite my brush with death. My eyes settle on the chair beside the bed. Abbie is curled up fast asleep under a blanket. She looks so peaceful and despite the dark circles under her eyes she is still as breath takingly beautiful as ever. *How long has she sat here with me?*

I desperately want to watch her sleep, but the need to clear my throat and get some water is unbearable. Abbie's eyes immediately open as

I try to cough and she flies from the chair to my bedside.

"Do you want some water?" Her face is full of panic and concern. I've never seen Abbie look so drained. I nod my head and attempt to smile at her, but I'm not sure if it worked. My brain and body parts don't yet seem to be on speaking terms.

After Abbie manages to get a few drops of water in me, my throat feels a little more lubricated so I decide to try talking.

"Hey baby. Miss me?" I manage to whisper in a voice that sounds like it belongs to a forty-a-day chain smoker rather than me.

Abbie smiles and a weak laugh falls from her lips as silent tears roll down her face.

"You have no idea. I thought…" She sniffs and picks up my hand linking her fingers with mine. "I thought I'd lost you." She looks at me with such heartbreak. None of my injuries compare to how much it hurts to look at her like this.

"Never." I raise a weak, shaky arm to brush my thumb over her cheek, wiping away her tears.

"Do you remember what happened Jake?" She leans further over the bed and runs her fingers through my hair and along my bandaged forehead gently.

"I crashed the car." Images of the accident flood my mind. It's not a night I'm going to forget in a hurry. "Was anyone else hurt?" A sudden wave of panic washes over me. I know I caused the accident. If I hurt other people too, I'll never forgive myself.

Abbie shakes her head. "No, it was just you. The other car barely had a scratch. Your car was crushed though Jake." A grief-stricken sob escapes her. "They had to..." She can't finish her sentence through her tears.

"They had to cut me out. I vaguely remember. I was in and out of consciousness then. The last thing I remember is being stretchered into the ambulance."

Abbie reaches for a tissue and wipes her face, still not letting go of me with her other hand. As if she's scared she'll lose me if she doesn't keep hold of me.

"How long have I been here?" I'm nervous about the answer. *How much time has passed while I slept?*

"Sixteen days. I've slept in here with you every night. I only left once the whole time and that was because the doctors insisted I went home to shower and get more clothes." An expression I can't place passes over her face, but before I can make sense of it, it's gone.

"You've slept in that chair for over two weeks?" I try to sound stern, but my voice is not capable of variation yet.

"There was no way I was leaving you, Jake. You don't know what it's been like." Abbie takes a deep breath and looks straight into my eyes.

"None of that matters now. You're alive and you're awake, that's all that matters. We're all going to be fine." Abbie leans over and plants a soft kiss on my cheek.

*What is she talking about 'all of us'? I thought she said no one else was hurt?*

Before I get a chance to clarify what she means the door swings open and Harry appears. He's wearing a ridiculous goofy grin on his face, but I don't miss the fact that he looks utterly exhausted too.

"It's about time, Sleeping Beauty," he jokes as he makes his way over to the bed clutching a punnet of grapes.

I smile at his idiotic joke. "Hey man," I croak.

"Wow Jake, you really need to cut back on the cigars bro, you sound terrible."

I try to roll my eyes, but it makes my head hurt.

Abbie gives my hand a squeeze and steps back from the bed. "I'll leave you two alone for a minute. I've got some calls to return, but I'll just be outside."

As Abbie turns and leaves, she and Harry exchange nods of greeting and knowing glances. The kind of look only people who have gone through a shared trauma can understand. *What have I put everyone through?* I may have been the one in a coma fighting for me life, but it seems those around me have dealt with an equal share of pain, if not more. I was blissfully unaware of my pain up until today, they have been fully aware of theirs.

"I brought you grapes. That's what you bring sick people right? Why is that? Do they have magic healing powers I don't know about?" Harry jokes putting the punnet on the side.

I chuckle, but it tickles my raw throat and makes me cough and splutter.

"You had us all worried, man." Harry looks at his shoes as if they are suddenly the most interesting thing in the room. Serious Harry is a rare creature. You have to respond just right so as not to spook him.

"I know. I'm sorry. I don't fully understand all the things I need to apologise for yet, but you should know that I'm really fucking sorry all the same. Thank you for taking care of Abbie. I haven't had a chance to talk to her properly yet, but I know that you would've done."

Harry nods and clears his throat. Firmly pushing down any emotions that were threatening to show themselves.

"She's one tough lady you got there. I'm not going to go into the details, that's for her to decide... but she's been through the ringer these past few weeks man."

I nod but don't really know what to say. I doubt I'll ever fully appreciate what she's been through.

"Just so you know. I've handled everything with the band and the press. You don't need to worry about any of it. We can discuss it properly when you're well. I'm so fucking glad to have you back, man." Unable to pull me in for a hug due to my wires and machines he settles for a fist bump to my shoulder.

"Thanks Harry. I owe you big time."

"That you do my friend, that you do." Light-hearted Harry is back in full swing and he gives me a salute as he heads for the door. "You need your rest and I need to get laid. I'll be back again tomorrow."

For the first time since I woke up, I'm alone and it's quiet. I take the opportunity to try and organise my thoughts and process what's going on. *I can't believe this has happened.* I was driving home to tell the woman I love that I want to marry her and leave the rock star life behind and instead end up fighting for my life in hospital. I still don't really know how serious my injuries are. Thankfully my brain is functioning normally which I gather is nothing short of a miracle. I have no idea if I can walk, but I can feel my legs so I hope that's a good sign.

I close my eyes and take a few deep breaths focusing really hard on different body parts to try and establish what hurts. My head is by far the worst pain, closely followed by my throat and chest. My left leg feels uncomfortable but nothing compared to the other pain elsewhere. *I wonder if I can have any more pain killers yet?*

A gentle knock on the door brings me out of

my thoughts and Abbie steps quietly into the room.

"The doctor will be around to see you soon. Everyone's been amazing." Abbie's voice is so weak. It's like all the life has been sucked out of her.

"How are you doing, Abbie?" I ask her seriously.

"It's meant to be me asking you that." She sighs and perches on the edge of my bed. She slides her hand in mine and I hold on to her as tight as I can.

"Tell me," I urge.

"They said you were unlikely to ever wake up. I almost had to face the prospect of switching off the machines." She watches my thumb trace little circles across the back of her hand instead of looking directly at me.

I don't react at first. *How do you react to being told you almost didn't make it?* I let the seriousness of my situation start to slowly sink in.

Abbie looks up at me through her wet lashes. "But then somehow you beat the odds. A miracle happened and you came back to us, just like I asked you to."

"You know I'd do anything for you, baby. Including coming back from the dead it would seem." Abbie lets out a small laugh at my attempt at humour.

"You know I was coming back home to you, don't you?"

Abbie nods. "Harry told me. I've got so much I need to say to you." She leans over so our foreheads are touching and closes her eyes.

"Me too, baby. I'm so sorry for everything I've put you through." I breathe her in just enjoying the closeness and warmth.

"You don't need to be sorry. None of this is your fault."

"It was my fault! The accident happened because I wasn't paying attention and I wouldn't have even needed to be driving home if I hadn't been such a dick about plans for after the tour. All of this is my fault!" I'm so angry with myself now that I hear it all out loud.

"Ssshh, Jake, it's alright. Don't get yourself worked up. You need to rest. Everything is ok now. Nothing matters except you, me and…"

The double doors swing open before Abbie can finish her sentence and in walks a nurse.

Abbie lets go of me and returns to her chair. Her shoulders visibly sag and she looks agitated. Whatever she was about to say is clearly important to her. I make a mental note to make sure I revisit that conversation at the earliest opportunity.

The nurse gives me more pain killers and checks all my readings. She fiddles and twiddles with buttons and tubes in my periphery while I watch Abbie. She's sat in the chair so as not to get in the nurse's way, but she's fidgeting with something in her pocket and looks nervous.

"There you go, Mr Greyson. You should be more comfortable for a while now. Can I get you anything else?" the nurse asks pulling my attention away from Abbie.

"No. No thank you."

The nurse leaves and quietly closes the door behind her.

"Nothing else matters except you, me and what?" I repeat Abbie's words back to her waiting for her to fill in the blanks.

She swallows hard before looking up at me and coming over to the bed. She removes her hand from her pocket placing a pregnancy test on the edge of the bed.

"Our baby."

# Chapter 26

## *Abbie*

Jake has been awake for seven whole days. One blissful week of having him back with me, watching him get stronger every day. I haven't been able to put into words how thankful I am that he's ok. I don't think I've really processed it yet. I'd lost all hope. I honestly thought I was going to have to say goodbye forever. But then somehow, he managed the unimaginable. He came back to me. Not just me, us. I'm still not used to the fact that I'm an us and not just a me. I like to think it was the news that we were going to be a family that finally brought him back, but I guess I'll never know.

To say Jake was shocked by the news would be an understatement. He just stared at the pregnancy test for ages and couldn't string a coherent sentence together for a while as he tried to make sense of what I'd told him.

Eventually though, his poor battered brain wrapped itself around the information and he grinned like a Cheshire cat.

"I'm going to be a dad!" he said in disbelief. Then he repeated it over and over, louder and louder "I'M GOING TO BE A DAD!" I don't think either of us have stopped smiling since.

Jake has been making such good progress that the doctors have agreed to let him home today under certain strict conditions. I've never been very interested in Jake's money, but it has certainly put my mind at rest that we have been able to afford the best physiotherapists to come and work with Jake when we go home. He is well on the way to making a full recovery, but he is very weak and has damage from his injuries that needs strengthening.

Jake is in his hospital room dressing to go home with the help of one of the nurses while I talk to Dr Cartwright about his discharge. He's arming me with prescriptions, dressings and physio charts ready for us to leave. I'm deep in concentration studying the medications I need to know about when Dr Cartwright looks up at the doorway.

"Mr Greyson, how lovely it is to see you up and about."

I turn to see Jake walk slowly through the door, steadied by the nurse who has been helping him this morning. Seeing him looking so much like himself again takes my breath away. His hair is wet from the shower and he's wearing a tight white t-shirt, which despite the bandages still wrapped around his torso, shows off his sculpted figure perfectly. The bandage from his head has gone, just the remnants of healing stitches remain. He flashes me an irresistible smile and puts one hand in his jeans pocket trying to act casual as if walking away from a near fatal car accident is just your average day.

"Thanks Doc. Please, call me Jake." Dr Cartwright shakes Jake warmly by the hand. Jake has asked him numerous times to call him by his first name since he woke up, but Dr Cartwright is far too polite and old-school for that.

"Now listen, Mr Greyson. You must rest and do as you're told while you're healing. I don't want to see you back in here anytime soon. You're a very lucky man to have stared death in the face and walked away. Please don't do anything reckless." Dr Cartwright gives Jake a stern look over the top of his glasses, but can't hide how much he's grown to like him.

Jake grins and nods. "Yes, sir."

"No wild parties, no fast cars, no alcohol with that medication, Mr Greyson and definitely no physical exertion that is not directly recommended by your physiotherapist."

Jake flashes me the most wickedly naughty grin and raises his eyebrows. A gesture that does not go unnoticed by the good doctor.

"Enjoy the rest of your life, Mr Greyson. It's been a pleasure."

"I can't thank you enough for what you did for me." Jake shakes him firmly by the hand.

Dr Cartwright gives Jake one final nod farewell. "All in a day's work, Mr Greyson. Take care of yourself."

With that he turns and heads off down the corridor, probably to go and save someone else's life. Leaving us free to start the rest of ours. Complete, in one piece and together.

"You know I have no intention of behaving myself when we get home, right?" Jake whispers in my ear.

I smile in spite of how ridiculous his suggestion is. "You'll do as your told and rest."

"Baby, using your teacher tone will only make me misbehave more." He nuzzles into my neck with his nose and trails soft kisses below my ear. It's the first time he's been able to kiss me properly since the accident and his lips leave a trail of blazing fire across my skin. I'm so hyper aware of his touch. I don't know whether it's because it's been so long since I've felt him or whether it's my pregnancy hormones taking over, but either way it feels incredible.

"Come on, let's get you home."

\*\*\*

Home for the next few weeks is going to be Harry's parents' house. My house isn't big enough and has too many stairs. Julie insisted we move in with them while Jake recovers as she could set us up with a downstairs bedroom and en-suite. Once she found out about the baby, she wouldn't take no for an answer. She insisted that

I would need help to look after Jake as I would be tired myself. *She's not wrong. I'm exhausted!*

Jake was happy to accept as it's the only place that's ever felt like a home to him. It will give us a chance to make some proper plans for our future and find a place of our own. Over the past week we have discussed the band, my career and the baby at great length and Jake is only too eager to give up his rock star lifestyle to start our family here in the UK. I will possibly continue teaching again after the baby is born, but for now Jake needs me and so will our baby so I have taken indefinite leave until then.

Jake sleeps most of the way home and I have to resist the compulsion to keep checking his breathing as I drive. He's been given the all clear, despite how badly the odds were stacked against him. There's no reason to think anything bad will happen to him as long as he rests. *And yet, I can't help but worry.*

As I pull onto the gravel driveway of Julie and Mac's house, I smile at the memory of first meeting Jake here. So much has happened to us since that night, but I remember it like it was yesterday.

"Jake, we're here, baby." I lean over and gently try to wake him with soft kisses along his forehead. He opens his eyes and smiles at me before pulling me in for a proper kiss. A *deep* kiss, one full of fire and passion. The type of kiss I never thought I'd get again. He buries his fingers in my hair and pulls me closer as his tongue dances with mine. Just as I start to get breathless and my thoughts take a totally inappropriate direction for the circumstances, he breaks away and grins.

I raise an eyebrow at him in question and in response he places my hand on his growing erection.

"It still works," he says smugly. I can't help but laugh.

"That's what you're pleased about? Not that you cheated death or the fact that somehow you can still walk and talk? You're over the moon that you can still get it up?" I laugh in amusement.

"I'm fucking over the moon! Now let's go inside and see what this baby can still do." He wiggles his eyebrows, gesturing at his now straining jeans.

I swat him playfully on the arm where I know he has no bruising. "We know exactly what it can do! The evidence is currently residing in my uterus!"

"No harm in making sure it's still fully functional." He teases.

"Not a chance lover boy, you have to rest, plus I have a have a sneaking suspicion we may have company."

Jake sighs and looks at me with a dead-pan expression. "You invited everyone over here to welcome me home, didn't you?"

"Yeah, maybe a little."

He chuckles and kisses the back of my hand. "I love you. Come on then, let's go mingle."

We spend the afternoon surrounded by those nearest and dearest to us. Harry and Louisa are here with Harry's parents who have laid on a lovely spread of tea and cakes. Julie is in her element hosting for everyone and fussing over Jake.

My parents are here too; I don't think Jake has ever been so mothered in all his life! Every so often he glances at me with a look of 'help me' as he is fed more scones and finger sandwiches by Julie and Mum. Some of Jake's ex-band members have come to see him too.

Sitting in the courtyard of the garden, under the exact same tree where I first met Jake all those years ago, I think I'm happier than I've ever been. Jake is alive and here, we are surrounded by people who love us and we are going to have a beautiful baby *together.* Life couldn't be any more perfect.

I close my eyes momentarily and tilt my face at the sky, enjoying the warmth of the sun on my cheeks and I smile. I feel Jake come and sit down next to me and wrap his arm around my shoulder.

"Thank you," he says, peppering my bare shoulder with kisses.

"What for?"

"All this. Being you. I'm the luckiest man

alive." Jake intertwines his fingers with mine and I rest my head on his shoulder. We sit in comfortable silence together absorbing the atmosphere and enjoying the closeness of each other.

Everyone looks happier and more carefree than they have in weeks, like the clouds have finally lifted. I think I might even detect a shift in the way Harry and Louisa are looking at each other today. Maybe it's just me feeling all sentimental and soppy because of my own circumstances, but it looks a lot more like love than the usual lust in their eyes.

When everyone has left for the evening, Julie ushers us off to our bedroom that she has had specially adapted to make life as easy as possible for Jake while he recovers. She won't hear of us helping with the tidying up. *I think she secretly likes it.* Besides Jake does look increasingly tired after all the socialising he's done this afternoon. This is the longest he's spent out of bed since the accident.

Jake stands at the foot of the bed and beckons me to go to him with his finger. The look he's giving me is smouldering. I swear he could melt cast-iron with that look. This Jake is a far cry from the mischievous joker in my car this afternoon and yet I love them both in equal measure. I do as he asks and close the gap between us. He slowly reaches around and pulls the band from my ponytail letting my hair fall freely around my shoulders. Then without looking away from my eyes, he slides my off-the-shoulder dress down and it falls to my feet.

He tries to pull his t-shirt off and over his head but winces when he lifts his arms too high.

"Here, let me," I offer gently as I carefully roll the t-shirt up his ribs and over his head. I trace my fingers across the one remaining bandage that is still wrapped around his chest. We go back to staring deep into each other's eyes as I tentatively start to unwind the bandage and remove it. There is something slow and sensual about the way we are together tonight, as if it's for the first time again. I still can't believe he's really here and that I can hold him again. I unbutton his jeans and let them fall to the floor before he sits on the edge of the bed. I can't deny how turned on I am right now and how much I want him, but I'm nervous of hurting him.

"Jake, you need to rest. It's been a big day," I say, but he pulls me onto his lap so I'm straddling him and nuzzles my neck.

"I was asleep for over two weeks. The last thing I want is more sleep. I want my beautiful girl to make love to me." He looks at me with so much need. "Please, Abbie."

*Game over. A girl can only put up so much resistance in the name of common sense.* I don't think I'll ever be able to deny this man anything.

"Before I do. I need to tell you something. Promise you won't be mad?"

Jake furrows his brow. "Surely we've had our

share of shocking news this year? It's not triplets is it?" He jokes as he runs his hands over my bare stomach.

"No." I laugh. "At least I hope not!" I pause, and take a deep breath before continuing. *I don't know how Jake's going to take this.*

"When you were in hospital. I honestly thought you were going to die... I asked Harry to find someone who could track your dad down." I start to hurry my words, nervous of what he's going to say.

"Before you say anything, I know how you feel about him and I do understand, but the thought of you dying and him not getting the chance to say goodbye or not even knowing about it was too much for me to bear."

I run my hands through his hair and try to read his face for a reaction, but he's not giving much away. He's just listening, waiting for me to go on.

"They didn't have any luck until after you had woken up. Now that you're stronger, the decision is yours. I have a phone number for him in my purse. Whether you choose to use it or not is entirely up to you and I will respect your decision either way." I stop rambling and wait for his reaction.

"Wow. That's a lot to think about." He rubs his hands up and down my bare arms and pulls me closer. "Of course, I'm not mad. How could I be mad at you for loving me enough to do that?"

Jake holds me tight and runs his fingertips up and down my spine while he processes what I just said.

"Mind if I think about it?" he asks.

"Of course not."

Jake places his finger under my chin and guides my lips to his. Goosebumps scatter across my bare skin as his tongue melds with mine and he lays us both back on the bed.

"Now, where were we…?"

# *Epilogue*

## *Jake*

7 months later...

"Where are we going?" Abbie asks impatiently as I park the car at our destination.

Pregnancy has made her feisty and I fucking love it. I promised her a romantic day out together before the imminent arrival of baby Greyson and I intend to deliver. Much to her annoyance I made her sit the entire journey blindfolded by a silk scarf so as not to give away the surprise.

"You'll see," I step out the car and retrieve the picnic basket from the boot before helping Abbie out of the car.

She is so heavily pregnant now that manoeuvring is a challenge for her. Despite what she thinks, she is still absolutely breath-taking. She's wearing a flowing white top and jeans. It makes me smile to see the plectrum necklace I gave her is now once again a permanent feature around her neck.

Once Abbie is on her feet, I untie the scarf

allowing her to see where we are. It takes a moment for her eyes to adjust to the bright summer sun. She smiles when she realises where we are. I've brought her back to the stream where I took us for a picnic on her seventeenth birthday. *So much has happened since that day.*

I take Abbie's hand and pick up the picnic basket with the other.

"I do hope there's whipped cream in there," she teases, referring back to the last time we were here.

"Oh, you bet baby." I wink at her and we start our slow stroll along the stream to the same spot by the willow tree. It's every bit as beautiful here as I remember it. The sun is reflecting off the water making it sparkle and a colourful mix of wild flowers are growing along the grassy banks.

After spreading the blanket out and helping Abbie to get comfortable I lay out the picnic for us to enjoy.

"So, have you had any more thoughts about a name yet?" Abbie asks, helping herself to a fresh strawberry.

We found out some time ago that we are having a girl and have been pondering name ideas ever since.

"No, not yet but I've decided it doesn't matter. If she takes after you then she's going to be a hottie and therefore never allowed out so she won't need a name."

Abbie laughs at me and rolls her eyes. "Over-protective much?"

"I'm kidding. I did actually have an idea. I thought maybe we could name her Alice... after my mum?"

Abbie's eyes glisten with tears. "That's a lovely idea, Jake, Alice is a beautiful name." She grabs my hand and places it on the side of her bump where it feels like the baby is doing cartwheels. "I think Alice likes her new name."

I reach into the picnic basket and pull out the promised can of whipped cream.

"Let's see what Alice thinks of this!" I flash her a wicked grin. *She knows exactly what's coming.*

"Oh no you don't!" Abbie protests. "I can't run from you this time!"

"Exactly."

I pounce on Abbie and pin her in the long grass as she laughs and screams. Her feeble attempts to fight me off do nothing to slow me down. After months of gruelling physio, I am almost back to the same level of strength and fitness I was before the accident.

I lift her top up exposing her beautiful bump and kiss it all over.

"Jake, stop it!" Abbie can hardly breathe between the laughter and strain of trying to keep me away.

I take the lid off the can and draw a heart shape with the cream on her stomach.

"AAAAHHHH that's so cold!" Abbie screams and I think Alice must agree. I can feel her jiggling around all over the place in there as I lovingly lick all the cream from Abbie's flawless skin. *What did I ever do to get this lucky?*

After we've eaten all the picnic food we can manage and spent the afternoon lazing in the sun, I decide it's time to get to the real purpose of our trip here today.

"Come on, let's go for a walk. I have a surprise for you," I say, as I help her to her feet.

"Jake, if you think I'm going to have sex with you at nine months pregnant in the middle of a field you are sadly mistaken."

I laugh out loud at her sudden crankiness. "As tempting as it would be to lay you back down and take you right here in the grass, that's not what I was planning."

We collect up the picnic things and head in the same direction we did all those years ago. Just as we turn the corner, what I want to show her comes into view.

"Do you remember this house?" I ask Abbie as we approach the white cottage with the beams. *I know full well that she does.*

"Yeah," she says smiling. "It's so beautiful. Like it belongs in an English holiday brochure."

"Do you remember what you said to me when you first saw it?"

"That I wanted to live in a house like that one day," she answers as we come to a stop in front of the white picket fence.

I turn to face her and take both her hands in mine. "Today is that day, baby."

Abbie gives me a confused look as I reach into my back pocket and produce a small black velvet pouch and place it in the palm of her hand.

"I don't understand…"

"Open it," I urge her.

She pulls the strings on the pouch and empties the contents into her hand. She gasps when she sees it's a door key with a diamond ring attached to it.

"Abbie Grace Daniels…"

"Oh my God!" She interrupts. She is visibly shaking with nerves or excitement; I can't tell which. *Maybe both?*

"I have loved you since the moment I met you. You're everything I ever wanted and now it's time for me to give you everything *you* ever wanted."

"You already have," she says quietly, trying to hold back tears.

I take the key and separate it from the diamond ring.

"This is our house now, baby. I had Harry look into it soon after I came back and it was just a matter of time, waiting until it became available. It's been ours for a few weeks, but I was waiting for the right time."

Abbie opens and closes her mouth several times, unable to find the right words.

"I can't believe this, Jake. This is incredible."

"I'm not done," I tell her as I get down on one knee. Holding the diamond ring out in front of me between my thumb and forefinger I look up at Abbie who now has tears streaming down her face. *I hope to God those are happy tears! Why is this so terrifying? I've virtually died and come back to life and yet this is the most fucking scared I've ever been!*

"I've rehearsed a thousand different versions of this moment in my head and now that we're here, I can't remember any of them. I guess what I really want to say is that I will spend the rest of my life trying to rock your world the way you have mine, if you'll let me."

She smiles a knowing smile at my familiar choice of words.

"Abbie...will you marry me?"

"Yes! Oh my God, a million times yes!"

I slide the sparkling rock onto her finger and press my forehead against her bump.

I had never known for sure if we would ever get our happy ending. All I had was blind hope and determination, but despite all the obstacles thrown in our path, here we are almost nine years later. As overwhelmingly happy as I am right now that we made it to this point; there's one thing I know for sure.

Real love stories don't end with a proposal, that's just where they start.

B CROWHURST

# Acknowledgements

There are a multitude of people I would like to thank for their support and input into this labour of love.

Firstly, I would like to thank my family and friends for their unwavering belief that I could make this happen, that means more than you will ever know.

Secondly, I would like to thank my beta readers who gave me the confidence to finish the book. Without your feedback, praise and constructive criticism this book would not exist, so thank you.

I would also like to give a huge thank you to Author Bunnies, not only for their editing input but their ongoing support throughout this process and going above and beyond in their plight to help me bring my book to life.

Another huge thank you goes out to author TL

Swan and her group of Cygent Inkers. Your support, inspiration and help has been invaluable and I couldn't have done it without you.

Last but by no means least, I would like to thank *you*, for choosing to read my book. Without an audience I would have no reason to write so thank you for taking the time to read my book, it means a lot and I hope it brought enjoyment to you.

Coming Soon...

# Welcome
# to Paradise

Summer 2021

# Never Miss a Release

If you would like to know more about B Crowhurst and future releases, here are some ways to keep up to date:

* Sign up to my newsletter via Facebook.

* Follow me on Facebook and Instagram.

* Find me on Goodreads.

Printed in Great Britain
by Amazon